# DEDICATION

To my husband of fifteen years, Paul. You are truly my own Mr Darcy. Without your love and support I would have never found the courage to complete this journey. *Thank you!*

# TABLE OF CONTENTS

# ACKNOWLEDGMENTS

While I would love to personally thank each person who has read the original version of this story online, I know such a task is not possible. Every comment written, and every nudge I received was what gave me the courage to eventually pursue publishing this story. So to all my readers – *Thank you!*

There are three ladies I would like to acknowledge by name, the first being Brenda. In her quest to draw new authors out of the woodwork she began a writing challenge on her forum. It was with her encouragement that I first put pen to paper – or rather, hit that first keystroke – thus beginning this journey. She has been behind me from the start and has reassured me every step of the way. I cannot effectively express how much I appreciate her friendship and guidance. *Thank you, Brenda!*

Two others who deserve my personal gratitude would be my editing team – Linnea and Anita. Both of these ladies were willing to take on the enormous task of helping a new writer, and for their time and patience I am truly grateful. When they signed on none of us knew where this story would even lead, and yet they have stuck with me through it all, giving me wonderful feedback and ideas along the way. They have both become so integral to this story that I know it would not be the same without their help. So to both of them I must give a heartfelt – *Thank You!*

# PROLOGUE

**Friday, September 27, 1811**
**Hertfordshire**

*here am I?"* Elizabeth Bennet groaned aloud in frustration as she turned to gaze over the landscape, hoping something familiar would catch her eye. For years she had asserted that she possessed such an intimate knowledge of the area surrounding Longbourn, her family home, that she could never become lost, but that declaration proved to be mistaken today. She had explored further today than ever before, and in so many different directions, and now she was truly lost.

Elizabeth thought it would be a great adventure to see what lay on the other side of the river she saw in the distance from her window every morning. For years she avoided this area because of having to cross where it was too wide and where the currents were harsh, but a bridge had just been built. She was uncertain if they would finish in time before the weather became too cold for her to explore, but they did. As the sun peeked from the horizon this morning she set out to discover this new area with great delight, exuberantly walking along new paths and daydreaming.

It was the daydreaming that proved to be her undoing. She was now turned around and unsure of which way to go. Usually the position of the sun would help her, but when she followed where she thought her home should be, she discovered unfamiliar wood.

At first, this was an adventure she had looked forward to for ages, but now she just wanted her father's strong arms around her once again. As tears began to well in her eyes, she remembered what Reverend Hughes said in his sermon last week. '*We need not be terrified of the unknown places we traverse, because God is always with us.*'

Elizabeth knew just what to do. She bowed her head and prayed, calling out to the only one who could settle her heart better than her father. She prayed for the Lord's guidance and protection. Immediately she felt a great relief as peacefulness settle over her. Somehow she knew everything would work out well.

Off in the distance, along a ridge of trees, she spotted what she thought might be a familiar tree. With a determined lift of her chin she fixed her eyes on the distant ridge and set out in that direction. As she approached the tree, with its wide open branches and large canopy of leaves, she realized this tree was so very unique that she could not possibly forget it. Unfortunately, it was not familiar to her. *Where should I go? In which direction should I travel?*

Elizabeth decided she needed to clear her mind, and the rumbling in her stomach gave her something else to focus on for a few minutes. She saw some wild bushes around, so she decided to see if any of them had edible berries. Luckily, her Granny Bennet had taken her under her tutelage and taught Elizabeth everything she could about the local plants, pointing out which could be used for food, which would be best for medicine, and most importantly, which could harm you if eaten or even touched. Elizabeth might be lost, but at least she knew how to survive!

Finding an elder bush, she held the corners of her handkerchief together and filled it with the sweet berries, then she sat down to contemplate her dilemma while she ate her fill.

With a full stomach, a clearer mind, and renewed hope, she turned back to the distinctive tree to see if it would lend its branches to her plight. Shedding her bonnet and gloves, for they would only hinder her climbing and be ruined, she found a sturdy branch that was low enough and swung up into the tree with practiced ease.

When Elizabeth was younger she was considered the best in the neighborhood at hiding games. What the other children did not know was her favorite hiding places were up above their heads where they never thought to look. She would watch as they went here and there, looking under bushes and behind benches. Many times she nearly gave herself away stifling a snicker while watching them from her perch as they searched. They would finally give up and go inside, and within a few minutes she would see her father come outside. He would slowly stretch his limbs and meander towards the back of the garden where Elizabeth's favorite climbing trees were located. He would never look up at her, for that would surely give her position away, but he would situate himself under the tree in which she was perched and say, "They have gone now, Lizzy. Come on down, and we shell go in for some tea and biscuits."

*Ahhhh, her father...she loved him dearly!* He was the one person in her family who truly understood her. She had a dry wit and loved to read of ancient philosophers and debate their positions. She and her father would spend hours going through texts and discussing the merits and faults of each tome. When they tired of reading they would turn to playing board games – their favorite being chess. He had such a strong, calming presence to those around him. What she would not give to have him ride up right now and rescue her from her dreary day!

In the distance she heard the familiar sound of horse's hooves as they galloped through the fields. She immediately began to scan the horizon. *Could it be my father coming to save me once again? Where is he? Which direction do I need to run to find my salvation?* From her treetop perch, she spotted the far-off silhouette of a lone rider. Scampering down the tree and grabbing her gloves and bonnet, she rushed off, hoping she could get to the rider before he was gone.

When she came across the rise of the hill that separated her from the rider she pursued, she slowed to a walk. The rider had stopped and was letting his horse graze while he stretched his arms above his head and looked around at the beautiful autumn landscape. Elizabeth did not recognize him. *How far have I come? Am I so far that this person will not know how to direct me home? It matters not*, she thought. *This gentleman is my only hope and all I can do is pray he is able to help!*

Slowing her pace and her breathing, for she did not want to appear the hoyden to the stranger, she placed the bonnet back on over her dark chestnut curls and began pulling on her lace gloves, being careful not to damage the intricate stitching. Her sister Jane had worked hard for several months last year to make these for Elizabeth as a gift. Elizabeth was so taken with the fine stitching that she would only wear them to church on Sundays, but Jane told her that she had made them to wear any day. So she began wearing them as much as she dared. She did not want to ruin them, but she knew that relegating them to only Sunday gloves was not what Jane intended, and she loved her sister so much that she wanted to please her. *Soon it will be too cold to wear them outside on my walks,* she thought. Chuckling a bit under her breath as she pulled herself back to the present, she squared her shoulders and found courage to face this unknown gentleman, with hope that he would be able to help her. Her courage rose with every step she took towards the stranger.

He had been riding for hours across Netherfield's lands and beyond, unable to determine what had kept him on his horse speeding over fields, jumping fences, and fording rivers. It was almost as though someone were calling to him. It was not an audible voice, but he could feel the pull with his soul. *Who needs me so much that their spirit is calling to me?* He knew no one in this area other than his best friend, and he had gone back to London early this morning to escort his two sisters and brother-in-law to his new home. *Who could it be?*

Deciding to give his horse a well-deserved rest, he slowed his mount. Looking around at the beautiful autumn leaves and breathing in the crisp air, he slid down and stretched his sore back and arms. He loved riding, but some days he felt too old for such long rambles. Fitzwilliam Darcy was only seven and twenty – would be eight and twenty in two days — but he felt the enormous burden of his responsibilities weighing him down. With everything that had happened in the last few months, he was in great need of a rest. It was for this reason that his family insisted he visit his friend, Charles Bingley.

Today of all days he could not remain inside. This was the sixteenth anniversary of the passing of his mother, and he felt her absence keenly. As he stood here in the midst of this unfamiliar land, his mind began to wander to the hours he would sit beside his mother's bed as she lay there, too weak to even dress and go to her sitting room. His fondest memory was the day she spoke with him about his future and the young lady he would one day marry. She cautioned him to choose wisely and find someone who could teach him to appreciate the joy that comes in laughter; someone who would keep him young as he aged. At only eleven years of age, he promised his mother that when he met such a young lady, he would carry her off and marry her as soon as may be. Lady Anne Darcy laughed at her son's exuberance to do the right thing immediately and she added that perhaps he should wait a respectable amount of time for the young lady to fall in love with him first. Darcy was never a child given to much joviality, but she realized that it was what he needed most in his life. His mother was sick off and on for many years, and she saw the way it affected her much-loved son. He needed someone with whom he could laugh, and she knew she would not be there much longer. She prayed daily for God to cradle him in His hands when the inevitable happened. Until then, she would try her best to show him that even with difficulties in life, he could still have joy.

Lady Anne passed away just a few months after their discussion. She had given birth to his baby sister five months earlier, and her body never recovered. He was heartbroken. She died just two days before his twelfth birthday. *Sixteen years ago today,* he thought as he watched his horse graze.

Her death was only the first of many difficulties he would face at a young age. His father only lived seven and a half more years and died without warning while Darcy was in his first year at Cambridge. It was a dreadfully wet spring. It drenched the Derbyshire area, and the flooding it brought was devastating to many of Pemberley's tenant families. Darcy's father tried to save the life of a girl who was stuck in a tree with the swelled river rushing by below. The girl was saved, but another felled tree being swept downstream by the rushing river struck his father. George Darcy was rescued from the river, but he would never wake again.

Darcy was away when the tragedy took place, and for the longest time he could not believe it had actually occurred. It did not help that the flooding prevented him from returning home for the funeral. His family urged him to stay and complete his studies, and in a matter of weeks he was finally able to go back home at Pemberley, only to a home he did not even recognize. Darcy and his eight year old sister, Georgiana, were all alone.

Their Uncle Hugh, the Earl of Rosebery, would be their guardian until Darcy's twenty-first birthday, but with his own estate, Dalmeny, just twenty miles away he would be needed at home to oversee the extensive work needed after the floods that also caused much damage there. The earl did what he could to find a suitable steward, then he left his nephew to see to the daily needs at Pemberley. They exchanged enough letters to warrant a personal delivery man to go between the two estates nearly on a daily basis, but the earl was confident in Darcy's ability to run Pemberley just as efficiently as his father before him had done.

Darcy was so busy during those first few months that he did not even realize how much time had passed until the day of his mother's death loomed in front of him. He missed her so much it hurt. He knew his father had missed her too, and it comforted him a little to know they were no longer separated by life and death. He knew they were in heaven looking down on him, and he sometimes felt as if they were guiding him.

*Yes, that is it,* he thought suddenly. *That is exactly what I feel – as if they are guiding me today.* He had felt this way quite often in the beginning, but after a few years he no longer experienced it as frequently. Today, he could feel it again. *I hear you Mother and Father. What do you want me to do? What is so important that you are drawing me out today into the Hertfordshire countryside?*

He scanned the horizon and saw a lady come across the top of the rise in front of him, walking his direction. She was breathtaking! He caught himself staring at her as she stopped and replaced her bonnet over dark, chestnut curls, and pulled on her gloves. She had a faraway look on her features, and he dearly wished to know what memory made her chuckle slightly. She shook her head as if trying to clear her mind, squared her shoulders, and began walking towards him again. Fitzwilliam Darcy knew she would soon change his future.

As she came closer to the stranger, Elizabeth felt as if she knew him. *Where could I have seen him before? Maybe when Jane and I visited Aunt and Uncle Gardiner in London? No, I do not recognize his face, but there is something familiar.* He had the most exquisite, piercing green eyes she had ever seen.

He bowed and asked in a clear baritone voice, "May I be of service to you, madam?"

"Yes, I seem to be lost. If you could please tell me where I am, I would be most appreciative?" she queried with a curtsied.

A shy smile appeared on his lips, "I would take great delight in assisting you,, but I am not from the neighborhood and do not know the area well. Perhaps, if you could tell me where you need to be, I can help you?"

She tilted her head ever so slightly at his familiar accent. "My family lives around here, and I went out for a walk in an unfamiliar direction, and seem to have lost my way. Do you know the way to Meryton from here?"

He furrowed his brow as he thought. *Meryton... Meryton... was that not the little village Bingley said we passed through on our way to Netherfield Park?* "I might be able to help you. Unless my memory has failed me, my friend and I passed through the village of Meryton a few days ago on our way to my friend's new home, Netherfield Park."

Elizabeth was excited to hear a familiar name, "Oh, Netherfield Park is but three miles from where my home, Longbourn, is located. Do you know in which direction that would be?"

"As a matter of fact I do. May I escort you?"

She raised one eyebrow, and with confidence, replied, "I do not see how it would be fitting, sir, as we have yet to be introduced. If you would just point me in the proper direction I would be most grateful."

Chuckling at her impertinence, he pointed behind himself to the left, saying it was about five miles away and that he was glad he could be of service.

Elizabeth thanked him and began to walk back home.

Darcy could not help but turn around and watch as she walked away. *Thank you Mother, thank you Father. You have chosen well.*

# CHAPTER

## I

The days passed and still Elizabeth could not put the stranger out of her mind. She thought she recognized him. When he spoke she could not determine where she had heard that accent before, but it was very familiar. Oddly enough, she was drawn to him and could not determine why.

*He mentioned he was visiting his friend who recently took up residence at Netherfield Park, so he may well be at the Assembly tonight, she told herself. He may even ask me to dance. Perhaps.* She sighed and completed her preparations, hope rising in her heart at the possibility of meeting him again this evening.

"CAROLINE, if you do not hurry we *will* leave without you!" Charles Bingley bellowed through his younger sister's door before he huffed and went downstairs to wait with his other guests. Caroline was not happy with the area in which he decided to lease an estate, and she was determined to make his life here miserable in hopes that he would remove to Town again. According to her the village of Meryton was not grand enough and lacked the class and sophistication she required. *Perhaps Louisa and Hurst will return to London sooner than planned and take Caroline with them,* he thought morosely. Bingley was a patient man, but his sister, younger by two years, was determined to test his every resolve. Now that she was four and twenty years of age he was more than ready for her to marry and be out of his care.

Their mother did her best to keep the flights of fancy in her younger daughter's mind from taking root, but she passed away when Caroline was only eight years of age. Both Caroline and their older sister Louisa were soon sent to boarding school. It was not the most prestigious of institutions, but they did cater to the landed gentry which their father, Thomas Bingley, and likewise his daughter Caroline, coveted so.

Louisa, being fourteen at the time, was well suited with the structure of the classes, and, when the time came for her to leave school, she found her place fairly easily, her friends helping to facilitate her way in society upon her eventual marriage.

Caroline, however, was taunted by some of the girls, and in response she built a false identity of being among the top of society's families. Over the years, she began to believe it herself. The sweet little sister Bingley loved slowly disappeared, and in her place was now a vicious, conniving woman whose one goal in life was to marry into the upper crusts of the gentry class. She had few friends of her own, and most of his friends refused to extend invitations any longer that included her. Bingley was grateful his closest friends — Fitzwilliam Darcy, and his two cousins – still endured her presence. He would hate to lose the most important friendships of his life over his manipulative younger sister and her machinations and constant attempts to attach herself to whomever she deemed worthy of her time.

Bingley and Darcy had met at one of the orientation classes for the new boys when the thirteen year old Bingley began at Eton. Darcy was a year ahead of him, and both boys having lost their mothers, there was an instant connection. Bingley soon gained a reputation for being a gregarious and exuberant individual – the complete opposite of his serious, soulful, and quiet friend. Darcy's father was grateful Bingley came into his son's life. He felt that, somehow from above, his wife had a hand in the boys meeting. After his first year at Eton, Bingley was invited to Pemberley for summer break, and from that time forward every school break was spent at Pemberley or with Darcy's cousins, Alex and Fitz, at their home, Dalmeny. Darcy's father had some contacts at the school, so the next year, and in subsequent years to follow, the boys were roommates at Eton and later at Cambridge.

Bingley's father and grandfather worked hard and invested in well-established industries and businesses in order to save as much money as possible, with the hope of one day buying into the gentry and erasing the taint of trade off the Bingley name. But neither man would live long enough to see it come to pass. The family's hopes and dreams were hung on the shoulders of a young Charles Bingley when, at two and twenty years of age, his father passed away, leaving the Bingley legacy in his hands. When he received word of his father's passing, it was the end of a long, hard relationship. He hated to admit it, and would only voice it once to Darcy, but he now felt a relief that he could be his own man. He knew what the expectations were of him, but he and his father held vastly different views of the future.

Darcy and Bingley both believed the days of trade being a social black mark were soon coming to an end. They could see on the horizon a new age, and they wanted to be a part of it. Both were determined not to tie up all their holdings in land, and instead invested in businesses that would profit them greatly in years to come. After four years Bingley's endeavors paid off and the profits allowed him to begin down the road towards fulfilling his forefathers' dreams. His first step was in leasing this property and learning the basics of land ownership before purchasing his own estate, hopefully in the north, closer to his friends.

Caroline did not know her brother still owned factories, or that many of his *investments* were so closely connected to trade. If she did, she would have had a fit. There would be no safe crystal glass in all of England saved from her fury. No, Bingley was wise to not tell her, but sometimes he wished he could brave that front just to stay her tongue for a few short seconds. She truly was testing his every resolve recently.

*And now they were late.* Bingley was trying to make an impression in this new community, and *this* was not the impression he wished to make. He knew it was nothing more than Caroline wanting to make a grand entrance. Addressing his brother-in-law who patiently sat, waiting on Caroline, he asked "Hurst, perhaps Darcy and I should go on ahead and you and Louisa can come when Caroline is disposed to join us?"

"I am amendable to such a plan," Hurst replied. "At least it would save your carpets from being worn through," he tipped his head indicating Darcy, who was pacing so furiously he did not even hear their conversation.

"Thank you. Hopefully she won't keep you too long," Bingley said as he turned to collect his hat and his friend.

*Will he come? No one from Netherfield has yet to be announced. Perhaps Charlotte will know if they will be here tonight*, Elizabeth mused to herself before turning to find her best friend, Charlotte Lucas. Charlotte's father, Sir William Lucas, was the local magistrate, and if anyone knew of the newcomers intentions, it would be him. He felt it was his duty as magistrate to know what each and every person was doing at all times. To Sir William, even the smallest bit of intelligence was not gossip, but necessary for him to best fulfill his duty to the community.

Seeing her friend halfway across the room, she turned that direction, calling out when she was close enough to be heard, "Charlotte!"

Charlotte, hearing a familiar voice, turned around. "Elizabeth! My, you look pretty tonight! Just *who* are you dressing to impress?"

Elizabeth knew Charlotte would be able to read her face, so she tried not to blush. "No one special; I was just wondering if you knew whether the new residents of Netherfield Park will be joining us this evening? I thought if anyone knew, it would be you or your father."

"Yes, my father would never let *that* bit of gossip slip by without his knowledge, *would he?* Well, you can rest assured your wish shall be granted," Charlotte said with a wink, "Mr Charles Bingley and his party should be here tonight. My father has gone on about it for days now, since he went to pay his call on Netherfield Park and invited them to join us."

"It is not *my* wish Charlotte, I was just curious," Elizabeth said while surreptitiously eyeing her mother, who was sitting over in the corner with Lady Lucas gossiping about the latest scandal to hit their neighbors. As if there were not enough single females around these parts, now it seemed there was a female cousin coming to live with the Long family of Haye Park after the young lady's parents died. The Long's would now have four young ladies of marrying age in their household.

"Yes, I see what you mean. Dear Elizabeth, what would they do without gossip to bring them together? I fear some days your mother and mine would not get along so well without it!" Charlotte quipped.

"'Tis true Charlotte, 'tis indeed true! Theirs is a friendship born of time and held together by their common love of the neighborhood's interests. Perhaps one day that will be us."

They laughed, then turned when they heard the first notes of the music ring through the room, alerting everyone that the first dance was about to begin. Neither lady had promised this dance yet, but there was a group of young men making their way through the crowd and to the ladies now. Charlotte's younger brother, Jonathan, had just returned from his Grand Tour. He immediately acknowledged Elizabeth and asked if she would favor him with a dance. Being just three years older than Elizabeth, the two grew up together and were good friends. Elizabeth and Lucas got along so well that for years Mrs Bennet and Lady Lucas secretly hoped one day their families would be united by the marriage of these two. Neither Lucas nor Elizabeth, however, wished for such a union. They each wanted to marry for love, and while they were great friends, they could never see each other as lovers.

After the first set, Mr Lucas was leading Elizabeth off the dance floor when there was a commotion at the door. All eyes turned to see two young gentlemen enter. One was very slender and tall with blonde hair. His face bore a friendly smile and he looked as if he was there to enjoy the pleasures of the evening. Behind his right shoulder stood the gentleman Elizabeth could not forget. He was taller than his friend by a full head, with a slightly larger frame than his slender friend. He did not have a smile on his face, but Elizabeth could see his vibrant green eyes searching the room for something — *or someone. Is he looking for me*, she wondered?

Darcy was nervous. He did not know her name, but he would never forget her face. She was the most beautiful woman he had ever met. *Will she be there tonight? Will she dance with me? I wonder — what is her name? Julia? No she does not look like a Julia. Lucy? Susan? No, those do not fit her either.*

He was unable to keep his agitation from being seen easily while in the confines of the small carriage, and his friend Bingley leaned over and patted his shoulder to get his attention. "Are you all right, Will? Is there something wrong? Did you receive some news from home today?"

Bingley only called him '*Will*' when he was worried about him, and he was touched to have such a kind-hearted friend. Darcy shook his head, "No, no, everything at home is well... as well as it can be, I suppose. No news today."

*What could it be*, Bingley thought? *He has been agitated for a few days now. He was well when I left the other day to go retrieve Caroline, Louisa, and Hurst from Town, but upon my return I noticed he was fidgety and has not stopped pacing since. What happened while I was gone? I will have to ask Mrs Nichols if she knows of anything. Yes, that is it, if anyone knows, my housekeeper will.* Bingley knew he would get nothing more from his friend, but he had his ways of finding out from others who were more observant than he himself could ever hope to be. Sometimes the most knowledgeable people were the servants who everyone forgot were always there in the shadows, and Charles Bingley was not above using them to his benefit, especially with the recent changes in Darcy's life. Bingley was under strict orders from Darcy's cousin, Colonel Richard Fitzwilliam, to let him know immediately if he was needed. This was to be a relaxing retreat from the pressures of the last few months which had nearly destroyed his friend. *I will have to watch you carefully tonight,* he thought.

The carriage stopped and the two men went into the Assembly Hall. They heard music coming from the double doors at the end of the entrance hall as they stopped to give their gloves, hats, and coats to the servant in the cloak room. By the time they approached the doors the music of the first dance had ended, and they stepped in to see all eyes turn towards them. Bingley loved to meet new people, and his face showed his exuberance. He was excited to be introduced to his new neighbors and find his place among their society. Darcy was not as easy in social situations and his personality tended more towards being unsocial, especially when it felt as if every eye in the place was sizing up his bank book and assets.

Bingley turned around, patting him on the shoulder, and under his breath, said *"Be brave Will,"* before he sauntered off to find Sir William Lucas.

Darcy stared down at his hands, wringing them in nervous contemplation. *Be brave. Be brave. Yes, thank you for the encouragement my friend,* Darcy thought, taking a deep breath. As he raised his eyes to search the crowd, he saw most of the faces turn from him and follow Bingley. *All except one set of dark brown eyes.* His eyes locked onto hers, and he felt a familiarity he had never felt with any other person since his mother. *I have to find out who she is. I must dance with her.* Turning to follow his friend in his search for Sir William Lucas, he hoped the dark haired young lady would be introduced to him soon.

Sarah Johnson

# CHAPTER II

"Elizabeth! Oh, where is that girl! How she tries my nerves at times such as this," Mrs Bennet exclaimed, waving her fan excitedly.

"I will go find her, Mama," Jane answered sweetly, as she turned to locate her dearest sister amongst the crowd. Knowing Elizabeth had just danced with Jonathan Lucas, she determined Elizabeth would most likely be found with the Lucas' on the other side of the room.

Jane saw Elizabeth standing in a daze on Lucas's arm. She went up to her, gently shaking her shoulder, "Lizzy, what is wrong? You look pale." Turning to her sister's escort, Jane replied, "Mr Lucas, perhaps you could retrieve some punch for my sister?"

"It would be my pleasure Miss Bennet. I will return shortly." He turned to make his way through the crowd to the table that held the drinks.

Jane guided Elizabeth over to some chairs and the ladies sat. As Jane tried to calm Elizabeth's shaking hands she could not help but wonder, *what could have caused such a reaction in Lizzy? I have never seen her like this before.*

Jonathan Lucas returned with a glass for each lady, and Jane's loving touch and some punch seemed to calm Elizabeth's nerves and put some color back into her cheeks. As their empty glasses were set aside, she spoke softly, "Lizzy, Mama was looking for you. Let us go now and see to her needs."

Elizabeth and Jane could not have been any more opposite. Jane was a bit taller than her sister, and had Susannah Bennet's golden curls and slate blue eyes. She personified *serene* and exuded a peaceful confidence. If Elizabeth were to describe her older sister in one word, it would be *elegant*. Jane's figure was everything gentlemen desired in a lady. Unfortunately, the gentlemen who had admired her so far did not catch her eye in return. A few spoke flattering words, and one even tried his hand at poetry, but none touched her heart. Jane Bennet might have been a bit naïve in her view of the goodness of others, but she would not marry without a mutual love.

Both Jane and Elizabeth went to stay with their Aunt and Uncle Gardiner in London three of the last four Seasons, and yet they were still not married. Susannah caught the eye of Henry Bennet very quickly and was married at only eighteen years of age. Why her much older daughters were not so blessed yet was sometimes baffling to the mother of five girls. Her one goal in life was to see them wed to worthy gentlemen, and so far she had not accomplished that with any of the three who were out. Tonight would be her chance; new to the neighborhood were two gentlemen, and she was determined to turn her daughter's eyes towards them before any of the other neighborhood ladies could capture their attention.

Jane and Elizabeth joined their mother just as Sir William Lucas began making his way towards them with the two strangers. Mrs Bennet fussed over the girls' posture and brushed a few invisible wrinkles from Jane's dress. Then, smiling, she stood all too eagerly waiting. Mr Bennet, having seen his wife from across the room, escorted their third daughter, Mary, over to join his family, taking his place at his wife's side. A gentle squeeze of her hand calmed her agitated nerves and Susannah could feel the smile on her face relaxing into a more affable welcome. "No need to scare the poor gentlemen, now Susannah," Bennet chortled in his calming way. How he knew when she needed him most was beyond her, but she was ever so grateful for his presence at her side this evening. She squeezed his hand back in thanks as they quietly waited.

While Jane's porcelain skin and golden locks may have come from her mother, her quiet and serene presence came from their father. Elizabeth, on the other hand, had his quick wit and his dark curls and skin. She best resembled her Granny Bennet, her father's mother. There could not be two sisters who were so very different, yet they were the best of friends and shared many confidences with each other. When one needed something, the other was quick to be there to provide it. What Elizabeth had not shared with Jane yet was her encounter with the stranger who was walking towards them now with Sir William Lucas. She was glad for her father's presence beside her mother. *Perhaps he could keep her from having a fit of nerves and scaring off these most becoming gentlemen,* she thought. Her breath caught when she noticed *his* bright green eyes were now looking directly at her.

"Sir William, it is good to see you tonight," Mr Bennet said with a slight bow as his friend stepped up with the two gentlemen in tow.

"Mr Bennet, capital, capital! Nice to have you join us here for this month's dance. You missed a great one last month, but I understand your horse threw a shoe. Your lovely girls were surely missed by the local young gentlemen. The turn out here tonight is much better than last month I dare say." He indicated to the room with his hands. He then turned towards the gentlemen with him, "These gentlemen behind me have asked to be introduced to your lovely family." Mr Bennet nodded and Sir William began the introductions.

Elizabeth looked past Sir William and into the brilliant eyes of the gentleman she had thought constantly about for the last four days. She was lost in a daze of memory and swimming in deep pools of green. Suddenly she felt Jane squeeze her hand and realized the gentleman she had been staring at had asked her to dance. "Oh... yes, I'm sorry. Yes I am free this set," she smiled in reply.

*Elizabeth. Her name is Elizabeth. Somehow that fits her.* Darcy was lost to his own wanderings for a moment. He felt the slight pressure of her hand on his arm as he led her to the dance floor.

He was brought back to the moment when he heard her say, with a coy smile, "I am sorry sir, but I did not catch your name. In this crowd I could not hear properly."

He shook his head a bit to clear the fog that had settled over his mind, "My name? Oh — yes, my name is Fitzwilliam Darcy." With a small contented smile on his face, he whispered just loud enough for her to hear, *"And you are Elizabeth."*

She smiled back at him and saw his eyes dance with merriment. *I wonder if he feels as drawn to me as I am to him? I cannot describe it. It is almost as if I am falling and falling, but at the same time I feel like warm, soft feathers are all around me cushioning everything. Is this what falling in love feels like? I do not know, but somehow I want to find out if it means he will be by my side.*

Neither felt that their dance was lacking even though no words were spoken by either one of them. Hands came together, they twirled around and down the line, in and out of each other's grasp, and yet their eyes never left the other. When the music stopped and both realized everyone around them was leaving the dance floor, Darcy turned to offer his arm and asked if Elizabeth would like a drink. She answered no, and he led her back to her older sister and his friend on the side of the room nearest the fireplace.

While Darcy and Elizabeth were dancing, Bingley and Jane were further down the line, each watching the couple whose eyes never left the other. Bingley realized he was staring and cleared his throat to get his partner's attention, "So, Miss Bennet, you are the eldest in your family?"

Jane, shifting her focus back to her companion, sweetly smiled and replied in the affirmative, "Yes, I am the eldest."

"I am the middle between two sisters. We were late because of my younger sister, so Mr Darcy and I came on ahead and my brother-in-law should be bringing my sisters along shortly. I am ever so glad we came ahead, as I now have this opportunity to dance with you," Bingley could not help but grin.

"I am glad you did Mr Bingley," Jane said calmly, looking down so she did not miss a step in the dance. When her eyes came back up to her partner's face, she caught herself smiling just like him. Jane felt that perhaps she had finally found someone worthy of her time, and set about quietly, in her own way, getting to know this most affable man in front of her. When the dance ended, neither one wished to end their conversation, so Bingley led Jane over to a less crowded area of the room. A few minutes later, Darcy walked up with Elizabeth on his arm, and all four amicably chatted through the next dance set.

---

Susannah Bennet was lost in her own thoughts, watching her two eldest daughters on the other side of the room. Each was seated next to one of the two gentlemen from Netherfield Park, and all were laughing. She smiled sweetly as she felt her husband's presence come up behind her. "You have done well tonight my dear," she heard him whisper in her ear as he gently placed his hand on her shoulder.

Turning, she replied, "Yes, I think for once our daughters may have found worthy gentlemen; and here in our own neighborhood, no less."

Bowing slightly while raising her hand to his lips, Bennet asked, "Since you seem to be at leisure at the moment with finding dance partners for our lovely daughters, would you favor me with a turn about the dance floor, Mrs Bennet?"

"Are you certain, my dear?" she said with great concern.

"Have I ever asked something I was not completely prepared to accomplish, Mrs Bennet?" Squeezing her hand, he assured her, "I shall be well my dear. Now will you favor me, or must I find another with whom to dance this set?"

A small giggle escaped her lips as Susannah agreed and turned to accompany him to where their neighbors were lined up for the next set.

When Henry Bennet first laid eyes on Susannah Gardiner, he felt as if he had been hit physically – she was beautiful! She had golden curls, and slate blue eyes. He could get lost in her eyes, and found himself just staring at her when they were first introduced. She was lively and had a bubbly personality, and he very quickly saw the treasure on the inside of her that others easily overlooked. Despite her father being a country solicitor, he knew she was just what he needed.

His family was not in agreement with his decision, especially since, for over two hundred years, there were only daughters of gentlemen added to the family. He and his cousin Thaddeus Collins had nearly come to blows when Collins insulted Bennet's bride. Bennet, though, did not care what any of his family thought. He had lived out his youth and had been looking for several years for a bride. He knew what was and was not available to a man of his small fortune. He might be of the gentry, but he was not wealthy. His father had depleted the funds of Longbourn, and it would take years to regain what had been lost over just one generation of mishandling. At two and thirty years of age, he had looked for many years for a lady who could be his helpmate, and he found her in the young and vivacious, eighteen year old Susannah Gardiner. Not needing his family's approval, he had married her quickly.

His mother, Rose Bennet, was wary of Susannah for several months, but after watching her only living child with this young lady he had chosen, she finally concluded that they were a perfect match. Bennet kept her nerves at bay, and Susannah added joy to his life. Against the rest of her husband's family, she gave her approval of the match. She found that Susannah filled a place in her heart left empty by the four children she had birthed but never had the opportunity to see become adults. Susannah's own mother died when she was very young, and she learned a lot from Mrs Bennet in those early years.

After years of marriage and life with children, Henry and Susannah grew closer in some ways, but in other ways they grew apart. Henry would sit in his study avoiding the noise of having six females in the house, and Susannah would parade around trying to garner his attention by flitting and fluttering noisily from here to there and back again. Some days it was quite comical to the outsider how they treated each other. It would seem they could not stand each other at times, but they each knew there was love deep down.

That all changed two and a half years ago. Bennet was in a carriage accident, and the possibility of him losing his life so easily projected the two to a new level in their relationship. Together, they had been through so much over the years, and they did not wish to miss out on more just because of letting life get in the way. So they changed their habits and began having breakfast together every morning and time alone every evening for just the two of them.

Susannah's nerves were in constant turmoil since she lost a baby nearly thirteen years ago. It was their long awaited son, but he was born too early and did not survive. What was worse, the birth was so traumatic on Susannah's body that she was unable to have any more children. It devastated the couple. Without a son, their home would be entailed away when Bennet died. While they loved their daughters, Susannah could not see in them the hope for the future she had seen in their son. She missed him terribly every day, even though he was not in their lives very long. For ten years the effects of little Luke's death loomed over them. However, when Bennet's own life was almost lost two years ago, they knew they must renew their devotion to each other. Henry loved Susannah, and

Susannah loved Henry, and they would not let anything else from the past intrude upon their happiness or their future again.

Seeing the faraway look in her eye as he led her across the room, Bennet knew what she was thinking. He squeezed her hand again, bringing her eyes back to his, and he smiled broadly at her. She cleared her mind of her memories of the past, and with a loving look at the devoted husband by her side, smiled and lined up for the dance. Bennet's calming presence beside her reminded Susannah that while they would like to see their daughters married and well settled, they agreed that only affection would do for them. Could Jane and Elizabeth find such regard for these gentlemen? She had high hopes that they were worthy of her daughters' love.

Sarah Johnson

# CHAPTER

## III

Caroline was angry. She was more than angry — she was *furious!* She had been left behind! *The nerve of him to leave me! How could he! He has gone too far this time,* she thought. She refused to put up with such treatment!

David Hurst sat in the corner of the drawing room, drink in hand, and seemingly forgotten by his wife and her sister on the other side of the room. Hurst and Louisa had waited a respectable amount of time, and then he cancelled the order for the carriage to be readied. *If Caroline was going to be this late, then they would just not go.* Not being inclined to dancing himself, this did not upset Hurst in the least. He was happy to go for Bingley's sake, but he would prefer to be upstairs, with his lovely wife, and without Caroline this evening. Bingley and Darcy were gone for over an hour when Caroline decided to appear downstairs, and she did not take the news well. Perhaps she would give herself a headache with her raging and retire soon, and then they could sneak past her door and hide out in his room.

No such luck would befall Louisa and David Hurst tonight. Caroline would rail and rage for two more hours before Bingley and Darcy returned. When they refused to come into the drawing room and instead retired to the billiards room where they could hide from Caroline and have a nightcap, Hurst decided to sneak out of the door closest to where he sat and join them. *Poor Louisa,* he thought, *I will have to tell Mrs Nichols she deserves a breakfast tray with a pink rose and her favorite chocolate indulgence tomorrow morning for having to put up with her sister tonight.*

Hurst sought out the housekeeper to pass on his request, and then he went to find his brother-in-law. The men enjoyed a quick game of billiards and a drink, all the while listening to Bingley talk of *the angel* at the dance. Each having been worn out by their respective activities that night, they soon retired. Hurst might

not have danced and talked the night away with two *lovely sisters*, as Bingley and
Darcy had done, but he felt as if he had been through a war listening to
Caroline. On his way past Bingley' study, he asked his brother-in-law if he could
borrow his desk for a minute. He quickly wrote Louisa a note, found the closest
servant to deliver it to his wife, then went upstairs to await her in their
chambers. Caroline had given them separate rooms, but Louisa preferred to
share with him. Over the years, he grew accustomed to her presence by his side,
and he knew he would never get to sleep if she was not with him tonight. He
counted himself lucky that, although he did not know his wife well before they
were married, he had ended up with the better of the two Bingley sisters. He
was not sure what he would have done with himself if Caroline had been the
bride his father chose. He shuddered with that thought, and climbed the last of
the stairs.

After passing the note off to two other servants, one footman was finally brave
enough to interrupt Miss Bingley in the drawing room to deliver the note to
Mrs Hurst.

"Excuse me madam, I have a note for Mrs Hurst," he said as he opened the
door, holding out the silver tray.

"A note? Who would send you a note at this late hour, Louisa? Give that to me,
and get out of here!" Caroline barked at the lone footman.

"Caroline, since I have not read the note, I cannot tell you who has sent it; if
you will give it to me, I will find out." Louisa said with as much patience as she
could muster.

Caroline acted as if she did not even hear her sister. She was holding up the
note to the light of the candle to see if she could read through the paper. When
that did not work, she sighed, tossed it back onto the tray, and with an
exaggerated, very unladylike yawn, she bid Louisa good night, said they could

return to their conversation tomorrow morning, and swept out of the room with a flourishing swoosh of her dress.

Louisa kept her mouth closed, but just barely. *Tomorrow morning I plan to sleep in, dear sister, and YOU will not be with me!* Louisa opened her note, and ran her finger along her husband's scrolling penmanship. She loved the way he wrote, so masculine and perfect. She silently chuckled at the words on the page, and stood to retire for the night. Passing the footman who had delivered the note, she handed him the coin her husband thought to place in the note for such a brave soul, then turned to retire to the loving embrace of her husband, David.

Elizabeth heard a whisper at her door, *"Lizzy... Lizzy, are you awake?"* She lit the candle on her bedside table and went to open her door.

"Mary? What are you doing still awake?" Elizabeth pulled her into the room so they would not wake the others.

"I am sorry if I disturbed you, but I just could not sleep with Lydia's snoring. May I sleep in here with you tonight?"

"Lydia?" Elizabeth asked with a confused look on her face. "Why is Lydia in your room?"

"I do not know for certain," Mary rubbed her cold arms, "all I know is, when we returned home from the Assembly, she was in my bed. She mumbled something about Kitty being mean to her and that she was never speaking to her again."

Elizabeth rolled her eyes at her youngest sister's antics, "Oh those two!" Pulling Mary with her they curled up in her bed. "The nights are getting colder and I am certain my room is the draftiest room in this house."

"It's much colder in here than in my room." With a sly smile, she conspiratorially whispered, *"Perhaps we should make Lydia sleep in here and you and I can go to my room instead!"*

"Now there's the Mary we all love," Elizabeth answered with a grin. "What was amiss with you tonight? You did not look as if you were too pleased with the Assembly. I know dancing is not your favorite pastime, but you seemed almost despondent tonight."

Mary looked down at her hands, and quietly answered, "I happened to overhear Jonathan and James Lucas discussing the dancing. Jonathan was encouraging his brother to ask me to dance, and James answered that I was *'not tolerable enough to tempt him'.*" Mary was wringing her hands and she felt tears welling up in her eyes.

"Oh, Mary! How terrible!" Elizabeth answered while pulling her sister into a tight embrace.

"I know I am not as outgoing as you or as poised as Jane, but how am I ever to find a husband if even the neighborhood gentlemen will not favor me with a dance?" Mary said as she began to weep. She pulled the thick glasses off her face and tried to stop the flow of tears with the sleeve of her nightgown.

"Oh Mary, I am so very sorry. If I know Jonathan, he was likely playing the concerned older brother by reminding James of his duty to dance more since there were more ladies than gentlemen there. I think maybe James has a little more maturing to do if that is how he thinks of you. Perhaps his time at Oxford has not been the best spent yet." Putting her finger under Mary's chin to raise it, she looked into her sisters brown eyes, "You are just as lovely as any other member of our family, even with your glasses, and I dare say what you and I lack in stature we more than make up for in personality which is not easily forgotten. We may not have Jane's blue eyes and blonde hair, but we aren't the Longs either," Lizzy said with a wink.

Mary tittered slightly while drying her eyes once more and replacing her glasses. The Long girls were pretty, but they had noses that were... well... long. All the neighborhood girls, even the Longs' themselves, jested about their noses.

"Thank you Lizzy. You always seem to know just what to say to bring me cheer."

"In all seriousness, Mary, one day a gentleman will catch your eye. He will think the best of you, and will love you for who you are. Until then, just have patience. I know Mama was married at only eighteen years of age, and she can sometimes be effusive about us being married soon, but she would never want to urge you into a marriage that did not form on love and respect." Mary nodded her head in acknowledgment of what Lizzy was saying. "And just remember, Papa is fourteen years older than Mama. Do not limit yourself to only those few in this neighborhood who are your own age like Mr James Lucas. Next season it is your turn to go visit Aunt and Uncle Gardiner in London, and who knows who you shall meet then! Perhaps your *knight in shining armour* is yet to be introduced to you! Patience, my dear sister; after all, I am one year your elder, and Jane is three years your elder, and we are not married yet, are we? And we have each been to London *three Seasons*!"

"Maybe not *yet*, but I saw how you were looking at Mr Darcy tonight, Lizzy. Do you care to tell me what you think of him?" Mary queried in her skeptical manner.

Elizabeth shifted to her back, put her hands behind her head, and cuddled further down into the mattress. "He is the most interesting gentleman I have ever encountered, Mary; so quiet and soulful, yet strong, and he has a very dry wit. He has a depth to him that I have never seen in another gentleman before. The few times I have seen him, I have felt drawn to him somehow."

"*Few times?* Just how many times *have* you seen him Lizzy?"

With a small chuckle, Elizabeth told Mary of her adventure the previous week and how he saved her from *certain doom*.

Mary laughed, "The way you tell it Lizzy, he was your *knight in shining armour* who rode in on his white steed to save the day!"

"As a matter of fact," Lizzy said while wiggling her eyebrows, "he did ride a white horse!"

Both girls broke out in laughter so boisterous they were nearly in tears. They soon heard a small knock at the door and Jane poked her head in, "Shhhh... what has you giggling so at nearly midnight?"

"If you come and join us here on the bed, we have some interesting stories to tell you Jane," Mary said confidently. Elizabeth just shook her head in amusement and scooted over to make more room for her sisters. *I have a feeling it will be a late night for us,* she thought.

<hr />

The gentlemen awoke earlier than the rest of the house. Darcy was just finishing a small repast with Bingley when a servant delivered a letter to him. He quickly finished his coffee and excused himself, intent upon reading the missive from his aunt it in the quiet of the library.

He settled into a chair and broke the seal. He was nervous to find out how his sister, Georgiana, was faring, but he could hardly bring himself to read it for fear of it containing unpleasant news. He remembered Bingley's encouraging words from the night before at the dance — *"Be brave Will."* He unfolded the letter and began.

*September 29, 1811*
*Pemberley, Derbyshire*

*Dear Darcy,*

*I know you are in dire straits to learn if this letter contains distressing news, so I will assuage your fears immediately and tell you — it does not.*

Darcy could feel the instant release of tension in his shoulders and he took a deep breath as he let the opening words strengthen him. *Georgiana is not worse,* he thought hopefully. He lifted the pages and once again read his aunt's words.

*Now I can write of what I most desire you to know.*

*Happy birthday, my dear nephew! I trust you are beginning to settle in there and have been acquiring some much-needed rest? You worried us all these last months. Are you enjoying yourself, Darcy? I pray daily for your complete recovery.*

*There has not been much change to report with regard to Georgiana. She still remains in her rooms. Dr Foxx has proposed we begin this next month with urging her to do more than is her habit, and your uncle and I have been working out the details of how we are to accomplish such a task. I must say, we are placing a large amount of hope on the new pianoforte you ordered in hopes it will draw her out again.*

*Speaking of the pianoforte, it was delivered late yesterday. Oh my – it is such a beautiful instrument! I sat with Georgiana while Alex and Fitz helped position it in her sitting room. Your sister was eager to hear the tones coming from the other room as the strings were tuned, and when Fitz picked her up and carried her in to see it, she was captivated. She sat on the bench for at least half an hour, lovingly inspecting everything she could. I pray it is a good sign of her continued interest in the instrument.*

*It easily fit beside the large window, just as you thought it would. It has been placed just perfectly so Georgie can see out into your mother's rose garden while she is playing, though with the weather turning colder there are not as many blooms.*

*Alex intends to give a little concert today, and we will encourage Georgie to practice as much as she can, as Dr Foxx believes it will strengthen her hand. I am certain she will grow strong enough to write you a short letter again soon. Her grip is getting better, but the quill is still awkward in her fingers, and she does not wish to write to you again until her script is more legible. It brings a smile to her face when she receives your letters though. She sleeps with them under her pillow every night, and they are all worn through with how often she pores over the words you write to her. She has been very worried for you. She says you are all she has left, and she does not wish to ever see you as you were when you left Pemberley. It frightened her so; it frightened us all I must say. We are here now, so your place is to rest and get well while we help your sister with her recovery.*

*Fitz received word this morning that he is needed back in London, so he will be leaving tomorrow. I believe Alex will be going with him, but your Uncle Hugh and I will, of course, be staying here with Georgie.*

*I pray we soon find the motivation your sister needs to continue on this long and arduous road to recovery. Perhaps she would enjoy going to Town for Christmas? It may be best for her as there is a broader range of masters and tutors. She mentioned just the other day that she wishes to learn German, however Mrs. Annesley does not know enough to teach it with confidence. Perhaps a master can be found to encourage this new venture.*

*It has been a long year, but everything will be well, my dear nephew. Everything will be well.*

*With all our love,*
*Helen Rosebery*

*p.s. Georgie started crying when she saw your gift for her. She said only you would give her a gift on your birthday! Thank you!*

Darcy folded the letter and placed it in his pocket. *Yes dear Aunt, everything will be well! If you only knew!*

He moved to the desk in the corner and wrote a letter in return to his aunt, as well as one to his sister. He was unsure what to say about the lady who had consumed his thoughts since coming to Hertfordshire, so he decided to leave that out of his letter – for now.

When the task was completed, he joined his friend, suggesting they take a ride and, perhaps, make a call on *certain neighbors* whom they met last night at the Assembly.

Jane and Elizabeth awoke earlier than Mary, so they went to Jane's room to dress.

"Did you see Mama and Papa dancing last night, Lizzy?"

Elizabeth stopped brushing her hair, and answered with a sweet smile, "Yes, I did notice. It is the first time they have danced since..." she got choked up and could not finish.

Neither could imagine what life would have been like now if the accident had not taken place. They were the only two out in society when it happened, so they each remembered far more than their other sisters did regarding their lives before the accident. Their mother had calmed tremendously, and their parent's relationship had been strengthened through the experience, but it was an emotional road for them all.

Jane hugged Elizabeth from behind, both looking into the mirror with a faraway look to their eyes as they each remembered the day two and a half years ago that changed their family forever. "We must not allow ourselves to become maudlin over the past," Jane said quietly. "I have an idea that is sure to lift your spirits. We have not taken the time lately to go see Mr Gouldings horses. Perhaps we can find a few extra treats in the stable. I am certain our sisters would like to join us."

"Yes, from what Mary said of Lydia last night, I think she and Kitty need an outing. Perhaps Papa will allow us to stop for some ribbons on our way through Meryton?" She put down the brush and turned to give her sister a hug, "Thank you Jane."

"For what?"

"Thank you for not allowing me to become downhearted about Papa."

"Well, as Granny Bennet used to say, *'think only of the past as its remembrance gives you pleasure'*."

The two completed their toilette and received permission from their father to go on their outing, including stopping in Meryton on their way home. They all dressed and soon descended the stairs, Kitty and Lydia eagerly discussing ribbon colors while Mary, Elizabeth, and Jane followed behind.

Hearing voices in the sitting room, Jane asked the housekeeper, "Does my mother have a visitor, Mrs Hill?"

She smiled as she helped the eldest into her pelisse, "Yes indeed; Mr Bingley, from Netherfield, and his friend, Mr Darcy, have come to call." At Elizabeth's blush, the housekeeper asked, "Would you like me to inform your parents that you are ready to leave now?"

"Oh, yes," Lydia squealed. "Perhaps they will see fit to introduce us to their guests," she said in a giggle.

Elizabeth looked askance at her younger sister, "If Papa felt the need to introduce you, he would have called for you. No, I will go in myself and inform him." She tied her bonnet and began pulling on her gloves as she stepped into the sitting room. All eyes turned toward her and she tried not to stare as Mr Darcy stood, along with Mr Bingley. She stepped to her father's side and laid her hand on his arm, "It is not necessary," she said as she saw him trying to stand as well. "I just came to tell you we are leaving for our walk."

Mr Bennet patted Elizabeth's hand as he quietly replied, "Thank you; I am quite sore after dancing last night."

"Yes, I imagine so."

Darcy, overhearing how fatigued their host was, offered, "My friend and I were just leaving as well. May we escort you on your walk, Miss Elizabeth?" He turned to the father, "That is, if it pleases you, sir?"

Elizabeth could not help but smile as she replied, "On behalf of my sisters, I thank you sir, but it is not necessary."

"Necessity is not always the force which pushes us into action, though, is it?" he said with a smirk.

Mr Bennet could not help but feel his daughter had met her match with this gentleman. "I thank you for your offer, Mr Darcy. I am sure my daughters would appreciate the company on their walk, and we can finish our discussion on the morrow when you return." He turned to Elizabeth and smiled, "Mr Darcy and Mr Bingley have been chess champions for several years at their school and club, and Mr Darcy has challenged me to a game."

She chuckled, "Are you certain it was not *you* who has challenged *him*, Papa?"

"Well, it may have been as you say. Either way, he and Mr Bingley are to return tomorrow for a match."

Elizabeth turned to the visitors, "You may have quite the battle on your hands as my father rarely loses."

Darcy chided, "Nor do I, Miss Elizabeth."

The two men took their leave and followed Elizabeth out of the room. Kitty and Lydia were introduced to the two gentlemen and soon the group was on their way.

Susannah took her husband's arm and helped him stand, "I insist upon your retiring, as you are clearly in need of rest." When he started to say something she put her finger over his lips as a mother would a small child, "Now, I will hear none of it. You did more at the dance last night than your leg is used to doing in a week's time, and I will see that you rest this afternoon."

Bennet kissed the tip of her finger that lay on his lips, "How can I argue with such sound reasoning?" He took his cane in one hand and put his other arm out for his wife, "Care to join me?" He could not help but feel loved when she looked back at him with those bright blue eyes that drew him to her the first time they met.

Sarah Johnson

# CHAPTER

## IV

If you will all wait right here, we have something to gather before we leave on our walk," Elizabeth said as she and Jane turned towards the stable. They returned with a brown paper wrapped bundle, and the group started out on their walk.

The two youngest Bennets walked ahead, eagerly discussing the flowers that lined the walk and enjoying the bright sunshine of the autumn day.

"Would you allow me to carry that for you, Miss Bennet?" Bingley asked.

"Yes, thank you, Mr Bingley."

He took the package from her, "It is not heavy, but it is an awkward shape. What, may I ask, is in here?"

Elizabeth grinned, "Why not see if you can guess, Mr Bingley?"

He felt the package, turning it this way and that and trying his best to determine what it was. Finally he shook his head, "I have not a clue. Maybe my friend will have more luck."

The package was passed to Darcy, and he stopped walking, closing his eyes as his hands examined the contours of the brown paper. Lizzy saw a small smile creep onto his face as she started seeing recognition on his demeanor. "I believe it is fruit – apples, a few pears, and some root vegetables – maybe carrots and beets?"

"Very good, Mr Darcy! I am impressed with your astuteness. Yes, apples, pears, carrots, and beets. We are taking these treats to our very *dear friends*."

"Would your *friends* happen to be horses, Miss Elizabeth?"

Chuckling, she again smiled at him, "Why, yes, Mr Darcy they are." The group turned to continue their walk, the two eldest taking the arm of the gentleman beside her as it was offered. "They are very dear to our family, as they helped save our father's life after a terrible accident a few years ago. When we have the time, we like to visit them and give them a few extra treats."

Jane and Mr Bingley kept on chatting amicably about their walk, while Mr Darcy grew very quiet. Elizabeth silently studied the darkness that came over his face, and wondered what affected his demeanor so.

After a few minutes, he turned to her and asked, "Was your father badly injured, Miss Elizabeth?"

"Yes he was."

"Would you mind telling me about it?"

Nodding her head in assent, Elizabeth looked at the ground as she spoke of the accident, "It happened two and a half years ago, and if it were not for a friend of Dr Jones' that he asked to help, I doubt my father would be able to walk today." Looking up at him, she continued the tale. "He was returning from town after a storm when the horses were spooked and lost their footing, sliding in the mud. The carriage rolled over several times and my father was pinned underneath. Sir William Lucas and his son happened to see the accident take place and they immediately rallied the neighbors to help free my father. The horses we are going to visit were used to pull the carriage off him that day.

"Along with some other injuries, his leg was broken in several places. Dr Jones said he was unable to set the leg, so he asked if we would allow him to call in a surgeon friend of his who had dealt with similar types of injuries while in the Army. After examining his leg, Dr Robertson determined there were several fractures in need of being realigned, but he was confident they were clean breaks and would heal if properly set." She looked into the eyes of her companion as she continued, "Many surgeons would have just amputated his leg, Mr Darcy, but not Dr Robertson. It has been a slow healing process for my father; for over a year his bed had to be moved downstairs, as he could not make it up the stairs. He has just recently begun riding his horse again, and when he and my mother danced at the Assembly last night, it was the first time since the accident."

With unshed tears in her eyes, she watched his face as he struggled with some unknown battle. Feeling he needed to open up about something, she asked quietly, "Mr Darcy, do you know someone who has also been hurt?"

Slowing the pace, somehow he knew she could help him accept what had happened. Almost inaudibly, he answered, *"Yes... my sister."* His voice cracked and his eyes filled with unshed tears. Elizabeth quietly rested her other hand on top of the arm with which he was escorting her. He felt the strength and compassion she possessed in her simple touch.

"When you are ready, Mr Darcy, would you please tell me about her?"

He nodded his head in acceptance of her request, and took the handkerchief she held out to him. He dried his eyes and handed it back to her.

Clearing her throat, and stepping up their pace, she smiled up at him and asked, "So, what do you like to give your horse for a special treat?"

He took a deep breath and gently shook his head to clear his mind, chuckled under his breath at her attempt to change the topic, "My horse seems to like parsnips and celery best. He also loves raspberries, though I do not allow too many at a time. My sister spoiled him on those when he was young."

"Your sister sounds like a very sweet person."

"Yes; she is the best." He was appreciative of the way she was able to turn his thoughts to a more positive memory of his sister.

As the group continued down the road, speaking of the weather and the local attractions, Mary quietly listened to the banter back and forth between the two couples. *I hope to one day find someone with whom I can be just as at ease.*

"Oh, look at that pretty pink ribbon, Kitty," Lydia's enthusiastic cry brought her sister's attention to what she saw from several feet away. Lydia and Kitty were not out yet, but they loved to refashion bonnets and help their older sisters re-trim their dresses. Lydia had been given a dress Jane wore years ago, and she had been looking for the perfect pink ribbon to accent it for many months. She excitedly spoke with the clerk about the price and how much she wished to purchase.

"Are you certain you would not be more comfortable outside with Mr Bingley?" Mary asked Mr Darcy.

"Oh, no, I am perfectly content in here, thank you."

"Do you shop for ribbons often then, Mr Darcy?" Mary quipped with a wry smile on her lips.

Chuckling, he answered, "I have guardianship of my younger sister, and have spent many a day going from shop to shop with her. I do not mind accompanying you and your sisters here today. It actually brings back fond memories."

"I would say your sister is truly blessed then, sir, to have you for her guardian." Elizabeth answered.

Looking down, he murmured, *"Sometimes I wonder."*

"Mary… Mary, do you think this color would go well with Jane's new bonnet?" Kitty called as she held a ribbon up to the bonnet in question. Mary excused herself to inspect the ribbon more closely.

"Mr Darcy, I do not know what has brought you to our neighborhood, but I hope you are able to put behind you whatever sadness has been dispensed upon your family. If I can do anything, all you need do is ask. I would love nothing more than to see you smile." Realizing what she just admitted to this man she barely knew, Elizabeth blushed bright red.

He seemed not to notice her discomfort at her own statement, and simply replied, "Thank you Miss Elizabeth; thank you."

"You, sir," she said smiling, "will have to start living by my grandmother's philosophy to *'think only of the past as its remembrance gives you pleasure'*."

He chuckled under his breath – *I could learn a lot from this young lady.*

After they finished with their purchases, they again congregated together to begin their walk back to Longbourn. They strolled along the country road, strewn with the last buds of wild flowers, and spoke about the weather and how long they thought it might stay nice enough for such ventures out of doors. When they arrived at Longbourn, the gentlemen took their leave and rode off towards Netherfield Park, promising they would return on the morrow for a chess match with their father and that they hoped to see the sisters again as well.

"Mr Bingley, I believe it is your turn, sir," Bennet said, clearing his throat loudly after his opponent had been staring out the window for several minutes.

Focusing his attention back to the game, Bingley apologized and made a very amateurish move of putting his queen in play too early. Bennet countered, putting his opponent in check, and within one more move he had won the game. Not seeming to care much for chess today, Bingley rose from the chair and walked over to the window with the pretext of stretching, but he was fooling no one.

"Mr Darcy, I hope you are more of a challenge than your friend over there, or I shall grow bored very quickly." Bennet joked.

A small smile formed on his lips as he shook his head at his friend and took his seat across the board from Mr Bennet. "I am not as easily distracted as my friend. I believe I am ready for you, sir."

The first few moves were chosen quickly by both, but the game finally slowed down as each of them tried to determine which moves would warrant the best outcome. Darcy, having played many different people he did not know well, had the advantage over Bennet, but the older man was not willing to give in so easily. A knock at the door halted the game as Bennet called for the person to enter.

Mrs Hill opened the door, stating, "Mrs Bennet thought you and your guests might like some tea, sir." She put the tray down on the table, then turned to hand him the note her mistress had also sent to her husband.

"Thank you Mrs Hill, and thank Mrs Bennet for her thoughtfulness as well," Bennet could not help but smile. The housekeeper left the room and he turned back to his guest. "If you will excuse me for just a minute, sir," he said holding up the note in his hand.

"Take all the time you need," Darcy answered as his attention was once again focused on studying the game board in front of him.

After reading the note, Bennet announced, "Well, Gentlemen, I am instructed to extend an invitation to join us for dinner this evening, if you are not otherwise engaged?"

Turning from the window, Bingley answered with a smile, "No sir, I cannot think of anything we have planned for this evening. We would be delighted to stay; thank you. May I use your desk to write a note to my sister explaining our change of plans?"

Concentrating on his chess game once again, Bennet waved his hand over towards the desk, "Go right ahead, Mr Bingley. If your family would like to join us, please extend the invitation to them as well."

"Thank you, sir, I will ask if they are engaged." Bingley quickly wrote a note to his sister Louisa, and Mrs Hill was called to dispatch the stable boy to Netherfield Park immediately. When Bingley stepped back over to the window he noticed that the object of his attention, Miss Bennet, was no longer outside picking flowers with her sister. He wandered back over and sat down to watch the game in progress.

An hour later, as the last moves on the chessboard were being fought out by the two well-matched players, Mrs Hill again knocked on the door and delivered another missive, this time for Mr Bingley.

Reading it, Bingley replied, "My younger sister is not feeling well, so the invitation has been declined by my family." Bingley caught Darcy's eye, knowing as his friend did that Caroline was simply not interested in extending her friendship to anyone in this neighborhood.

After another half an hour, Bennet could feel his leg begin to ache, "It seems this is a draw, Mr Darcy. Neither one of us is willing to concede; however I must say you have been a very inventive opponent. I thank you for your time and attention, sir." Turning to face both men, he continued, "If you do not mind though, I will turn your entertainment over to my wife and daughters." Rubbing his leg, he quipped, "If I am to be worth anything this evening, I will need to rest for a little while."

"Miss Elizabeth mentioned you had difficulties due to an accident," Bingley answered. Looking outside and seeing the eldest three Bennet sisters again in the garden, he smiled, "Perhaps we should stretch our legs with a walk amongst your fine garden, sir."

Mr Bennet looked over Bingley' shoulder out at his daughters, "A fine prospect it is, Mr Bingley. My wife and girls love their flowers. I am certain they would appreciate your presence on their afternoon stroll. Thank you, gentlemen; I have greatly enjoyed our chess games, and look forward to future matches."

Bingley and Darcy left Mr Bennet's study through the door leading out into the garden, and quickly caught up with the three sisters. "Miss Bennet, Miss Elizabeth, Miss Mary," Bingley addressed them as each man bowed. "May we escort you on your walk through the garden?" Bingley beamed as he held out his arm to Miss Bennet. *She is gorgeous; simply an angel,* he thought. As the couple walked off, oblivious to the others in the group, Mr Darcy offered one arm to Miss Elizabeth and his other arm to Miss Mary.

They strolled along, Darcy telling Elizabeth of the chess game against their father, until Mary stumbled. Mr Darcy was quick to catch her arm, no harm coming to her, but she thought it best to sit while the others continued their stroll. Mary watched the two couples and could not help but smile at the attention both these gentlemen were giving to Jane and Elizabeth. Remembering what James Lucas said at the Assembly, that of her being *only tolerable,* she could not help but smile at the couples. *Neither of these gentlemen would dare say something so insulting about one of my sisters,* she thought. A bird flying overhead pulled her attention from the couples. She reached into the inside pocket of her cape and pulled out her book, thumbing through the pages until she came to where she had stopped reading earlier. She was soon lost within the pages of her novel.

Louisa entered the drawing room with her mending basket in hand. "Good afternoon, Caroline," she said with a smile as she saw her sister sitting there.

"Where were you all morning, Louisa?"

*Hiding from you! No, I cannot be so rude,* she thought, *however much I wish to do just that.*

"Well?" Caroline said, impatiently drumming her fingers on the arm of her chair.

"I slept later than usual, and when I did finally arise, I spent some time catching up on my correspondence."

"If I had known you were to be so engaged, I would have gone with our brother and Mr Darcy to make some calls this morning. They came back just a short time ago, and neither one will answer as to who they were visiting every day this last week."

*Hmmm,* Louisa thought to herself, *could these neighbors be the Bennet sisters?* "If you had come down earlier yesterday, you could have met some of the neighbors yourself, Caroline. I had a lovely visit with Mr and Mrs Bennet and their daughters."

44

Caroline rolled her eyes at her sister as she stood to leave the room. "Yes, so I heard – *all five* of their daughters. Lovely indeed! If *this* is how you are to be today Louisa, I will find my own entertainment. There has to be something to do in this forgotten wilderness." Huffing loudly, she went to the music room to practice the pianoforte, hoping Mr Darcy would hear her playing and be impressed with her newest challenging piece.

Louisa sat mending a shirt until she saw her husband's head poking around the door frame. When he spied her sitting on the couch alone, he stepped in to greet his wife. "Good afternoon, my dear."

Smiling as he leaned down to kiss her cheek, she replied, "Good afternoon to you as well, David."

"I was certain I heard Caroline in here, but I now see it is just you."

"Oh, she was here, but she did not prefer my company any longer. I think I heard her playing the pianoforte a few minutes ago, so I believe you are safe for now."

"What has put her in such a snit today?" he asked as he sat down near his wife.

"My brother and Mr Darcy called on *some neighbors* again this morning, and they refused to discuss with Caroline who it was when they came home a little while ago."

"Ahhh, I wonder if it was *the lovely Bennet sisters,* whom you had the pleasure of meeting yesterday?"

"I was wondering the same thing."

"Hmmm... maybe it's time I go track down my brother-in-law, and find out what pleasures they have been up to this fine morning. Take care my dear, you know how Caroline reacted last time your brother showed any interest in a country gentleman's daughter that *she* did not hand pick for him. If his interest in Miss Jane Bennet is anything like it seems, we could be in for some hard times ahead with Caroline."

"I know," she said with a sigh. She looked up from the shirt in her hands, "I was thinking – perhaps we should go visit your family for the Christmas season? It would give us a reason to be away from Caroline, and you know how she is at that time of year. We have stayed in London for the last three winters because of her, but I feel that this year we would do best to be gone for a while."

David Hurst looked at his wife's concerned face and determined that, even if it were not to visit his family, he would take his wife away from her sister for a while. "Yes, that does sound like a good idea. I will write to my father about their plans, and hopefully we will be able to join them." He said gently, kissing her cheek before he stood. "Well my dear, I am off to find that brother of yours. Maybe I can talk him into going shooting this afternoon."

# CHAPTER

## V

Bingley leaned over and whispered in his sister's ear, exasperation clearly heard in his voice, *"Louisa, why did you have to invite Caroline?"*

"I did not *invite* her; she decided to come along on her own. I did not want to insult the Bennets by not returning their call after such a lovely time the other day. *What was I to do?"* she whispered back, hoping Caroline was far enough away in the carriage to not hear them. Fortunately her husband was keeping Caroline's attention with one of his stories.

"She will insist we only stay for a half an hour, at most, and I had planned to stay longer today," Bingley complained.

"Why did you not ride instead? We could have returned home in the carriage with Caroline and you and Mr Darcy could have stayed longer."

"I did not want to smell of horse today," he pouted.

"You could have brought one along so you could return later."

Bingley groaned in frustration. "I wish you had suggested that *before* we left Netherfield."

Louisa tried to stifle her chuckle, but she just couldn't.

"What is so humorous?" Caroline asked.

"I am certain she was just listening to my story," Hurst offered, smiling at his wife.

"Yes, my husband's story," Louisa nodded her thanks for his quick response.

Caroline immediately changed the conversation. "Mr Darcy, we have not seen much of you these last few weeks even though you are a guest in our home."

"Caroline," Bingley warned, "he is *my* guest and *I* have seen plenty of him since we came."

"Charles, I am not trying to be rude, but I find it odd that five of the last eight evenings he has excused himself early for *business*. I know he is a busy man, but it just seems a little extreme to me." Her false smile oozed with disdain.

*Why does she think she has the right to question me? She has no say so in my life,* Darcy thought. Fixing his fierce glare on Caroline, and making her shrink back in her seat, he answered frostily, "I have had a great deal of *business* to take care of lately."

"Oh, look, we are here," Bingley said to the stony silence of the carriage. *Thank God*, he thought to himself.

"There is a carriage coming this way," Kitty announced to the sitting room as she entered and sat down.

"Oh, my! Do you know who it is?" Mrs Bennet's eagerness beamed.

"No, I could not tell. Perhaps it is Mr Bingley and Mr Darcy once again," Kitty eyed Jane and Elizabeth as they both blushed.

Mr Bennet joined his family in the sitting room. Upon entering, he saw Lydia peering out the window, and he sat beside his wife as he cleared his throat. No words were needed; Lydia turned back to her seat and folded her hands properly with a look of contrition on her face. She and her father had been talking lately of the comportment of a young lady, and what he expected from her as she neared the age of her coming out. She had a few years still to go, but his expectations were quite high. She had just recently been allowed to share a bedroom with Kitty and to sit in on some calls with her mother and sisters, and she did not wish to be moved back to the nursery again or totally barred from what small society she was allowed. Bennet gently squeezed his wife's hand as a showing of his presence beside her, and he felt Susannah immediately calm.

"Mr Bingley, Mr Darcy, Mr and Mrs Hurst, and Miss Bingley, sir," Mr Hill announced as five people stepped through the door. Elizabeth stood to welcome the visitors and was taken aback at three of the members of the party. She had noticed the resemblance of Mr Bingley to his sister, Mrs Hurst, when they called on Netherfield a few days ago. However, the men did not join them for tea, so this was the first time she saw them standing side by side. When her gaze fell to the unknown lady in the group, she immediately knew it to be Mr Bingley's other sister, as she was nearly identical to them as well. She was shocked. Never before had she observed three people who looked more alike! They were all tall and slender, with his sisters almost as tall as Mr Bingley himself, and they had the same color of light blonde hair and blue eyes. The most noticeable difference was that Mrs Hurst and Mr Bingley both had smiles on their faces, while Miss Bingley wore a scowl. Mr Darcy and another man stood behind the siblings, and she guessed this other man to be Mr Hurst. He was the same height at Mr Bingley, but not as slender, and he had light brown hair. Her eyes fixed upon Mr Darcy, and she smiled seeing that he was watching her reaction.

Introductions were made and everyone took a seat. Darcy sat in a chair near Elizabeth, and the smile on his face, though slight, was a sight to see. In the two weeks since she had first encountered him, he became an integral part of her day. She could see herself falling in love with this man. He was extremely tall, with broad shoulders, but his eyes held such compassion and they drew her in. It was almost as if some force she could not control was pulling the two together. Thinking she might be falling in love, Elizabeth mentioned this feeling to Jane one night, certain her sister would confirm her suspicions, but Jane did not understand what she meant. Jane said she found Mr Bingley to be amiable and of course he was nice looking, but what Lizzy described was not at all what she felt. This baffled Elizabeth as she was certain her sister was falling in love with Mr Bingley. If what Jane felt was truly love, then what was she feeling? She did not understand it; Elizabeth only knew that when she looked into those bright green eyes of the man sitting near her, she felt as if she was just where she belonged.

Caroline Bingley curtly avoided even the simplest of acknowledgements and sat down in a chair near Mr Darcy. Mrs Hurst and Mrs Bennet spoke of some recipes Louisa promised to bring from their cook, with Mr Hurst interjecting his own opinions on ragout into the conversation. Caroline rolled her eyes at her brother-in-law; she just did not understand him at all. How Louisa could have ever found him worthy of her hand was beyond her. She looked over again and saw Louisa sitting there with a smile on her face and a genial air about her. She could not believe her sister was enjoying the association with these people.

Turning towards the group of ladies sitting nearby, Caroline decided she would show Mr Darcy how well she could handle those below them in society. Interrupting the conversation already in progress, she asked, "Miss Elizabeth, do you ever go to Town?"

Turning towards Miss Bingley, Elizabeth answered, "My sister Jane and I have gone three of the last four Seasons, and our family has gone a few times over the years to visit our relatives there."

"Oh, you have relatives in town; would I happen to know them?"

"I do not know, they do not live near Grosvenor Square, and Mrs Hurst mentioned the other day that is where she and her husband reside. Where is it you reside Miss Bingley?"

She ignored the impertinent question back to her. "Just where do your relations live if not on the most fashionable side of London?"

"Gracechurch Street."

"Oh? And where exactly *is* Gracechurch Street?" Caroline sneered, knowing full well where it was.

"Near Cheapside" Elizabeth said with a raised eyebrow.

Caroline answered with her nose in the air, "No, you are correct; I would never go to that area of Town."

Mr Darcy cut into the conversation, "It is a shame Miss Bingley, as I have found the best warehouse for imported goods is in that area. The name is *'Gardiner's Goods'*."

Elizabeth beamed, "That is my uncle's warehouse, sir."

"Your uncle is Edward Gardiner?"

"Yes he is."

"I have known the Gardiners for many years. Mrs Gardiner grew up close to where my family estate is located. I am surprised I have not seen you or your sister, as I often visit their home when I am in Town," Mr Darcy said with a smile.

"I am surprised too, Mr Darcy; I have never heard them even speak of you," Elizabeth replied.

"Well, we mostly associate in a business sense, so perhaps that is why he has not mentioned me."

"That may be. My uncle does not like to mix business and family life," Smiling, as she thought of her uncle, she continued, "He says when he comes home he hangs all his problems on the tree outside so they do not intrude upon the harmony of his home."

"That sounds like something he would say."

Caroline, feeling left out of the conversation, once again interrupted, "Do you play an instrument, Miss Elizabeth?" Not seeing a pianoforte in the room, she felt certain the answer would be no.

"Yes, I do, Miss Bingley. My sister Mary and I play the pianoforte, and my youngest sister Lydia is learning the violin."

Feeling defeated in her attempts to make Elizabeth Bennet appear inferior in front of Mr Darcy, Miss Bingley excused herself and went to sit beside her sister for the rest of the call.

Mr Darcy continued the conversation without even noticing Miss Bingley's absence, "I am impressed with Miss Lydia's attempt to play the violin. It is a difficult instrument to master, and most people tend to favor something easier."

"She has always said she was drawn to the feel of it in her hands. I have heard a few master violinists while in Town, and with practice, I think she has the potential to be as good as they are. Unlike me, she is a diligent student and puts the time into her practicing. As a result she is able to perform with much passion."

Remembering the evening entertainment he and Bingley enjoyed when they were invited to stay for dinner, Darcy could not help but say, "You forget that I have heard you play, Miss Elizabeth, so you cannot convince me you are not impressive." Looking down at his hands, sadness came over his features and he whispered, "I miss listening to my sister play the pianoforte and the harp."

Elizabeth felt compassion in her inner-most being for this man in front of her. He had not yet opened up about what had happened with his sister, but she hoped he would soon find the peace he needed.

The half hour call soon came to a close, and the visitors took their leave, with the men promising to return on the morrow to join a shooting party Mr Bennet was planning with a few of the neighborhood men.

The following day the Lucas family descended upon Longbourn with the arrival of the other gentlemen who would join the shooting party. Jonathan Lucas could not help but smile as his youngest sister, Maria, was whisked away by Kitty and Lydia with talks of new fashion plates from London to admire. He turned to his eldest sister and, seeing the sadness in her eyes, he implored, "Charlotte, I know something is amiss, and I understand you are not willing to speak with me about it, but please promise me you will speak with Miss Elizabeth."

"I will be well, Jonathan. Do not fret for my sake."

"I will always fret for your sake, as you are my dear sister. Please, speak with her. She has a way of cheering you as no other can do."

"I promise," she said quietly with a nod.

Lucas turned to join the other men gathering on the side of the house. He watched his sister as she spoke with Mary then she went into the pleasure gardens. He hoped she would be in better spirits when they returned.

"Lucas, it is good to have you back in the neighborhood," he heard one of the neighbors call out. He turned to join the others, leaving his sister's care in very capable hands.

"Charlotte!" Elizabeth saw her best friend walking towards her in the back garden. "I did not expect you today."

"Since my father and brother were coming to shoot, my mother and I decided to call. Kitty and Lydia immediately captured my sister's attention with some new fashion plates from your aunt in London, and our mothers are fussing over some detail in the kitchens, so Mary told me I could find you out here."

"We have not had a tête-à-tête in quite a while."

"Yes, not since before the Assembly," Charlotte answered with a raised eyebrow.

Groaning, Elizabeth smiled, "I knew you were going to ask about that." Pulling Charlotte towards the rear of the garden where they would be alone, Elizabeth continued, "I shall tell you all. You will not believe the tale I have for you."

The two friends occupied a bench near the rear of the garden and the story of how Elizabeth had come to be lost, and who saved her from *certain doom* began to unfold.

"But, Lizzy, you are never lost," Charlotte said unbelievingly.

"I know; I have a reputation in the neighborhood for always knowing where I am, but I went a bit further than I intended. You know that new bridge they built past the Walter's farm?" When Charlotte nodded her head, Elizabeth continued. "I have always avoided the area past the river because of having to walk so far to get around to the other side, but with the new bridge I thought it would be a fabulous new adventure. I was so caught up in finding new bushes and trails that I was not attending which way I had gone, and I found myself lost. I tried to find my way back by following the direction of the sun, but I only found unfamiliar wood. When I had finally stopped to calm down and think, I saw Mr Darcy riding his horse across a field. After he pointed me in the proper direction, and I walked about a mile or so that way, I began seeing familiar territory again. I think I was just lost because of not being able to see over that ridge."

"Well, I am glad you found your way home. Was your family worried about you?"

Chuckling, Elizabeth answered, "My father said he was going to give me another hour before he rode out to find me. He had also heard the bridge was finished, and he thought I had walked in that direction."

"He knows you well, doesn't he Lizzy."

Looking into her friend's eyes, Elizabeth asked, "What is wrong Charlotte? I can see that you are downcast, so do not try to deny it."

Standing to pace, Charlotte was uncertain if she wanted to tell her friend, but with the promise to her brother, she knew she could not avoid this discussion. She sighed, and began her tale, "With my birthday last month, I am now seven and twenty. I do not see any prospects in my future, and I do not wish to be a burden on my family. My brother is working hard to turn Lucas Lodge into a profitable property, but I doubt it will ever be as large or as gainful as Longbourn. My family cannot afford a Season on Town, and yet the war has taken most of our local young gentlemen from us." Tears now flooded her eyes, "I do not want to be forever alone, Lizzy."

Pulling her into a hug, Elizabeth's heart broke for her friend. Charlotte was the oldest single female in the neighborhood at seven and twenty, and some of the matrons would not let her forget. How could Elizabeth convince her dear friend she was not an old spinster and that one day she would meet a gentleman worthy of her hand? Charlotte's parents had an amicable marriage, but they were not a love match as her own parents. Charlotte said for years that all she wanted was a comfortable position, claiming that love was entirely up to chance.

Elizabeth was unsure what to say to calm her friend's fears, but she could distract her, at least for a few hours. She handed Charlotte a handkerchief and lifted her chin, "Enough of these tears. You know my feelings on this subject, and I will not let you become maudlin, especially not today when I have a new area to show you."

She could not help but laugh as she took the handkerchief from her friend and dried her eyes. Elizabeth threaded her arm through Charlotte's, and with a smile from each, they walked off on a new adventure. As they passed the grove of trees, they plucked a few apples and watched as the group of gentlemen that had formed the shooting party all rode across a field in the distance. "How far do you think you can walk today?"

Laughing, Charlotte answered, "Not as far as you."

Elizabeth chuckled, "At least I will not be lost again."

***

Jane and Elizabeth retired that night, and Jane quietly listened as her younger sister expounded on her deep feelings for Mr Darcy. "Oh, Jane, my heart breaks for his pain. I do not know what has made him so sad, but I want to mend it just to see that pleasant look upon his face. When he smiles at me, my stomach feels as if I have fallen from a high perch in a tree and I can almost feel my heart beating through my chest."

Jane smiled at her sister, "Lizzy, do you think you might be in love?"

"In love? I do not know what love feels like Jane, but Granny Bennet used to tell us we would know when the right person came along, and I am certain he is the right person." Elizabeth sighed and hugged her pillow. "What about you. Are you in love?"

With a dreamy look on her face she whispered, "I have no experience in love, so it is hard to say. I know Mr Bingley is the most amiable gentleman of my acquaintance. I am comfortable in his presence, though I do not have the depth of feelings you describe. Perhaps I do *not* love him." She sighed heavily, "How am I ever to know?"

Elizabeth sat up and fixed her eyes upon her sister's, "Jane, please do not compare my own feelings for Mr Darcy to your feelings for Mr Bingley. You have not known him long, and with time you will come to know your own heart in the matter."

"Oh, Lizzy," Jane said hugging her sister. "My heart says that I could very easily love this man."

"Do not let it overwhelm you; just take your time and I am certain you will find what you most desire."

The two laughed and spoke for a few more minutes, then settled down to sleep. Jane contemplated what Elizabeth said of not comparing her own reactions to those of her sister's. The two had spoken several times of the deep feelings Elizabeth held for Mr Darcy, and Jane was beginning to wonder if Mr Bingley was truly who she desired, especially without such strong emotions on her part. However, one thing she was certain – her sister and Mr Darcy would soon come to an agreement.

# CHAPTER

## VI

Rain kept the erstwhile visitors away for three days, and Jane and Elizabeth were trying not to stare out the windows with forlorn looks on their faces. Each found the days seemed to be brighter when *certain gentlemen* from Netherfield Park came to call. They hoped the rain would let up soon and allow them to visit again. Elizabeth was always uneasy during storms, and her nerves were on edge after three days of the downpour. While she was anxious to see the gentlemen, she was ever glad they did not choose to brave the weather just to visit.

When one particularly loud clap of thunder startled her, she felt Jane's hand squeeze hers. She had always reacted so to storms, but could never determine why. It was her sister's quiet presence that seemed to calm her the most though, and she appreciated Jane being at her side now.

Jane saw the color wash out of Elizabeth's cheeks and felt it might be best to distract her, so she asked, "What did you think of Miss Bingley last week when we met her?"

Elizabeth shrugged her shoulders, "I cannot say I know much of her. She did not speak long with me before she found another conversation more enjoyable."

"Mr Bingley speaks very highly of his sisters, so I am sure you are wrong! She would not knowingly be rude to you – I am certain of it."

"Jane, I know this shall truly shock you, but not everyone is as pure in thoughts as you are. Some people despise others for no particular reason, and I fear Miss Bingley does not wish to have our friendship."

"Oh no! Elizabeth, you cannot be correct."

The two were interrupted when Lydia came bounding into the room. "Does anyone want to play a game of charades, or perhaps perform a play with me?"

"No, thank you," Jane said with a sigh, "I must finish this mending." She looked down at the article in her lap that she had not put one stitch into for close to ten minutes.

"I will, Lydia, if we put together a play," Kitty said with as much enthusiasm as she could muster. It did sound like a pleasant pastime, but she was so tired today. Standing, she grabbed Mary's arm, "Come with us, Mary; we may need your pianoforte skills."

"All right, but I get to choose my own music," Mary answered, eyeing Lydia, who preferred a different style.

"I will agree to such terms only if I get to choose your costume," Kitty replied. Not much could motivate her today, but for fashion, she would do just about anything.

Chuckling at Kitty's sudden enthusiasm, Mary left the room to retrieve her music.

"Come on, Lizzy," Lydia whined, "you make the best voices for the men!"

Elizabeth could not help but laugh at her sister's methods, "Thanks Lyddie. I will join you, but only if I get to choose the play."

Grabbing Elizabeth's hand, Lydia pulled her excitedly to Mr Bennet's study to choose a book. "I have read all but two of William Shakespeare's plays. Can you choose one of those? PLEEEEEEASE!"

With a cocked eyebrow, she stopped, turned to her sister, and said, "I believe it is time we introduce you to Plato and Aristotle!"

"No, Lizzy, please! I cannot stand those philosophical writers! They make my head hurt." Lydia countered.

"I will make a deal with you," Elizabeth stopped to see if Lydia would agree first. When she nodded her head, Elizabeth continued. "If you can convince Jane to join us, then I will choose *'Much Ado About Nothing'*."

"Oh, do not worry, I will convince her," Lydia bounced away to retrieve her eldest sister.

After all the girls converged in the sitting room, needed items in hand, they sat down to organize who would play which role. Just as they were dividing up the parts, Mr Bennet entered. "Ahhh, I see you did convince them to put together a production — well done, Lydia! If you do not mind, I have asked Mrs Hill to bring some refreshments; I thought I would have a nice afternoon tea with my daughters before I lie down to rest."

The next hour they all spoke of their parts, deciding which music compositions would be played and when, while they enjoyed biscuits and tea with their father. Before he retired, he told them how much he anticipated their performance this evening, and he left the room with a smile on his face. Realization dawned that the days of all his girls being at home was soon to come to an end. Even though his eldest two had been out for years, he had not prepared himself for them to truly be gone. Now that they had two excellent suitors vying for their attentions, he knew these gentlemen would win their hearts and hands soon enough. Jane and Mr Bingley might stay around the neighborhood; after all he had leased Netherfield Park. If Elizabeth married Mr Darcy though, he anticipated they would not see much of her, as his home was in Derbyshire, several days travel away. He felt a pang in his chest at the thought of losing his girls. Just as he was stopped in the middle of the hall, he felt his wife's hand gently touch his arm. He turned to her, and she could see the raw emotions displayed on his face. He hugged her tight, almost crushing her.

"Henry, is everything well?"

"Yes, my dear. I was just being overly emotional about our daughters and their futures. I will miss them greatly when they are all gone." He loosened his hold on her, and took her hand in his. "I dearly wish we could have had more children."

Tears stinging her eyes, she touched his cheek, "I know, Henry; I know." They had always spoken of having ten children, joking that Susannah would teach them very ill on the pianoforte. She was not very musically inclined, though she tried when she was younger. She had stopped playing after her own father embarrassed her at a gathering by pointing out her inadequacies to all there. Bennet was there at her side to escort her out for some fresh air, and he determined in his heart that he would never treat his own children in such a fashion. Susannah smiled at her husband, "Just think though, once our girls marry and move away we will then have the opportunity to be grandparents."

Chuckling at her enthusiasm of their future, he kissed her hand and they both retired to rest.

As the autumn days slowly passed, Bingley and Darcy spent a part of most days at Longbourn, when the weather permitted. Darcy continued his chess games with Mr Bennet and Elizabeth would often join them. Bingley was too distracted to care about winning, and soon was no longer asked if he would like to join them. He instead spent his time in the sitting room or in the garden with other members of the family, mainly Miss Bennet. There were many walks in the garden and to nearby places, and meals were often shared by all.

On this particular day Miss Elizabeth and Mr Darcy were eyeing each other across the chessboard and enjoying a debate about a particular piece of literature. Neither would forfeit their side of the argument and both were quite enthusiastic in the repartee they shared.

Darcy could not help but be distracted by the lady who sat opposite him. She was not only beautiful and accomplished, she was also determined and could hold her own against him. She reminded him of his father in a way, and he felt a connection to her that was so deep he could not explain it to others. He knew there was no need to search any longer – he had found his perfect mate in Elizabeth.

As the game ended, with Elizabeth winning, Bennet suggested they join the rest of the family for tea. They entered the sitting room, and Elizabeth saw Mr Bingley and Jane talking in the far corner. A small smile played on her lips.

Noticing where she looked as they sat, Darcy asked her, "Miss Elizabeth, would you mind if I asked you an intrusive question?" Not certain where this was going, she warily answered in the affirmative, and he continued. "I do not claim to be a great reader of people, and it has been pointed out to me many times that even my own disposition can be difficult for others to comprehend."

"On the contrary, Mr Darcy; I find you a very cordial gentleman with great depth of character."

He could not help but smile at her compliment. "Thank you." He turned to look towards his friend. "My question is of your sister," he indicated Jane's direction with his head. "I do not wish to intrude, but my friend has had some difficult times in the past. He has not had his mother or father to rely upon for most of his life, and unfortunately, his sister, Miss Bingley, has been trying to convince him of some ideals I am not at all certain are true. He does not realize how manipulative she can be sometimes." Elizabeth looked down at her hands, seeing where this conversation was going. "She has nearly convinced him that your sister's serene countenance is evidence that she has no regard for him."

Elizabeth thought for a moment before answering, "I do not claim to know her reasoning, but Miss Bingley is not the only one to point out such a deficiency about Jane. My dear friend, Miss Lucas, has said the same on several occasions in the past."

Darcy looked back to the couple as they chatted, "I am not asking you to reveal any sisterly confidences you may have, but I would be most obliged if you would answer this for me in any way you can." He looked back at her, "Does Miss Bennet have *any* special regard for my friend?"

A small smile slowly appeared on her lips, as she turned to the gentleman sitting near her. She met his eyes, and saw the need for a positive answer in them. "I cannot reveal all, Mr Darcy, but I *will* say I would not be worried for your friend if I were you."

Her answer eased his mind, "Thank you. I did not wish to see Bingley get pulled in by his sister's manipulative ways and break Miss Bennet's heart if she did care for him."

"You care for my sister's heart then," Elizabeth said with a sly grin.

With a raise of his eyebrow, he answered her, "She has become *like a sister* to me; I do not wish to see either of them hurt," Darcy answered, winking at Elizabeth.

She found her heart beating faster as it dawned on her the implications he hinted at in his answer. *Could the attention he was paying her truly indicate he cared for her? That he regarded her above all others?* Elizabeth knew in that moment her heart truly did belong to him, all he need do was ask. *Would he ask?*

As the visit came to a close and the two gentlemen left, Elizabeth and Jane went upstairs to speak of all their hearts could think upon. Elizabeth told Jane of her conversation with Mr Darcy, and Jane could not imagine Mr Bingley's sister to be so cold hearted. Naïve with regard to Caroline Bingley Jane might have been, but she realized she would need to show more of her feelings if she ever hoped to marry the one gentleman who had touched her heart. Unlike those in the past who had told her only that she was beautiful, Mr Bingley engaged her in conversation. He went out of his way to get to know her, and she had, in some ways, shut him out by not being open with her own newly developing feelings. Jane hoped she had not lost her chance at love and happiness. She determined that she would be more open with Mr Bingley in the future.

---

*Pemberley, Derbyshire*

"Hugh, I just do not know if she will be ready to travel before Christmas," Helen Fitzwilliam exclaimed to her husband.

Being the Earl of Rosebery, his duties would require his presence in Town soon and he did not wish to leave the ladies behind at Pemberley. He sighed deeply, "Perhaps if the doctor would try…"

"Dr Foxx said *if* she puts in the effort she should be able to travel soon, but Georgie is just not pushing herself to recover as she needs to be and no one can make her do this; she has to decide to do it on her own."

"I know, my dear, but perhaps something will motivate her soon, otherwise my duties will take me from you both."

Their conversation was interrupted by a scream emanating from their niece's sitting room down the hall. Both looked at each other, dropped what was in their hands, and ran from the room.

"What is wrong? What has happened? Did you hurt yourself?" A frantic Rosebery cried as he hurried into her room. Both halted immediately when they saw the smile on Georgiana's face.

"HE HAS *MET* SOMEONE! LOOK," she cried out, waving the letter in her hand, "he has MET someone! OH, I am so happy! He wants me to get well soon so I can travel to meet her!" Georgiana beamed.

Rosebery's smile nearly matched that of his niece. "You will have to work hard, but I am certain you can do it Georgiana."

"Of course I can do it – *he has MET someone!*" she squealed with glee.

"There you go, my dear," Rosebery said quietly, leaning down to his wife's ear, "She now has a reason to put in the effort. We had better go read Darcy's letter and see what he has to say; I have a feeling we will be traveling quite the distance next month. Georgiana is a Fitzwilliam; once an idea is set in her mind, there is no changing it."

"Hmmm, yes, *the Fitzwilliam stubbornness*; I know all about *that,*" Lady Rosebery smirked.

"As if the Alexander's were any less stubborn; after all, my dear, once your eye was fixed upon *me*, nothing could stop you from winning my heart," Rosebery winked at his wife.

"Very true, my dear, very true," she winked back at him as she went over to their niece, embracing her then taking a seat to hear all Georgiana had to say of her brother's letter. Rosebery left the two ladies, intent upon opening the letter Darcy sent to him, and hoping it would answer some questions about this *special someone*.

---

Darcy sat in the library pretending to read when a footman interrupted him with the delivery of a letter. When he saw it was from his sister he broke the seal eagerly, and read.

> *October 24, 1811*
> *Pemberley, Derbyshire*
>
> *Dear William,*
>
> *You have met someone? That is all the information I am to receive from you? Who is she? What is she like? How old is she? Does she have any brothers or sisters? What does she look like? So many details, and you have left them all out! I cannot believe you write to tell me you have met someone, and that is all you say...*

Darcy chuckled while reading the letter from his sister. *It is not long, and it is a bit hard to decipher in places, but she has written!* A small smile stayed on his lips as he remembered all she had been through and all she was still overcoming. He was more proud of her than he could ever express!

Standing, he folded his letter and placed it in his pocket. It was a good thing he thought to order a special carriage a few months ago to better accommodate Georgiana's current needs; it looked like she had enough incentive now to work towards the goals Dr Foxx set for her. *Thank you Elizabeth; you have inspired what no one else could in my sister on her road to recovery.*

Darcy quit the library and returned to his room to write a letter in return and to settle some much needed business if Georgiana were to visit. He began making a list in his mind, and nearly ran into Mrs Hurst when he came around a corner. "Oh, pardon me, Mrs Hurst. I was not attending."

"That is quite all right Mr Darcy; no harm came to me," she answered, smoothing her skirt. He quickly apologized again and retreated down the hall. *What a dramatic change he has undergone since coming here to Netherfield Park,* she thought. *No doubt it is the influence of a certain local gentleman's daughter!*

Sarah Johnson

# CHAPTER VII

**D**arcy could not sleep. He knew he needed to speak with someone, and he knew who that someone must be. Rising before dawn, hoping a rigorous morning ride would help calm his nerves, he raced along fields, jumped fences, and wandered along Hertfordshire's autumn beauty for two hours before he finally went to Longbourn.

A knock at the door startled Bennet out of his sleepy haze. After a fitful night, he had given up on rest hours ago and come downstairs. Calling out for Mrs Hill to enter, he was presented with a calling card. He did not expect his early morning visitor until later in the day when they planned to go shooting. Mr Darcy, with dark circles under his eyes and windblown hair from his ride, was shown into his study. The young gentleman looked worse than Bennet was sure even *he* appeared this morning.

"Have a seat, Mr Darcy," Bennet waited until his guest took a seat before he chose his own seat. He had been watching this gentleman for several weeks now, and he was quite certain he knew where this conversation would be going. As he sat down, he could see every emotion playing out in the eyes of the young man who sat before him. In sheer size, Mr Darcy was the tallest gentleman Bennet had ever met – *he must be at least 6'4"*, he thought. He had broad shoulders, dark features, and looked an intimidating figure. However, what he saw in his green eyes was a young gentleman much in need of his father and mother. Darcy had revealed to him once that both of his parents died years ago, but that was all he said. Mr Darcy was very private about his affairs, and Bennet could see this was going to be an enlightening conversation.

Mr Darcy did not seem to be speaking, so Bennet decided to start them off. "What brings you to Longbourn so early today, sir?"

Twisting the ring on his little finger in agitation, Darcy seemed to not hear him. Bennet kept watching him, and after a minute or so Darcy looked up. "I have something I feel that I need to speak with you about, sir." Bennet acknowledged him with a nod, and Darcy continued. "I need to ask a favour of you — because of your own personal experience, but first I must unburden myself of a rather sordid tale; one of which no one outside of my closest family knows."

"If you feel you must, then please do. You are at liberty to tell me anything. I promise to keep your confidence in the matter."

"Thank you, sir." Darcy sat forward, resting his elbows on his knees and looking down at his hands entwined together. He sighed deeply, then began. "When Bingley and I were younger, we spent some weeks in Brighton with friends. We had a pleasurable time and have each spoken of that trip as being one of our favorites for many years now. So, when my sister Georgiana's new governess, Mrs Younge, brought up the idea of a surprise birthday trip to Ramsgate, I thought it would be a pleasant experience for my sister as well. Unfortunately, I had business to complete with the spring planting and was unable to join her for some weeks.

"I received a few letters from my sister, and she talked of how much she enjoyed the seaside, but how much she wished I was with her as well. The last letter she sent came when I was extremely busy, so I set it aside and forgot about it until the following day. When I opened it, my heart nearly broke. The missive was written in a hurried manner and was terribly smeared, but contained only two words – 'Help me'.

"I immediately left Pemberley with the intention of riding straight through to Ramsgate, but not long into my journey I came upon an accident."

Bennet's whole body tensed when he heard the crushing words exit the young man's lips, but he continued to listen intently.

"Several carriages were stopped to help, and I intended to go on past until I saw something shiny in the grass. I do not know why, but I slid from my horse to see what it was. When I picked up the jeweled comb I immediately knew it was Georgiana's. I had given it to her only a few weeks before, and she said it was so pretty that she intended to wear it every day.

"The next few hours are a blur of activity as Georgiana was pulled from the wreckage and carefully moved to a local inn. She was unconscious for two days, but luckily, she did not produce a fever. The doctors said her injuries were severe but manageable and she should heal – just a broken hand and some cracked ribs that would take some time. The most severe of her injuries though was the damage to her legs. They were twisted under the carriage, and while she did not have any broken bones, as Miss Elizabeth said you had, sir, she had a great deal of muscle damage. Within a week we were able to remove to Pemberley and her recovery seemed to be doing well."

Bennet poured a drink and handed it to Darcy, who took a sip before he continued the tale. "We were back at Pemberley a month when Georgiana tried to get out of bed on her own. She fell again, causing more damage to both of her legs. The doctors were originally hopeful she would one day walk again, even if just a little, but after that incident they are now unsure if she will ever take another step.

"I refused to leave her side again. Not only did I feel I caused her injuries by allowing her to go to Brighton without me and trusting in someone whom I hired, but I felt I was at fault for her falling again as well. I refused to leave her side, and hardly slept or ate. Eventually my family forced me to leave Pemberley, saying Georgiana could not recover if I was causing her distress by not eating and sleeping properly. They felt we would both have a better time of things if I were to leave and let them take care of her in my stead. That is when I joined Bingley in London and shortly after that, here in Hertfordshire."

"That is quite the tale, and I can understand your reaction, but I would agree with your family that you need not cause harm to your own well-being for the sake of what cannot be changed."

"My uncle said nearly those same exact words."

Bennet smirked, "He sounds like an intelligent and caring individual." After taking a drink he asked, "Did you ever find out what took place to bring your sister to such a disastrous tragedy?"

"Georgiana would not confide in me for a long time, but eventually she told me what happened. Mrs Younge, her governess, had a friend who began coming around quite often, and Georgiana found herself uncomfortable around this man. He then began paying her more attention, even trying to convince her he cared deeply for her. Being young, Georgiana did not know what to do, so she asked Mrs Younge for advice and was assured Mr Wickham was an honourable gentleman and she would do good to secure him while she still possessed her youthful beauty. Georgiana knew this was not advice I would promote, so she made plans to join a friend's family who were also visiting in Ramsgate. The morning she intended to contact them, George Wickham kidnapped her."

Bennet could not help but suck in a breath as the shocking news was revealed. He closed his eyes, his face paling as he said simply, "Oh my!" He opened his eyes again to see Darcy's face pale.

"Yes, she is quite brave." He took a drink again before he continued. "My sister rode with him for two days trying to find an opportune time to get away, but he stayed by her side. She wrote me the note when they stopped for the first night and she left it on the desk hoping the servant would send it out after they departed. Finally on the third day she was able to get away in the carriage when they stopped and he stepped out of it without her. She has much experience with horses, but is not very familiar with driving a curricle. Mr Wickham somehow procured a horse and was trying to catch her when she lost control of the reins and the carriage rolled, trapping her underneath. She remembers seeing his face standing over her one more time." His voice became angry when he uttered, "He just left my sister there to die."

Bennet reached over and grasped Darcy's arm, "I know how hard this must be for you, but it will do no good to hold onto such anger. You must focus on your sister's recovery."

Tears welled in his eyes, "How can I? She was left there for hours before someone else saw the wreckage and stopped to help." The tears were now flowing down his cheeks and his hands were balled up in anger, "Georgiana was lying in the mud for hours, twisted under the carriage wheels. If only I had taken the time to read her letter, I could have prevented this catastrophe."

What Darcy said was almost more than Bennet could bear, and he found his heart breaking for this young man in front of him. How could he be put through so much in his short life? This was not the conversation he thought they would be having today when his visitor came in the door, but he could understand why Mr Darcy opened up to him.

Bennet knelt in front of the younger man and pulled him into a fatherly embrace. Darcy could not hold back the tears as his body shook; emotions he held in for so long were finally allowed to be released. After some time, he began to calm and the arms around his shoulders loosened. When the older gentleman struggled to stand from the kneeling position he had taken, Darcy could see the pain on his features. He put his hand out to help, "I am sorry, sir. I should never have..."

Bennet interrupted him, "Nonsense – I am just stiff from a long night with little sleep. You did not cause my pain, just as you did not cause your sisters pain."

Darcy helped him back to his seat, then sat again himself, "On some level I know what you say is true, but I cannot forgive myself."

"The Good Book says if you have any grievance against someone, you must forgive them. Reverend Hughes pointed out to me after my accident that the scripture could be taken to mean forgiving myself as well as others."

Darcy thought about what he said for a minute, then he finally spoke, "I will try."

"That is all I ask. Now, you mentioned a favour you would like to ask of me? What do you need me to do, Mr Darcy?"

"Darcy...please call me Darcy."

"Darcy." Sitting up on the edge of his chair, Bennet looked directly into the young gentleman's eyes, and asked with fatherly affection, *"What do you need from me?"*

"Sir, I wondered if you could speak with my sister?"

He was a little taken aback at such a request until Darcy explained further.

"I am hopeful she will be well enough to travel here soon to join me, and she could use your advice and encouragement. I have never been injured as she is; I have never been laid up in bed for months, unable to even walk without others' assistance, and neither has anyone else in my family. We do not understand what she has been through other than what we see her struggle with daily. With

Georgiana's diagnosis for her future being so grim, I know we need help, and I believe you could offer what none of us can give her." He looked down at his hands, and quietly continued, "She sees the way I look at her, and she shuts me out. I think Georgiana feels she will hurt me more if she unburdens herself to me."

"Yes, I can understand that; I did not wish to burden my family and friends either. It took a great deal of stress, and finally, after a particularly trying day, I just broke. After that, things seemed to be on the mend. It has been a long recovery, but if my journey can in any way help your sister, then I would be honoured to speak with her." Smiling, he continued, "I may not be an expert at understanding the female mind, but I have had enough experience, with my own girls and with this," he said, patting his leg, "that I may just be able to help you." He paused for a moment before adding "What of *you*, Darcy – how can I help *you*?"

"I just want my sister to be well again, sir."

"You cannot think you do not need help in healing also, son," Bennet said. "If I can recommend someone who has been where you stand, it would be my daughter Elizabeth. She can be very insightful and you need to unburden yourself to someone who can relate. Carrying around this anguish over your sister will only hinder your own happiness."

Darcy smiled, "Miss Elizabeth has a way of seeing the positive things in life, while still accepting the negatives that come along with it."

"Yes she does," Bennet agreed.

"She once told me her philosophy in life is to *'think only of the past as its remembrance gives you pleasure'*."

Bennet chuckled, "My own dear mother used to say the same thing. She and my Lizzy were alike in so many ways."

"I believe Georgiana could learn a lot from Miss Elizabeth's influence," Darcy said. "I hope they can become friends. Georgiana does not have many ladies she can go to in the family, only my Aunt Helen. My other family members are not as affable. I fear the woman I have exposed her to as a companion was not the best influence; I have much for which I need to atone."

Bennet looked at the serious mien of the younger gentleman, "Do not berate yourself over the past. You could not have known all that would take place, and if there is anything I have learned of your character from our chess games, it is that you agonize over every decision. I would dare to say you did the same with your sister's companion and were deceived by lies she told. That is not your fault, Darcy."

"I am trying to see it that way, but it is difficult, sir. If Georgiana could meet you and your family, I know she would learn."

"Is that all you wish to ask of me?" Bennet inquired.

"At this time, yes." Smiling and looking down at his hands, he quietly added, "However, in the near future I expect the need to speak with you again on *other matters* might arise."

"I imagined as much. My door is always open to you Darcy," Bennet said with a pat on the younger gentleman's shoulder. Darcy was encouraged from all they discussed. He had been struggling for weeks trying to decide whether to come to him with the details, and he was grateful Mr Bennet did not blamed him for the tragedy. He knew his family kept telling him he was not at fault, but he did not fully believe their biased opinions. Mr Bennet, however, was unbiased, and yet he had not blamed Darcy.

He took his leave, grateful for the opportunity to unburden himself of all he had carried these last few months. Though he felt better, he was still nervous for what the future held for his sister – and for himself.

Sarah Johnson

# CHAPTER VIII

urst entered Bingley's study and sat down across from his brother-in-law, leaning his cheek on his hand as he thought deeply about something.

"What is troubling you?" Bingley asked.

His brows furrowed, "I do not know. There is something our sister is planning, but I do not know what it is."

Bingley sighed, "What makes you say that?"

"I was on my way down the hall and saw her being sneaky, so I followed her. She disappeared into the library. Now, if there is anything I have learned about Caroline over the last ten years, it is that reading is not her favorite pastime."

"No, you are correct there." He thought for a minute before he stood, "Come, we will see what she is doing."

Hearing shuffling behind her, Caroline turned around, surprise on her features at seeing her brothers instead of Mr Darcy.

"What are you doing, Caroline?" Bingley asked.

Pointing to herself, she replied, "Me? Nothing... well, reading." She grabbed a book off the table beside her and held it up.

"I do not know what you are planning, Caroline, but whatever it is, it will not work. You *WILL NOT* disturb my guest – he is here to rest, not to be accosted by you. Since I know you do not enjoy reading, *especially Cowper,*" he indicated the book she held upside down in front of her, "you have no other reason to be in this room."

She raised her chin in defiance, "Since you shall know very soon anyway, I will tell you Charles." She walked to her brother in confidence. "While you have been dallying around with your country angel, Mr Darcy and I have been growing quite close, and I was to meet him here this morning for a private tête-à-tête. He said as much to me when I saw him earlier." She blustered at her failed attempt, hoping Bingley would not notice her falsehood.

"I find that impossible, Caroline, since he left before dawn for a ride, and you do not rise so early. Only the truth of what scheme you are about will assuage my curiosity."

Caroline looked from Bingley to Hurst, and seeing she would not get anywhere with either of them, she quickly slammed the book down on the table and walked with displeasure to the door. Finding they had locked it when they entered, she turned around to inquire about the key. She was met with her brother's red face, as he said in almost a growl, "Darcy does not care for you Caroline. He has never cared for you, and he will not marry without affection. You have set your sights too high with him, and you need to stop your attempts to gain his hand through whatever means necessary before you ruin your own reputation. He will not offer for you, and neither will I force him to if you choose to put yourself in a compromising situation to gain his hand."

Bingley unlocked the door and watched as his sister stormed out of the room and stomped down the hall. When he heard her footfalls on the stairs, he turned to Hurst, "Say nothing to Darcy."

Hurst shook his head, "I know he is distracted with what has happened with his sister, but the man needs to be alerted to what she is planning. It would serve him well to stay out of rooms alone."

Bingley ran his hand over his face, "I know, but I promised Fitz and Alex that I would not cause him more distress. Perhaps it is best, for now, that we keep an eye on our sister ourselves and alert them to the situation instead." He thought for a minute, then replied, "Yes, that is what we will do. I will write to them now and warn them of Caroline's new attempts."

"If you think it is best?"

"Yes, I do."

Bingley wrote his letter and dispatched it immediately. Assured of its arrival to Darcy's cousin before dinner, he and Hurst retired to the billiard room to play a few games.

Darcy felt better than he had in months. He was glad he finally decided to speak with Mr Bennet. He was a kind gentleman with much wisdom to share, and that was something Darcy dearly missed about not having his father around. Hearing the crack of the balls as he walked down the hall, Darcy ambled into the billiards room. Looking up from the table, Bingley and Hurst were glad to see the peaceful look on his face, and were both prepared to do whatever necessary to keep it that way. They knew their decision not to tell him of Caroline's attempt was for the best. "Care to join us for a few games before we need to prepare our weapons and go to meet Mr Bennet?" Bingley asked with a smile. Receiving an affirmative answer, Hurst set up the table for a new game while Bingley poured Darcy a drink.

---

Colonel Richard Fitzwilliam needed to retrieve some papers he had in a locked trunk at his parents' home. He made his way through the familiar streets until he reached the stone edifice on Cavendish Square that he knew so well. Entering through a side entrance to avoid the butler, he swung the door to the library open and wearily trod across the floor, glad his long, hard day was finally coming to an end.

"Bad news?" Alex asked.

Not expecting anyone to be in the library, he jumped. Noticing his brother, Fitz chuckled, "Oh, it's just you, Alex!"

*"Oh, it's just you, Alex,"* he repeated mockingly. "You say that like I should not be expected to be here."

"Well, it *is* the *library, Primmy,*" Fitz smirked at his older brother.

Alex cringed at the nickname he detested. It was bad enough to be the *Viscount Primrose* and all the teasing he received with such a title, but now because of the new Prince Regent, affectionately called *Prinny* by everyone, Alex had to endure more taunting than ever from Fitz these days. "Ha ha, *little* brother; watch it – I can still whip you, *Ricky!*"

Fitz chuckled at his elder brothers attempt to ruffle him with the childhood moniker, but he had learned long ago not to let it affect him. "Whip me at what, snowball fights? I have always ridden and fenced better than you, and even Charles Bingley can shoot more accurately..."

Their brotherly banter was interrupted by the butler's knock on the door, "Colonel Fitzwilliam, sir, here is your mail."

Chuckling and shaking his head that his plan of avoiding the staff had once again been thwarted, he replied, "Thank you Simms," and accepted the stack of correspondence. *If only they could teach the new recruits some of the natural instincts my parents' staff possess, then my job as an intelligence officer would be much easier*, he thought. He began thumbing through the stack as the butler retreated from the room. "Oh, look, a letter from Netherfield Park; express even."

"Good, I was beginning to wonder if we shouldn't hear from that quarter soon. I will pour us something to drink and you can see what it says." Alex stood to get the drinks, while Fitz settled into his favorite chair by the fire.

Alex handed Fitz his glass, listening to the barely audible mumbling as he quietly read the letter. "*WHAT?*" Fitz shouted, liquid splashing out as he nearly dropped his drink onto the table beside him.

"Oh no, what has happened now?" Alex asked, putting down his own drink and heavily dropping into the chair nearby.

With a worried look on his face, Fitz sat forward on the edge of his seat, carefully eyeing the letter in his hands. "I can't make out half of this mess – Bingley really needs to work on his scrawl." Shuffling through the pages of the letter, he replied, "It seems there is a local gentleman, *a Mr Bennet,* with what Bingley refers to as *'five lovely daughters',* and he says he and Darcy are besotted with two of them!"

Alex stood, his quick stride taking him towards the door.

"Where are you going?"

"To pack!"

"Pack! Why?"

"To go to Hertfordshire, of course."

"You're just going to show up at their door?"

"Do you really think Charles Bingley, or for that matter Caroline Bingley, would turn me away? I am the Honourable Alexander Fitzwilliam, Viscount Primrose and the future Earl of Rosebery — his sniveling sister would trip all over herself to accommodate me." Alex countered with a smile. "Care to join me, or do your duties to the crown keep you occupied at this time?"

Fitz wrinkled his brow, "Unfortunately, I cannot get away for a few more weeks; I wish I could though." He looked at his brother with an uneasy look, "From what Bingley says, Darcy seems taken with this family. Write and let me know what you think of them. I hope this turns out to be a blessing and not just someone taking advantage of our beleaguered cousin. He has had a difficult year, and deserves some respite, but I have never heard of these Bennets before now."

"Will do; I promised Georgiana before we left Pemberley that I would go visit Darcy soon anyway, so I might as well get on with that task." Alex smiled slyly as he left to pack and order his carriage readied for the morrow. Stopping at the door, he turned and asked, "Are you staying to eat, or should I ask Mrs Gibson to pack you something?"

"No, I have time to stay tonight. Perhaps later I can vanquish you at billiards."

"Oh dream on, little brother," Alex said as he left the room.

*A country gentleman with five daughters; Oh God, I hope this is good,* Fitz thought as he went to refill his glass. Finishing the letter from Bingley, he was intrigued by the last part that gave mention to some situation Bingley put a stop to regarding his sister. *She has been after Darcy for years,* he thought to himself. *Oh well, Alex is going there tomorrow, so he can hear all about what she has done now. I hope Bingley has finally put her in her place.* He sat back in his chair as he thumbed through the rest of his correspondence. Pulling out the letter from his parents, he took a sip of his drink, and settled back in his chair to read what they had to say.

Mrs Bennet came rushing down the stairs, waving her handkerchief, "Mary! Oh where could that child be now? I swear she acts more and more like Lizzy every day." She rushed into the sitting room, and seeing her eldest, asked, "Jane, have you seen Mary? I cannot find her anywhere and she has not chosen her dress for tonight!"

Standing to place a calming hand on her mother's shoulder and lead her to a seat, Jane answered, "Yes, Mama; she and Lizzy were arranging some flowers for the tables and they needed more crocuses. We saw some just the other day when we were walking near the wood and Mary volunteered to go for them." Jane's sensible explanation seemed to calm Mrs Bennet's fit of nerves.

"Well, perhaps since she is busy, you and I could look through her closet and see what she has for tonight," Mrs Bennet thought aloud.

Jane led her mother from the room, "I think she would love to wear one of my old gowns; maybe the light blue one from my second season in town..."

Henry Bennet heard them through his open door, and laughed to himself as their voices faded up the stairs. *Jane has such a way with her mother.* Stretching, his attention was brought back to the letter sitting open on his desk. He knew he would have to answer it soon, but he was not looking forward to such a task. He remembered his cousin, Thaddeus Collins, as a young man, and somehow he had a feeling this son of his, *William Collins,* was no different. The letter droned on about the supposed act of kindness Collins was extending in offering to come and *unite the family again through whatever means necessary.* Bennet was not sure he wanted to extend the hoped for invitation, and he was certain he would not like this man's idea of *whatever means necessary.* Maybe it would be best to put it off another few weeks. He shuffled through the stack of papers on his cluttered desk and finally found what he was looking for. Opening it, he thought, *this could be the way out! I hope Gardiner will have more news for me soon.*

Lydia poked her head into his book room, "Mama sent me to remind you of your promise to rest this afternoon so you do not get overly tired this evening when our guests are here. I thought we could have our tea upstairs today, if it pleases you?"

"I would prefer to have our tea here and I will lie down later. There is plenty of time for a short nap later, but first I would like to hear *your* thought on this new section you read from *Romeo & Juliet*."

Lydia smiled and with a sly grin, "I will go retrieve my book and see if there are any crumpets to be had with our tea!" She winked as she bounced out of the room.

Elizabeth had always been Bennet's favorite daughter to converse with because she was most like him in wit and sense. However, Lydia's cheery disposition was what helped him through the darkest of days after his accident. They bonded over biscuits stolen from the kitchen late at night, tea every afternoon, and a shared love of Wordsworth and Shakespeare. She would point out things no one else would have perceived from their writings.

Lydia was known to chatter on about inconsequential details on just about any topic, many times frustrating those who had to listen to her. He did not mind though; sometimes it was his only retreat from the mundane life that now tied him down. She never looked at him with pity as many others had; instead, she smiled with simple pleasure and enjoyed their time together with child-like exuberance. He came to love things about her he doubted he would have even had the eyes to see if he had not had the accident. As he waited for her to return, Henry Bennet once again thanked God for the blessings that came from such a trying experience.

Sarah Johnson

# CHAPTER IX

Mary was frustrated. She set out for the area in which they saw beautiful, pink crocuses just the other day, and was almost there when she tripped and fell, then she slid down a rain-slicked hillside and nearly landed in the river below. Her skirt was now covered in mud, her hair was a mess, and she was missing one glove and her bonnet. Worst of all, she also lost her spectacles. Thoughts of how she would possibly be able to make it back up the hill, or even more so, how she would return home safely, flooded her mind causing her heart to beat wildly.

She closed her eyes to calm herself, then crawled to the nearest object that resembled a tree, feeling its rough bark as she stood. Without her spectacles she could barely see the blurry shapes in front of her, but with practice she soon learned which objects were trees and which were to be avoided – such as the rocks she nearly ran headlong into. Ever so slowly she made her way up the hill, only sliding back down twice in her quest. When the ground leveled off she knew the road would be close. Remembering a fallen log along the side of the road, she slowly felt her way to it and sat down, crestfallen.

This was just not her day. It began with Kitty and Lydia irritated with each other, and they both snapped at Mary for no reason. Mrs Bennet's fretting due to their dinner party tonight upset Mary's regular routine, and the combination of all these things led to quite the headache.

In a showing of sisterly affection, Elizabeth asked for her help with the table arrangements for that evening, thinking it would calm her nerves, but then they ran out of crocuses. Elizabeth was not known for her hasty jaunts out of doors, so Mary offered to go instead, ensuring they could finish their arrangements in plenty of time to dress for this evening. What she did not count on was the root she tripped over, or the muddy slope she slid down when she lost her balance. Now here she sat, all alone — muddy, without her spectacles, and nearly in tears — pondering how she could solve this dilemma. *Why did I even step out of bed this morning? Oh, where is my knight in shining armour? Lizzy's appeared out of nowhere in her time of need,* she thought. *Where is my knight?*

Through the forest noises and the sound of the river beyond the tree line, she heard a horse as it cantered along. Not wanting to accidentally step onto the road and put herself in harm's way, she kept her seat on the fallen log and began waving her arms and shouting for help, hoping the person would notice her and stop.

Alex was not in the best of humour. He and Fitz were up talking far too late last night. He thought he would be able to sleep in the carriage today, but then there was a last minute problem with the wheel that would take until late in the afternoon to repair. Not wanting to delay his trip, he decided to ride on ahead to Hertfordshire on horseback, thinking he would enjoy the crisp, autumn air before it became too cold to ride comfortably such a distance. His valet would follow with his trunks in the carriage once the wheel was repaired.

It sounded like a good idea at the time, but now he wondered if he had truly gone mad. After getting a late start because of the carriage, he also became lost twice. Then when he came out of the inn after stopping for directions and a bite to eat, he found that the saddlebag in which he had packed a few necessary clothing items, had been stolen. He was speaking with the man in charge of the stables when he stepped too close to another man's horse. The nervous animal relieved itself, and, unfortunately, his clothes were soiled in the process. It was not a good day.

He now looked forward to arriving at Netherfield Park and getting cleaned up. It was lucky for him that he and his cousin were close enough in size, he being only slightly shorter by a couple of inches, that he would be able to borrow some clean clothes until his trunks arrived.

As he rode through the town of Meryton, he was glad to see a sign directing him to the right. According to his instructions, he was now within just a few short miles of his destination. Picking up the pace, he urged his horse onward. Nearly a mile outside of the small town he saw someone sitting on a log on the side of the road waving her arms and calling for help. *What could have happened to her,* he wondered, eyeing her particularly disheveled appearance. *I really do not want to stop again, but I know I must.* He reined in his horse and addressed the young lady, "May I be of assistance to you, madam?"

"Oh thank you for stopping!" Mary stood up from the log, but did not dare to take a step for fear of falling again. She did not recognize this gentleman's voice, but she knew he was her only hope at this time, so she pressed on with her request. "I seem to be having quite the day, and one thing after another," she said, while indicating the mess her dress and hair were in, "has led me to what, I fear, is quite the predicament, however, I will not bore you with the details. In the course of events I seem to have lost my spectacles, and I cannot see a thing without them."

Alex tried not to laugh at the dilemma of this young lady who seemed to have had a worse day than even he had. "I understand completely, madam," he said with a smile. "May I escort you home?"

"Yes, that would help tremendously, sir."

Alex jumped down from his horse and walked over to the lady. Bowing, he introduced himself, "Alexander Fitzwilliam, at your service, madam. Where do you need to go?"

"I am Mary Bennet, and I live about a mile from here. My father's estate is called *Longbourn.*"

"Pleased to be of service to you, then, Miss Mary Bennet," he said with a smile. *So this is one of the lovely Bennet sisters about whom Bingley wrote. I wonder if she is one that is spoken for already,* he thought. "If you will just hold onto my arm," he said as he lifted her hand to his outstretched arm, "we can proceed."

They progressed slowly, only managing to cover a few feet in a minute's time. As he helped her step, he realized it would be a long mile if they were to walk this slowly. "I know propriety says you should not, but I feel it may be in the interest of ease and time, madam, if you ride on top of my horse."

Mary froze, a terrified look coming over her features, "Oh no! I could not possibly!"

Seeing the look on her face, he knew this would be a precarious negotiation. "Are you frightened of horses, Miss Bennet?"

"Yes," she squeaked out, her hand grasping his arm more tightly.

"I do not want to offend your sensibilities, but would you be comfortable with my riding on the horse with you?" he asked with compassion in his voice.

"Are you familiar with the area? Perhaps you could go to my home and tell my father where I am?"

"Unfortunately I have never been here before, and with my sense of direction, especially today, I would most certainly become lost."

Mary swallowed hard, looked towards the ground, and contemplated the situation. After a minute, she came to realize there was no other way than to ride. He did not know the area, and she could not get back home without his assistance. Bravely squaring her shoulders, she looked back up into the blurry face, and quietly answered, "I understand it would be necessary to use your horse, sir, and I would feel much safer if you were to be on it with me."

Alex watched as emotions played across her face while she came to her decision. He could not imagine having to be in her situation, and he was amazed at her strength as she faced her fear and chose to ride. He helped Mary onto his mount, and with practiced agility, he jumped up behind her, wrapping his arms loosely around her and grabbing the reins. She sat rigidly as he guided the horse slowly down the road. "Where to now, Miss Bennet?" He asked with a smile, hoping his cheerful voice would calm her nerves.

Mary closed her eyes and tried to picture where they would need to turn to find the trail along the back garden wall, and described it for him. It would not do to show up at the front door on a stranger's horse, especially with him riding along with her. The path through the back garden was straight and lined with bushes that would help guide her along and keep her sure footed so she could easily find the door to her father's study on the back of the house.

As they slowly rode along, she found herself relaxing a little more. She was not sure which was worse though – being on a horse, a generally loathsome experience for her, or the feeling she had sitting here in this gentleman's arms.

In an attempt to calm Mary's nerves, Alex asked, "Is this trepidation of horses something you have always had, or did something happen to cause you to now fear them?"

Mary answered quietly, "I have always despised riding, sir."

"Ahhh, I completely understand then. My cousin is terrified of horses, and no amount of us goading would get her to ride when we were children. Now she prefers to drive her phaeton, though it took her many years to become comfortable with even that."

"I have been frightened since I was little. My sisters teased me into getting onto one, and once on it I realized just how high I was and fell off. It is not just horses; it is anything high that terrifies me."

"Well then, I understand why you were out walking, as it keeps you much lower to the ground." Feeling her relax ever so slightly as she chuckled lightly, he said, "It is now your turn to ask a question, madam. Any question will do."

"What brings you to our neighborhood, Mr Fitzwilliam?"

"My cousin — I came to visit him."

As they turned off the road and onto the windy, slightly downward path that would lead to the garden wall, the horse picked up his pace causing Mary to yelp in fear, stiffen, close her eyes tightly, and bury her head in her companion's chest. She did not even realize what she had done until she heard him trying to calm her.

Alex felt a tug in his heart when Mary buried her head in his chest. There had never been a lady before for whom he felt such compassion, and whom he wanted to protect as he did this lady. Stopping the horse, he ever so gently placed his large hand on her back and spoke into her ear, "*Shhhhh,* Miss Bennet, all will be well. I will not let you fall. Can you trust me? I promise to return you home safely. *Shhhhh*."

She felt herself relaxing in his embrace, and could not believe the compromising situation she placed them in by agreeing to ride with him. Embarrassed at her brazen actions, she finally lifted her face from his chest and found him looking directly into her eyes. He was close enough now for her to clearly see the emotions playing across his handsome face as his green eyes bore into hers.

"Can you trust me to return you home safely, Miss Bennet?"

She slowly nodded her head in acknowledgment of his question, and he broke eye contact to start the horse along on the path once again. She noticed, however, his arms were clasped more firmly around her this time. Mary slowly released the fabric gripped in her fists and turned to face forward again. She closed her eyes as they made their way along the path. When in his arms she felt like she belonged there, and that terrified her almost more than being on this large animal. She did not understand how a stranger she had known for only half an hour could make her feel so comfortable.

As they approached the entrance to the garden, Alex stopped the horse jumped down, helping Mary to the ground after him. Taking her hand in his, he bent over it, and replied, "Home safe and sound, Miss Bennet, just as I promised."

"Thank you, sir. I do not know what I would have done without you. You have been more help than you know."

"It was my pleasure, Miss Bennet." He answered with a deep bow.

Mary curtsied and turned towards the house. Alex stood there watching this brave young lady slowly make her way along the garden path. A few times he saw her almost stumble, but she caught herself again. He watched as she found a door and knocked. Upon it opening, she was gently encased in the arms of an older gentleman and led inside. Forgetting everything he had been through to arrive in Hertfordshire today, he joyfully jumped back up onto his horse and galloped back to the main road.

When he saw the fallen log upon which she sat when he first spied her, he reined in his horse, tied him to a tree branch, and began to look around for clues as to where Mary could have become so muddied. Hearing the river in the distance, he set off down the hill directly behind the log. Sliding in places, he finally reached the bottom, and quickly located her missing bonnet and glove. Fortunately, he also found her spectacles only a few feet away. Picking them up, he made his way to the river and gently washed the mud from the frames. He folded his handkerchief around the eyeglasses, and put them into the inside pocket on his coat for safekeeping. He grabbed her glove and determining that her bonnet was not worth saving, then slowly began to make his way back up the slope. Alex cursed under his breath when he slid back down several times, getting more muddied in the process. He now understood how Mary Bennet had become so disheveled, as his own clothes were soon covered in mud as well. He finally made it to his horse, rubbed as much mud as he could from the bottoms of his boots, and continued on his way in the direction of Netherfield Park. He could not help but think of the brave young lady with expressive brown eyes.

Sarah Johnson

# CHAPTER X

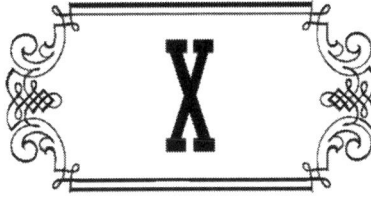

The crack of the balls broke the silence in the room. Darcy and Bingley both eyed the green baize table in front of them. Bingley had won the right to break this game, and that gave him the advantage. It was not unheard of for him to clear all six balls into the pockets in one turn. Charles Bingley grew up being the youngest and smallest of their group of four boys, but he learned early how he could use that to his advantage. In the game of billiards, Bingley had an advantage in that the table was low and Darcy must bend uncomfortably to make the shots. He could tell now, with their being on the seventh game of the afternoon, that Darcy's back was starting to ache, and Bingley was willing to use this to his benefit. Each gentleman eyed their opponent and the table, walking to different angles to see which shot would yield the best results.

A knock at the door interrupted their friendly game, and the butler handed Bingley a calling card. "Viscount Primrose to see you, sir."

He was surprised at the mention of the unexpected guest. "Thank you, Smyth; show him in here please and have Mrs Nichols prepare a room."

The butler left and Darcy leaned down to look over the table once again, "I wonder what Alex is doing here?" Mumbling under his breath, he added, "Probably sent by Fitz to spy on me."

"Sorry Darce, you know I was under strict orders to let your cousins know how you were faring." Lowering his voice, he said, "I guess I said a little too much in my letter and he decided to see for himself." Bingley looked contrite.

"What *exactly* did you say in this letter?" Darcy put his cue stick back in the rack, knowing that Bingley' next shot would end the game. "Don't tell me you said something about Miss Elizabeth?"

"Well, you know how I can be sometimes — I was so happy with my own fortune in finding my angel," Bingley ignored the rolling eyes staring back at him, "that I might have mentioned that you too were a bit... besotted."

*"Besotted!"*

"Oh, come on, Darcy; everyone sees it, so do not try to deny it!"

With a small smirk appearing on his lips, Darcy patted his friend's shoulder, "Well, I cannot fault you too severely, considering you are similarly *besotted.*" Bingley lined up his shot as Darcy continued, "I actually began about a half a dozen letters to my family, but did not have the nerve to send them. I took the coward's way out and sent Georgiana a rather vague letter, hoping she would pass the word on to the others."

Bingley chuckled at his friend, and was about to take his next shot when Mr Smyth again came through the door. "Viscount Primrose, sir."

Bingley put down his cue stick, and with a broad smile, went to shake his guest's hand. "Alex, it is great to see you again — come in, come in! Would you like a drink?"

"You are altogether too chipper for me, Bingley, but yes, a drink would be nice," Alex replied wearily.

"Well, Alex," Darcy eyed the mud smeared over Alex's clothes, as he stuck out his hand for a firm shake, "what exactly have you been doing? I am certain by your appearance alone there must be a story. My all too proper, dandy of a cousin, would never be seen in public covered in mud and smelling of..." Darcy stopped to sniff the air, "well, I won't say what you smell like."

Downing the drink Bingley handed him, Alex answered, "*A dandy!* I might like to be presentable, but I am no dandy! I will forgive your infuriating comments though, for now." He eyed the balls on the table, picked up the cue stick Bingley had laid down and leaned down to take the winning shot. "Yes, there is certainly a story to tell, however, if you two do not mind, I feel the need to clean up first. Since my valet has not yet arrived with my trunks, could I borrow some clothes, Darcy?"

"Oh, ho, now you also want to borrow my clothes? This must be one interesting story!"

Laughing, Alex turned to Bingley, "If you do not mind, I decided to take you up on your open invitation to visit at any time I had the opportunity."

"No, we do not mind at all; you are more than welcome here, my friend. We do have a social engagement this evening, but I doubt they would mind if we added one more to our party."

Bingley pulled the bell for the housekeeper, and the three men had one last drink while Bingley quickly wrote a note to be dispatched to Mr Bennet telling of an addition to their party. Mrs Nichols showed Alex to his room, while Darcy and Bingley retired to dress for the evening.

⁂

"Thank you, Foster; that will be all," Alex said to Darcy's valet, dismissing him after his help with removing the mud caked boots from his feet. "I think I can take care of my cravat well enough on my own."

"Yes sir," he answered. He laid the borrowed clothing on the bed and picked up the muddy boots. "I will have these cleaned for you, my lord," he replied as he left the room.

Alex took a deep breath, stretching his arms over his head. As he peeled the now dried and cracking, mud-caked clothes from his body, he thought of all that took place today. He gingerly pulled the handkerchief from his coat pocket. He opened it to look at the spectacles wrapped in their protective cloth. A small smile formed on his lips as he remembered the face on which these belonged. He could picture her wearing the round frames with thick lenses. Holding them up to inspect them more closely, he realized just how thick they were. *No wonder she needed my help, she probably could not even see her own feet without these.*

*Miss Mary Bennet* – somehow, he knew his life was forever changed in the short time from this morning to this afternoon. He gently wrapped the spectacles back up, placed them on the table with his watch fob, and went about the process of cleaning the stench from his body.

He was tying the last of the knot in the borrowed cravat when he heard a knock at the door. He opened it to see his cousin, and stepped aside as Darcy came into the room.

"What brings you to Hertfordshire, Alex? Is everything well with the family?"

Affectionately patting his younger cousin's shoulder, Alex looked into his eyes and replied, "Everyone is well, Darce. How are you faring?" No words were needed; Alex could read Darcy like he was an open book. He no longer saw the bloodshot eyes and hollowed cheeks that had been there the last time the cousins were together. Alex also noticed that his cousin's clothes fit a little better as well. It was clear his cousin was gaining back the weight he lost when he was not taking proper care of himself at Pemberley.

Alex was the one who insisted Darcy be sent away. Fitz was the one to approach Darcy, with the backing of their parents. Even though Fitz was physically much smaller than Darcy, the two had always possessed a special bond. When no one else could persuade Darcy to do something, Fitz could accomplish that goal. Darcy knew that once Fitz, ever the seasoned and hardened soldier, had decided something, nothing would stop him. After a rather unseemly meeting where Darcy came out with a bloodied lip, Fitz finally convinced his older cousin that Georgiana would do much better if Darcy were gone for a while. Darcy blamed himself for the tragedy that had struck his sister. *He had been the one to suggest the birthday trip. He had been the one that was too busy to go with her. He had been the one who did not check references on Mrs Younge.*

Alex could see all of this playing out in Darcy's eyes, and his deep voice cut through the thick silence of the room, with words that would finally be heard by Darcy, "*You were the one that saved her, Darce.* Stop castigating yourself – she is alive and doing well."

The next thing he knew, Alex was locked in an embrace that would have choked a smaller man. Darcy did not express his emotions often, but with the events of these last few months Alex was not alarmed at the unexpected embrace.

When Darcy finally let go, the two sat down. "So, Darce," Alex smiled, "tell me about these Bennets?"

A small smile formed on Darcy's lips, "Bingley told me he let that slip in his letter."

"Yes, Bingley is a good friend, is he not?" Alex smirked.

"I had every intention of writing to let you know, I just lost my nerve every time I tried. I did write to Georgiana, though," Darcy replied.

"Ahhh, yes, Fitz and I received a letter from Mother and Georgiana, and both were adamant that you had lost your mind completely. Georgiana wants details about this young lady who has caught your attention, and Mother wants to know if your father would approve of her. Tell me, what is her name?" Alex was secretly hoping Darcy would not say *Mary*.

Looking down at his hands and playing with his ring, Darcy answered softly, *"Elizabeth – her name is Elizabeth."*

Alex was relieved at hearing the name *'Elizabeth'*. He was most certain Miss Mary was not Bingley's preference either – he always preferred the taller, blonde, angelic look.

Darcy continued softly, "I have a feeling, if Father were still here, he would have chosen her for me."

Not wanting to get lost in the sea of new feelings and old memories again, Alex stood, "I am greatly looking forward to meeting your Miss Elizabeth. It is time we join Bingley. He will never forgive us if we make him late." He picked up the handkerchief wrapped spectacles and the watch fob from the table, and the two men went downstairs to find their host.

"Oh, Mary! What happened to you?" Elizabeth could not keep the shock from her face when she saw her sister's appearance as Mary held onto their father's arm and he led her up the stairs. Gently taking her other elbow, Elizabeth helped lead her to her room, and called for the maid to bring hot water and a tea tray. Bennet gladly turned over his emotional middle daughter to much better hands and retired to rest and dress for the evening himself.

Mary had told him of her adventure and of the stranger that stopped to help her. She indicated he was traveling towards Netherfield Park when he came upon her, and with the last name of Fitzwilliam, Henry had a feeling this man could be related to Mr Fitzwilliam Darcy – after all, Fitzwilliam was not *that* common a name. He was determined to find out all he could of this *Alexander Fitzwilliam* tonight.

Bennet stretched out on his bed, and soon found he was very tired. He was ever grateful for his wife's insistence he lie down this afternoon. She knew his needs better than he did sometimes. Although, he had a feeling today, it was partially her need as well. She was protective of him becoming too fatigued, and knew tonight he would be standing a great deal. This was the first dinner party of this magnitude they would host since before the accident. His wife was in her element. She was fluttering all around, and to those not accustomed to her it would seem she was all nerves, but he knew his Susannah — she loved to entertain, and she had been looking forward to this party for a long time. He had promised her that when he was strong enough to dance, they would once again begin entertaining, so he knew this was coming when he had asked for her hand at the Assembly four weeks ago.

Turning into a more comfortable position, Bennet closed his eyes for a short nap.

Hurst was dressed before his wife was ready, so he descended the stairs and was told the other gentlemen were in the billiard room. When he entered he could not help but smile at seeing the newest member to their party. He bowed, "Lord Primrose; I did not know you were to visit. It is indeed a pleasure to see you again, my lord."

"Yes, it must have been about two years since we were last in company. It is a pleasure to see you as well, and please dispense with the formalities. As I told you before, your brother here is too old and too good a friend for me to require you to be so formal."

"Shall I call you Primrose then?"

Alex cringed and rolled his eyes, "Only when the public setting necessitates such use of a title I have grown to despise. '*Alex*' will do when we are not in the company of others."

Bingley immediately spoke up as he handed his brother a drink, "Oh, the stories Darcy and I could tell you of Alex when we were all at Eton together. He was involved in more skirmishes over his name than anyone else I know. Why he hates it so I will never understand, but he has always insisted we use his first name when among friends."

Alex picked up the cue stick he held at his side and leaned down to examine the table in front of him. "If you had Fitz for a brother, you would understand why I hate that name. He has teased me since he first learned to speak." Alex missed the shot and took a step back for Darcy to take his turn. "My mother says his first word was spoken only to rankle me."

"If you were not so sensitive, he would have nothing about which to tease," Darcy jested.

Alex turned to Hurst, "You see what I must endure? Even my cousin is out to make my life miserable."

Hurst laughed, "We all have our family burdens to bear."

"Yes, and I would give anything to have yours rather than mine right now," Bingley replied. "Can you imagine what my sister will say when she learns you are visiting?"

Darcy patted his friend's shoulder, "Bingley, perhaps it is time you be more firm with her. Let her know this is your house, not hers."

"Yes, I will keep that in mind. It will be difficult, but believe me, I can garner the proper feelings if the need arises." He turned back to the table and began to place the balls in order again. "Come gentlemen; we have time for one more game before we must leave."

The gentlemen and Mrs Hurst were all waiting in the hall, coats, hats, and gloves already on, when Caroline finally appeared on the stairs. She was dressed well above the proper attire for a country dinner party. As she sauntered down the corridor she recognized Mr Darcy's cousin, Lord Primrose, standing with the group. When she reached the bottom of the stairs she curtsied deeply, "We did not expect you, my lord." Eyeing her brother for not telling her of his presence, she continued, "I will let Mrs Nichols know to ready a room for you."

"There is no need, Caroline, as I have already taken care of *my guests'* needs." Bingley was vexed with her attitude lately, especially after what she tried to say of Darcy just a few days before. He would no longer allow her to act in the position of hostess in his home; Louisa had already agreed to take over while they were in residence. "If you do not mind, I wish to leave immediately, as I did not want to be late this evening." He snapped his watch closed and turned and led the group outside.

Sighing at her brother's actions and pulling her cloak around her shoulders more firmly in an agitated manner, she followed Louisa out the door.

Darcy's carriage was larger than Bingley' and they were able to fit their group of now six inside comfortably. The ride to Longbourn was silent, each occupied by their own thoughts and hopes for the evening.

Bingley was no longer uncertain of Miss Bennet's regard after Darcy assured him he need not worry about what Caroline tried to convince him. He decided to pay close attention to Miss Bennet's eyes tonight and see if he saw in them any special affection for him. He was certain he would be able to tell, and if he did determine she cared, he was willing to go visit Mr Bennet tomorrow and announce his intentions towards this angel God had put in his path.

A small smile graced Darcy's lips as he thought about tonight. He knew from the moment he saw her that Elizabeth was the lady for him. He felt a pull he could not explain and he knew what he must do. Tonight he hoped to have a few minutes alone with her to ask a very important question. His meeting with Mr Bennet yesterday gave him assurance that her family perceived his attentions, and he hoped Elizabeth did as well. Remembering her eyes, and how they lit up when she looked at him, he was certain his addresses would be well received.

Alex looked down at his hands, remembering the face of the lovely young lady he rescued earlier. He could still smell the lilac fragrance she wore and his heart beat wildly at remembering the feel of her in his arms. She fit there so perfectly – he could not explain this sensation. He would return her spectacles and hope to have some time tonight to engage her in conversation. He wanted to get to know this young lady. What he dreaded was the possibility of being, once again, placed in a situation that could direct the rest of his life in unforeseen ways. Would she have told her father of their ride on horseback, or of their compromising position when she became frightened? He dearly hoped he would not be forced to offer for someone he knew so little about, but she did intrigue him greatly.

David and Louisa Hurst sat next to each other, both thinking of their conversation earlier. His family would be in Town for Christmas, and since they were trying to avoid having Caroline along with them, they discussed different possibilities for a trip elsewhere. Louisa was certain Bath would be too crowded. It was not to her liking anyway because of memories of their last trip there. So she proposed they go to Brighton. Hurst promised her he would look into that possibility. The two had been married now for nearly ten years, and a trip to Brighton was sounding better the more he thought of it. *Ten years,* he thought, *I could never have imagined what the last decade of my life would be like.*

Caroline looked around the carriage at the faces dimly lit by the lanterns moonlight filtering in through the windows. She was certain she would have been able to convince Charles to go back to Town before now, but he held onto his firm belief that Hertfordshire society was where he preferred to be. Caroline was rebuffed every time she tried to turn one of them to her way of thinking.

For three years now, she had tried to garner the attention of Mr Darcy, and she was incensed he was not only still ignoring her, but he was giving his attentions to *Eliza Bennet*, with her *fine eyes and pert opinions*. How dare she try to take what Caroline had rightfully claimed as her own! Caroline tried one last time just the other day to convince Mr Darcy what he was missing out on, but her efforts were thwarted by her brothers. Ever since then, Bingley was furious with her. If he could, she was certain he would have sent her back to London already. With a great sigh she knew what she must do – she must change her focus to another person and give up on this dream of being mistress of Pemberley. It was obvious that would never take place.

Her eyes happened to turn to the gentleman sitting next to Mr Darcy – his cousin, Viscount Primrose. He was nearly as tall, just as good looking, and more amiable than his younger cousin. Caroline was certain *he* would not be affected by these Bennets; after all, he was one day to be the Earl of Rosebery. He had an obligation to fulfill in whom he married, and a country gentleman's daughter without a substantial dowry was clearly below what society required for such a gentleman. There was no way one of the Bennet daughters would turn *his* head. She decided she would begin attaching herself to him. If she could not have his cousin, with his money and grand estate, then she would at least have a title; there was rumor he even owned a castle. Focusing her eyes on Alex, she made a decision that would, unbeknownst to him, haunt him for many months.

# CHAPTER XI

The carriage pulled up to the door and they disembarked. Caroline positioned herself in such a way as to be escorted by the viscount. *She would show these country nobodies who she really was.*

Caroline did indeed, once again, make them late, and the group entered to the rest of the neighborhood already ambling about. Mr Bennet, with Mrs Bennet and Mary on his arms, was close to the door and walked up to greet the newcomers. Having resorted to using her old spectacles, Mary could see better than without them, but objects were still a bit blurry. Mr Bennet promised his middle daughter he would lend her his arm for the evening, and tomorrow they would see if they could find her spectacles. If necessary, they would send off for a new pair from London.

As they walked up to the newcomers, Mary saw Miss Bingley hanging on the arm of the gentleman she met earlier. She felt her stomach knot.

Mr Darcy stepped up to make the introduction, "Mr Bennet, Mrs Bennet, Miss Mary, allow me to present my cousin, Alexander Fitzwilliam, Viscount Primrose."

Mary's eyes shot up to his – *a viscount! He never told me he was a viscount. Why did he only introduce himself as Alexander Fitzwilliam?* As he was *officially* introduced to her, she curtsied, and stared at him, unable to look away. He was a little shorter than his cousin Mr Darcy, but they were similar in build and had the same piercing, green eyes, dark hair, and handsome looks. She could easily see the family resemblance with the two standing next to each other, and she did not know why she did not notice it earlier today. She had hoped not to see the stranger again while he was visiting his cousin in the neighborhood, but now that she knew his cousin was Mr Darcy, she was mortified at the circumstances of their afternoon ride.

*There she is,* Alex thought as they came through the door. He saw her shy look as she walked up to their party on the arm of the same older gentleman whom he had seen meet her at the door this afternoon. He was not certain if she told her parents of their encounter earlier in the day or not, but soon enough he would know just how these Bennet's would react to the ripe opportunity he had lain right in their laps to attach themselves to a peer. When Darcy introduced him, he saw her face shoot up and meet his eyes. *Was that hurt he saw in her features? What happened that would cause such a reaction?*

"Welcome to our home, my lord," Mr Bennet bowed.

Turning away from Mary, Alex returned the bow, "I am honoured you have allowed me to join you at such late notice, sir."

Patting his wife's hand, he replied, "Any family of Mr Darcy's is more than welcome in our home, my lord." Turning to the group, Mr Bennet said, "We have a few entertainments planned after dinner." He added with a raised brow, "If you are brave enough to join in on one *particular* game my girls have devised, please let one of them know. It is sure to be an amusement you will not wish to miss."

Mrs Bennet threaded her arm through Mrs Hurst's and the two walked off with the intention of introducing her to all the neighborhood women. Turning once again to Alex, Mr Bennet quietly said, "My lord, may I have a moment of your time?"

Detaching Miss Bingley from his arm, he nervously followed the older gentleman and Miss Mary. With his rank and position amongst the Ton, more than one young lady had set her cap for him. He had spent years trying to escape entangling himself in sticky situations with unmarried females. He was certain that was why Miss Bingley had attached herself so firmly to his arm already this evening; he would have to speak with Bingley about his sister.

*Now I am certain Miss Mary has told her father of our meeting, but I am still unsure of how much Mr Bennet knows. Will he be upset that a stranger has ridden on a horse with his daughter, even if it was with good intention? We were discreet, but I cannot be certain we were not seen by someone else. With being unknown in the area, and what it could have looked like when Miss Mary buried her head in my chest, there is no telling what may come of the encounter.*

As they entered a dark paneled room lined with bookshelves, Mr Bennet led Mary to a seat. He turned and with a simple bow of his head, he said, "I believe I owe you my gratitude, my lord. My daughter told me of your coming across her this afternoon and helping escort her back home."

Relieved that this was evidently all she told her father, Alex looked towards Mary, who was looking down at the hands held tightly clasped in her lap, and again turned to Mr Bennet, "It was my pleasure." Reaching into his inner pocket, he pulled out the handkerchief, "After I helped Miss Mary home, I went back to see if I could find her spectacles. Here they are, sir," he said, holding out the wrapped frames.

With a smile, Mr Bennet received them, "I thank you, my lord. You have saved us from having to search for them ourselves tomorrow, or having to order another pair from Town."

"I am glad to be of service to you, sir, and to you as well Miss Mary." With a bow towards both, and a second glance at Mary, Alex walked back out to join the rest of his party. He was relieved he had not been caught in a trap after all. *Well, Fitz,* he thought, *I think Darcy has found an honourable and loving family after all.*

"Here you go, my dear," Mr Bennet handed the wrapped package to his daughter. "It seems you will no longer require my arm all evening, so if you do not mind, I will go find your mother."

"No, I do not mind," she said quietly as she accepted the spectacles from her father. She unwrapped them and put them on her face as her father left the room. The cloth in her hand had intricate embroidery along the edge and she could not help but finger the delicate threads that made the bright blue and yellow primroses. In one ornately decorated corner were the letters *'A.F.'* in gold thread. It was the most beautiful handkerchief she had ever seen, and probably the most costly, and yet he had wrapped her spectacles in it for her. Her mind was whirling. *Why did he go back to find my spectacles?* Remembering how it felt to be in his embrace, she blushed thinking of him taking the time to climb down that muddy slope, probably ruining his own clothes, just to help her. *Why did he not tell me he was titled though?* He puzzled her completely. Although she knew she should leave the handkerchief on her father's desk, for some reason she stuck it in her pocket and left the study. She could not clear her mind, and as she joined the others she saw him on the other side of the room, again with Miss Bingley on his arm, amiably chatting with Sir William Lucas and Mr Darcy. Determined to avoid him for the rest of the night, she went to find Jane.

The evening continued, and Mrs Bennet's dinner was enjoyed by all. Lady Lucas was heard commenting to Mrs Long that it would be the talk of the neighborhood for months.

The parlour games were a delightful addition to the usual entertainment, and many of the neighborhood's young people enjoyed playing the Bennet sisters' made up game. They developed the idea from their own rainy day pastime of a production of Shakespeare's *'Much Ado About Nothing'* a few weeks prior. Sir William Lucas and Mr Bennet were the chosen officiates, and the participants were randomly divided into teams of three. Each group would silently act out as many stories as they could, from the list given to them by the officiates, in three minutes time, with the audience guessing which work of literature was portrayed. Mrs Bennet's contribution as a prize for the winning team members, was an embroidered handkerchief for each person.

The audience roared with laughter as hats and scarves were tossed about and tripped over by the actors. They especially loved it when Miss Elizabeth and Mr Bingley decided to play opposite genders while acting out Romeo and Juliet. The team of Mary Long, Louisa Hurst, and Viscount Primrose had a last second win, beating the team of Elizabeth Bennet, Charles Bingley, and Charlotte Lucas by only one point with their rendition of *'Jack The Giant Killer'*. Of course it helped that Alex was so tall that he easily looked the part of the giant next to an extremely short Mary Long. Miss Bingley's team came in last place. After being coerced into playing, Miss Bingley felt it *beneath herself* to pretend to be something she was not, and unfortunately for her team, it cost them several points.

The new game was deemed such a success that the rules were written down to be used at future parties in the neighborhood.

Elizabeth and Mary stood by the fire having some refreshments after the games. They were soon joined by Miss Bingley.

"Good evening, Miss Bingley," Elizabeth said. "I hope you are enjoying yourself?"

Miss Bingley eyed her, "It is tolerable, for a country dinner, though nothing to those in Town."

"Yes, well, we do the best we can," Elizabeth smirked.

"I am sure you do," Caroline replied snootily as she turned to walk away and find her self-appointed escort once again.

Miranda Philips was standing behind two of her nieces, drinking her tea and looking around the room at her neighbor's and family gathered all around. Rage was starting to seethe on the inside of her; would nothing go right in her life? She had been trying one plan after another for years, and nothing seemed to affect her younger sister's family. *Why? Why did Susannah get all the good, and she get all the bad?* Once again envious of all she did not have, from the fancy teacup in her hand, to the honourable gentleman and children at her half-sister's side, she felt her heart beating faster as her eyes fell on her two nearby nieces once again. She saw a tall, blonde-haired lady walk up to Elizabeth and Mary; it was obvious the lady held her nieces in disdain, so Miranda stepped closer behind the group to hear what was being said.

*"Yes, well, we do the best we can,"* she heard Elizabeth say.

*"I am sure you do,"* the blonde-haired lady answered haughtily before she sauntered off.

*Hmmmm,* she thought, *I need to find out who this person is; she may be a potential ally in my new plan.* Keeping a small distance behind the tall, blonde woman, she followed her across the room. The lady walked up to an extremely tall and attractive young gentleman with dark hair. As the lady threaded her arm through his, Miranda saw the look on his face. It was obvious he did not enjoy her attentions. *Maybe this information would come in handy*, she thought. Miranda continued to track the couple until the gentleman was finally able to remove himself from the woman and disappear from her side. Who were these unknown people? She would have to visit someone in the neighborhood tomorrow and catch up on the gossip she had missed while she was out of town. Miranda continued to follow the blonde lady as she circulated the room.

Kitty and Jane happily helped their mother mingle throughout the rooms, making the guests feel as comfortable as possible. Mary and Elizabeth soon joined Charlotte and some others around the piano, both lending their masterful talents to the entertainment. Lydia was allowed to join in with the musicians, and those who had not heard her play the violin were quite impressed with her artistry. Mary was touted to be the most accomplished girl in the neighborhood, and it showed in her playing this evening.

Elizabeth noticed a certain pair of bright green eyes following her wherever she went when she was not on his arm, and her heart fluttered with thoughts of him.

Caroline watched Alex stop to observe the group forming around the pianoforte. *Who could have caught his eye? Surely not one of the simple people of little means in this small country town?* She looked at the group, but could not tell where his eyes focused. Coming up to his side, she leaned into him, "My lord, I can guess the subject of your reverie."

"I should imagine not, madam." Alex hoped his newly forming admiration for Miss Mary was not seen by Miss Bingley.

"You are considering how insupportable it would be to pass many evenings in this manner – in such society; and indeed I am quite of your opinion. I was never more annoyed! The insipidity and yet the noise; the nothingness and yet the self-importance of all these people! What would I give to hear your strictures on them!"

"Your conjecture is totally wrong, I assure you." He said with the straightest face he could muster, "My mind was more agreeably engaged. I have been meditating on the very great pleasure which a pair of fine eyes in the face of a pretty woman can bestow."

"I am all astonishment! Who has caught your admiration in such a crowd as this?" Caroline asked.

Looking at her, he said, "Why, the Miss Bennet's, of course," then he turned and walked away, disappearing before a stunned Caroline could catch up to him again.

Finally free of her clutches, he walked outside, listening to the music through the opened windows. If he stood in one certain place in the garden, he could see the group surrounding the pianoforte. His height gave him the advantage also of seeing the person seated at the instrument. He watched as Mary's face showed deep emotions and her fingers flew across the keys. There was something about her that drew him. The ladies he had met in the past barely held his attention for the length of a set of dances, and yet here he was hiding in the bushes to see the bright eyes of a woman who completely fascinated and intrigued him.

When the music stopped he made his way inside again, trying to avoid Miss Bingley, whom he heard speaking with her sister in the hallway. He saw his cousin standing alone in the corner of the room, so he procured two drinks from the table nearby and went to join Darcy, offering him a glass. "I see you are still as unsocial and taciturn as ever."

Smiling slightly, Darcy took the drink, "I do not know how I earned such a reputation; after all, I do dance and join in society's functions." Alex smiled at his cousin's response. "Have you heard from the rest of the family lately? How is Anne? Aunt Catherine will not write to me after our rather heated words back in the summer."

Finishing the drink in his hand, Alex replied, "Yes, as a matter of fact I heard from Aunt Catherine just a fortnight ago. Anne is doing better and is now able to go out of her rooms, though she still tires rather quickly." Looking his cousin in the eye, he said quietly, "I truly feared for her life this time, Darce."

"Yes, as did I."

Changing the direction of their discussion before both were caught up in emotions rarely displayed, Alex continued, "Taking up the majority of the rest of Aunt Catherine's ten-page letter was advice on how I could catch the perfect heiress with a large fortune, and just whom she had in mind for the position — a certain '*Miss Webb*'."

"I can imagine she is not one you would wish to join yourself to for life."

"I do not see how everyone has put up with her advice for so long without reproaching her as you did. She once wrote me of a gentleman's young daughter she had the nerve to call down in the streets and reprimand. Let me see if I can remember how she put it." Clearing his throat, he repeated his Aunt's words in her typical proud manner, "*She had no bonnet, and her dress was at least six inches deep in mud. How she could have thought to be out like that is beyond me. She looked almost wild.*"

Rolling his eyes at their aunt's actions, Darcy patted his cousin's shoulder, "I am just glad it is you now and not me." When Alex chuckled, Darcy exclaimed, "I do not see how you can laugh at her attempts."

"Simple," he said, "because I know she is afraid of my father and he would never force my hand at the whim of his sister's declarations!"

Alex looked out over the crowd, his eye stopping when he saw Bingley standing on the side of the room beside the striking blonde he had been introduced to earlier as Miss Bennet. He watched the couple for a minute, then tipping his head that direction, he quietly asked, "Is this serious?"

Turning to see where Alex indicated, Darcy replied, "He can't keep his eyes off her when she is in the room, and she is all he speaks about when she is not – *his angel*. Miss Elizabeth assures me that, even though her countenance is all that is serene, her heart has been touched by him."

"Ahhh, so you and Miss Elizabeth have spoken of them." His eyebrows rose as he eyed his cousin. Lowering his voice once again, he asked, "So what of you and Miss Elizabeth – how serious is that situation?"

Swirling the drink in his hand, Darcy looked deep into his glass, and barely audibly said, "Serious enough that, if given the opportunity tonight, I would ask for her hand." Looking up into his cousin's eyes, he smiled shyly.

"Well then, why are you standing over here speaking to your dull cousin; go find your lady love and propose to her!"

"I have your blessing then?" Darcy asked with a touch of anxiety on his countenance.

Alex replied with a lift of his brow, "Do you need it?"

"No, but I would like to know my family approve of who I have chosen to be by my side."

Thinking of all he had learned earlier about the integrity of the Bennet's, Alex smiled, patted his cousin's shoulder, and raised his glass in salute, "Well then, yes, Darcy, you have my blessing. I will tell the family how perfect she is for you, how she brings a light to your eyes that I have not seen since Uncle George passed away."

"Thank you, Alex. That is just what I needed to hear," Darcy said with a grin as he too lifted his glass to his cousin's.

"Good; now get over there and do your duty." Alex indicated with his head the direction Miss Elizabeth was standing with her father and a few others.

Putting down his glass on a nearby table, Darcy walked away towards Elizabeth.

Alex put his own glass down and stepped outside to get some fresh air. As he strolled along the garden path he saw a familiar figure sitting on a bench in the corner of the garden. He was just about to walk out to her when Miss Bingley once again attached herself to his arm. Sighing, he turned back towards the house. There was no way he was going to be caught outside with Caroline Bingley. She would make sure the situation was viewed in as bad a light as possible. He would have to find another opportunity to speak with Miss Mary before the night ended.

Mary had a message from her mother for Mr Darcy, and she saw him in the corner of the room speaking with his cousin. She had hoped to avoid *the viscount* after the disastrous introduction earlier, but there was no way around it now. Sighing, and quietly working her way through the crowd, she came up behind the two tall gentlemen and caught the end of their conversation ". . . *She had no bonnet, and her dress was at least six inches deep in mud. How she could have thought to be out like that is beyond me. She looked almost wild..."*

Mary gasped, her heart pounding so loudly that her ears began to ring. *I thought this gentleman to be all kindness this afternoon when he rescued me, and while riding his horse I felt so at ease in his embrace. He even went out of his way to find my spectacles. Now here he is telling his cousin I had no right to be out in such a condition? What right does he have to give his opinion of me so freely? He has no say in my life or what I do!* Mary was furious! Forgetting the message she was sent to pass on, she quickly turned away from the gentlemen, making her way back through the crowd. She grasped her cloak and went outside into the garden. A few guests ambled about as she found a quiet corner bench and sat down. *Her heart broke.* She did not know why she felt so at ease with this gentleman this afternoon, but now that she knew his true opinion of her, she would not make the mistake again of trusting him. Tears welled up in her eyes, as she heard the words repeatedly in her mind. She felt the sting of rejection once again, only this time it hurt much worse than when James Lucas said she was not tolerable enough for a dance.

# CHAPTER XII

Elizabeth was standing with her father when she felt a familiar presence come up beside her. She knew exactly who it was without turning her head. He leaned over to whisper into Mr Bennet's ear, to which Mr Bennet waved him on. He then leaned down and, gently taking her elbow, he asked if he could speak to her privately. He led her to Mr Bennet's study, and as he closed the door, she realized what he was about. She nearly froze in nervousness, but he caught her eye and she calmed immediately. She did not realize he had led her to a chair until she was seated and he was bent down on one knee in front of her, holding one of her hands in both of his.

Looking into his brilliant green eyes, she heard him say, "Miss Elizabeth, you must allow me to tell you how ardently I admire..." his voice slightly cracking. He took a deep breath, cleared his throat, and continued, "... how ardently I admire and love you."

Her eyes filled with tears, and he heard her whisper, *"You love me?"*

Darcy smiled, "Most ardently." He gently lifted the hand encased in his, entwining his fingers with hers, and continued, "Miss Elizabeth Bennet, would you please do me the honour of accepting my hand? Will you please marry me?"

She was so overwhelmed that she could not speak. Nodding her head in answer, she saw the biggest smile form on his face, showing dimples she had never seen before. As she looked into his eyes, she knew she had made the most important decision of her life. "Oh, yes; yes, I will marry you!" she was finally able to respond.

He lifted her hand to his lips, kissing the back ever so gently, "I love you, *my Elizabeth*."

As tears began to stream down her face, she felt him dabbing her cheeks with his handkerchief. She looked back into his eyes, and for the first time voiced her own feelings, "I love you too..." stumbling, not sure what to call him, but feeling that *'Mr Darcy'* was too formal for the situation.

Sensing her reason for stopping, he quietly said, "William; please call me William."

Meeting his eyes, she raised her free hand to cup his cheek, and replied, "I love you too... *my William*." The smile on his face said it all as he heard her give voice to those words. As tempting as her mouth was, he knew he would be lost if he kissed her, so instead he helped her to her feet and gently pulled her into an embrace.

She felt his arms wrap around her. She laid her cheek against his chest and felt a peace she did not understand come over her. As she closed her eyes, the arms around her feeling so familiar, she shuddered. *Where have I felt this before,* she thought?

He pulled back slightly, "Are you all right, Elizabeth?"

Not knowing why she had shuddered, but not wanting to frighten him, she answered, "Yes, William, everything is perfect. I am just a bit chilled."

He led her over to the fire, and once again drew his arms around her. "Is that better?" he asked, rubbing her back.

"Yes, much," she answered quietly, as once again she closed her eyes and let the comfort of his embrace engulf her.

This time he felt her arms wrap around his body in return. Closing his own eyes and laying his cheek against her dark curls, he slowly took a deep breath. *He had found where he belonged – at long last.*

The two stood entwined before the fire for a few minutes, and then Darcy pulled away, "I believe we must return to your father, Elizabeth." Relishing in the freedom to call her by her name, she once again saw dimples appear on his face.

"Yes, it would not do to have him find us like this," she smiled, "though I do not mind the privacy he has allowed us thus far."

Darcy once again clasped her hands. Bringing them up to his lips, he bestowed a kiss on the back of each. Then he threaded one of her arms through his and led her from the room.

When they joined the group again Mr Bennet looked into his daughter's eyes. At her smile he then looked up at the man at her side and nodded with a knowing look. He excused himself and the two gentlemen left for a few words in private.

"I see you were serious about the need to speak again soon," Mr Bennet teased while closing the door.

Looking down at the floor, Darcy nervously replied, "Yes, sir."

"Since I have seen the way you both were looking at each other, I conclude that her answer was positive?"

Smiling slightly, Darcy answered, "Yes, sir, it was."

"Good then, there is no need to get emotional about this. Welcome to the family, son." After a firm handshake, he asked, "When do you wish to announce this?" With a conspiratorial look in his eye, Mr Bennet pronounced, "The whole neighborhood is in my sitting room, if your desire is to announce it immediately?"

Shaking his head in amusement, Darcy answered, "I will not deny *you* the pleasure of announcing it whenever and however you choose, sir." Looking up into his soon to be father-in-laws eyes, he continued, "My *own* pleasure is solely in Elizabeth's response."

"Capital, capital." Firmly patting Darcy's shoulder, Mr Bennet smiled, "If you will wait right here, I do feel the neighborhood needs to be spared my wife's initial effusions. I will warn you, she may be quite... exuberant."

"I can understand completely, sir."

A few minutes passed and Mr Bennet again opened the study door, leading his wife into the room. Following directly behind them was Elizabeth. Darcy was caught staring at her radiant face.

Clearing his voice, Mr Bennet led his wife to a chair, and began, "My dear, I have learned of something this evening, and thought it best to inform you of this unexpected development in private."

Not knowing what was to be said, Susannah had a fearful look in her eyes. Her voice quivered, "Is everything well, Henry?"

Bennet leaned down in front of his wife causing her to look directly at him, "Yes, my dear, everything is well. It is more than just *well*." He indicated the two young people who were now standing side by side in front of the fire trying not to intrude upon the moment of privacy needed by the older couple.

Susannah looked at her daughter, then looked at the gentleman standing at her side. Noticing how close they were standing, her attention went to their clasped hands. Her eyes welled up with tears when she once again looked at their faces and saw them gazing at each other, love shining bright in their countenance. "Oh, Henry!" she quietly managed to say as her hand went to her mouth.

Bennet pulled a handkerchief from his pocket and placed it in his wife's hand before turning to the young couple, "I believe she has figured it out on her own."

Elizabeth squeezed Darcy's hand as she heard her mother's breath catch in an emotional, tearful sob. He released her hand, and Elizabeth went to hug her mother.

Bennet walked to the other side of the room, followed by Darcy. "Would you like a drink?"

"No, sir, I would prefer to keep my wits about me at this moment."

Bennet chuckled, "Well, if you do not mind, I think I might need something myself."

"Not at all, sir," Darcy answered, sitting down in the chair in front of Mr Bennet's desk.

When Susannah was better able to control her tears, she hugged her daughter back. "Oh, Elizabeth, I am so glad you found love."

This statement from her sometimes-flighty mother brought tears of joy. She laughed, and pulled her own handkerchief from her pocket. "If you do not stop, we shall both have swollen eyes for the entire neighborhood to see."

"We cannot have that, now can we?" Taking a deep breath, the two ladies stood and straightened their dresses. Putting her daughter's stray curls back into place, Susannah continued, "You are beautiful, Elizabeth. Mr Darcy has seen what we have had the privilege of seeing for twenty years, and I am happy you have found such a young man that clearly adores you."

Seeing that the ladies were now ready to rejoin the party, the gentlemen stood and offered their arms in escort. When Susannah's hand wrapped around her husband's arm, he grasped her hand and gave it a squeeze. He quietly whispered into her ear, and she nodded her head in response. Turning to the younger couple, he quirked his eyebrow and said energetically, "Let us see of what mettle you are made, Darcy." They left the study and began gathering everyone together for the announcement that was sure to top the list of gossip in more than just Meryton for weeks to come.

Mary saw everyone going back inside, so she stood to make her way back in also. As she came in the door she saw that they were all gathered, though she did not know why. Over the voices, she heard her father say, "If I can have everyone's attention please..." He waited a moment for the conversation to cease, then continued, "We want to thank everyone for coming here tonight. It has been a long time since we have been able to do this, and we are honoured to celebrate this special evening with all of our friends." Smirking to Sir William nearby, he said, "I do believe we have surpassed even last month's Assembly with this turn out." Everyone laughed, and he continued, "As I said, we are honoured you are here tonight." He looked down at his wife's face and squeezed her hand. "I promised my wife that when my leg was strong enough to dance, we would begin entertaining in our home again. Our family has been through a challenging past few years, but we are still proudly standing before you. I am grateful to God for the family I can continue to have around me on a daily basis. From the bottom of our hearts, we thank you for joining us here tonight." Grasping Susannah's hand, he looked into her eyes and they shared a moment. "Before some of you begin to leave, my wife and I have one last thing we wish you all to know. We are truly blessed with our family, and we are soon to be even more blessed, as Mr Darcy has asked for our daughter Elizabeth's hand in marriage." He indicated the happy couple standing at their side.

A roar of excited congratulations went up all around the room.

Caroline was standing in the back corner. With the crowd gathering about, she had been separated from the viscount, and the announcement left her speechless and unable to catch her breath. She felt herself falling and was caught and led to a nearby chair. The next thing she knew, the Hursts were by her side. Louisa handed her a drink, and Hurst said he would call for the carriage.

On the other side of the room, by the doors leading to the garden, Mary found herself surrounded by cheers of excitement and congratulations for her family. She was uncomfortable in a crowd and turned to go back outside. She stepped quickly, not seeing what was in front of her. Suddenly she felt herself hit a familiar chest. Alex caught her elbow and helped her regain her footing, then asked if she needed some air. She looked at him and curtly replied no before turning and pushing her way through the crowd in the opposite direction.

Alex was taken aback. *What have I done to offend her?* Thinking back through their sparse interactions throughout the evening, he remembered her shock at his being introduced. *Maybe she did not think she would ever see me again and is embarrassed by what happened this afternoon?* Alex walked off to find his cousin and offer his congratulations, his head full of questions, and his heart reeling.

The three occupants of the carriage were silent, each lost in their own thoughts of the evening. Ten minutes into the drive, Bingley spoke up, "Congratulations, Will."

"Thank you."

"You know, you make it very hard on the rest of us mortals. I was going to ask Miss Bennet if she would allow me to court her, but you just jump straight into marriage!" Bingley said, half-jokingly.

"Bingley, do not base your own choices on what I do. If you feel you are ready to ask Miss Bennet for a courtship, then do so. You need not jump in as fast as I have." A look of peace came over his face as he said, "I have known since the moment I saw her that I would marry Miss Elizabeth; there is something about her that completes me. I have not felt this way since my mother and father were alive. The day I first met Miss Elizabeth I was out riding and it felt as if my parents were leading me. I could not determine why I had to be out that day until she came across a hill, walking in my direction."

"So the Assembly is not the first time you met?"

Smiling, he shook his head. "No; I saw her two days before my birthday, the day you went back to Town to get your sisters."

"Ahhh," he replied, "that makes sense. I knew upon my return that something happened, but I could not determine what."

Alex spoke up, "I haven't heard you say you felt like your parents were leading you for quite a while Darcy."

"I haven't felt like they were for the last few years." Quietly he added, "Until last spring."

Alex patted his cousin's shoulder, "But now you feel they have led you to Miss Elizabeth?"

"I felt them as strongly the day we met as I did when my father had just died. When I looked up and saw her, it was as if she fit into a part of my soul that no one else could. Without even knowing her or her name, I knew I would marry Miss Elizabeth. I knew she had been hand-picked by my father and mother."

"I heard your father say many times that one day, when it was time, he would help you choose your perfect mate. She would be lively and quick-witted, and would make you see the joy in life, as he said that is what your mother always said you needed."

With a faraway look, Darcy replied, "Yes, Mother told me so before she died. I promised her I would find the right person and not just marry some heiress for money or consequence. Somehow I would find the right person," quietly adding, "and now I have."

"I am glad you have, Darcy; I am glad you have."

As the carriage pulled up the drive to Netherfield Park and the men climbed down from the equipage. "I am sure we are all tired, so if you do not mind, I will go check on my family and retire." Bingley held his hand out to his friend, "Congratulations, my friend. You deserve someone as special as Miss Elizabeth." He started to walk up the stairs, but turned back to add, "I will have Mrs Nichols ready the guest chambers in case any of your family wish to visit." He turned back around and left the cousins.

Alex started to follow Bingley up the stairs when Darcy's voice stopped him, "If you think you shall get away that easily, you are mistaken, Alex. You owe me a story, and since I doubt I will be able to sleep tonight anyway, I intend to make you stay awake and keep me entertained." Darcy passed him on the stairs, walking through the front door. Alex rolled his tired eyes, but smiled and followed his cousin.

As they each settled into a chair in the library, Alex looked over at his cousin. *I have never seen him so at peace,* he thought. He took a slow drink from his glass and put it down on the table. "So, where do you want me to start?"

"At the beginning would be good," Darcy sarcastically answered.

"Ha ha, Darce. All right, I will indulge you tonight, but only because you are too happy to remember much of what I tell you anyway." Alex went on to tell him of the adventures of his day, but left out *certain details* of his meeting Mary. He was not sure why she was so unfriendly towards him at the end of the evening, but she intrigued him, and he was determined to sketch out her character. She seemed such a genuine young lady this afternoon when it was just the two of them, but tonight she avoided him completely. Several times he tried to say a few words to her, and each time she rebuffed his efforts and left. He would figure her out, he was determined. If it took time, then that is exactly what he would give her – time. That he had in plenty. He was not needed back in Town for several months.

Sarah Johnson

# CHAPTER

# XIII

Elizabeth awoke drenched in sweat. Her heart pounded so hard she thought it would jump from her chest. With bleary eyes, she looked around and began to calm as she saw that she was safely in her own room. She had sept for only an hour, but knew she would get no more sleep tonight. She went to the bowl of water on her dressing table and washed her face, then pulled a shawl around her shoulders and curled up in her window seat. As she looked out over the dark, moonlit garden, she tried to remember her dream.

The little snippets of what she could recollect were very confusing – she thought she heard a thunderclap, and she might have seen a tree limb – everything else was unclear. However, one thing was very vivid. She kept hearing a conversation she and her Granny Bennet once had when she was five years old.

*"My Lizzy-Belle, come here and sit with your old Granny for a bit." Lizzy bounded over to her Granny and snuggled up beside her on the sofa. "Do you know what I have for you today? A special treat."*

*"A special treat? For ME?"*

*Laughing, she tapped the end of Elizabeth's nose, "Yes, sweet child, for YOU!"*

*Bouncing up and down on the seat, Lizzy enthusiastically asked, "What is it? What is it?"*

*With a gentle hand on her shoulder, Granny Bennet said, "Calm down, dear. We would not want to wake your sister upstairs, now would we?"*

Putting her finger to her lips and loudly whispering, Elizabeth shook her head side to side, "Oh, no, we shan't do that. Lyddie does cry a great deal."

Granny Bennet laughed, "Yes, my dear, some babies are a little more prone to crying than others. Now settle down here beside me, and I shall show you my surprise."

Rose Bennet reached over to the table and picked up a very old, well-worn book. "I was going through an old trunk of mine the other day, and I came across this book," she said, holding it out for her granddaughter to see, and allowing her to lovingly finger the smooth texture of the leather binding. "My own Grandmother used to read this to me when I was your age, and since Janie is gone this week, and you seem a bit down, I decided you would get to hear it from me first."

"Oh how fun! Thank you Granny," Lizzy said as she snuggled into her grandmother's arms.

Rose opened to the front page and quietly read, "Once upon a time, there was a widower who married a proud and haughty woman as his second wife. She had two daughters, who were equally vain. By his first wife, he'd had a beautiful young daughter, a girl of unparalleled goodness and sweet temper."

Lizzy interjected, "Just like Janie!"

Chuckling, she said, "Yes my dear, just like Janie; and just like you too."

As the story unfolded, Rose Bennet watched Elizabeth's expressive eyes. She was sad for the girl's loss when her father passed away, and was incensed at the treatment the poor girl received at the hands of her mean stepsisters and stepmother. "I would have run outside and hidden in my tree, Granny; then they would never be able to find me."

"Yes, they would not have been able to find you there. You are safe up in your trees aren't you, my Lizzy-Belle?"

Settling her granddaughter back down, Rose continued reading. The more she read, the brighter Elizabeth's eyes got; she was mesmerized by a fairy godmother and glass slippers, and when Rose read of the ball, Elizabeth stood and twirled around the room as if she were dancing in the ballroom with the magical couple.

*Rose finished the story, ". . . and they lived happily ever after." She looked down at Elizabeth who was now sitting on her knees on the floor, staring up at the book, and listening with intensity. "Did you like that story, Lizzy-Belle?"*

*With a dreamy look in her eyes, Elizabeth answered, "Oh, yes! One day I want to marry a prince and live in a castle!"*

*Rose laughed. Helped her granddaughter up onto her lap, she said, "Well, my dear, one day, when you are old enough, I will help you find the right gentleman. He may not live in a castle, but he will be perfect for you." Rose gently pulled her into a tight embrace and kissed her forehead.*

Elizabeth dried the tears from her eyes as she wrapped her arms tighter around her legs. She missed her Granny Bennet so much that it hurt. *I have found my prince, Granny, and I believe you would like him very much,* she thought. Fitzwilliam Darcy was the epitome of the kind of gentleman Elizabeth could imagine her Granny Bennet approving of.

She was lost once again in memories as she sat there watching the sun come up on what looked to be a beautiful autumn day.

"Madam, your mail." John handed Mrs Gardiner the stack of letters then retreated from the room.

Maddie took a sip of her coffee and asked her husband, "Have you decided what you will do yet?"

Edward Gardiner was distracted by the paper spread in front of him. "Hmmmm? What was that, my dear?"

"I asked what you will do, Edward. Last night you were still uncertain, and after your early morning visitor, I was not sure if you had decided yet," his wife asked.

Hearing the tone of her voice, he knew it would be best to put his paper away for now. He folded it, took a sip of his tea, and cleared his throat. "Well, I think Bennet will like the news I have for him. I need to write down what I learned this morning, and maybe hire out for a personal delivery courier. I would not trust this correspondence to the post."

Going through her stack of mail, Maddie was drawn to one letter in particular, "Oh my! Look at this mess," she said, holding it up. "It looks as if it may have been dropped." Examining it carefully, she said, "This address was put on very ill indeed, but I think it may be Lizzy's hand. It looks as if it has been redirected several times, no doubt because of the writing."

"You could just open it and find out who sent it, my dear," Gardiner smirked.

Maddie carefully opened the seal to find that it had indeed, been dropped in a puddle. The ink was smeared, and she was unable to make out more than just a few words in the greeting. "Well, this explains why I had not heard from our niece in a few weeks, but I cannot make any of this out. I will have to write Lizzy and let her know I could not read a thing from her letter."

"If you finish your reply by noon, I shall add it to the courier package I need to send to Longbourn," Gardiner said.

"Thank you, my dear; I will write to her this morning."

Mr Gardiner was passing the front door when he noticed an express being accepted by the footman. Thinking it may be from his brother-in-law, he stopped to retrieve the letter. After having correctly ascertained the sender, he returned to his study to read what was so important that an express charge was necessary.

October 31, 1811
Longbourn
Hertfordshire


Dear Gardiner,

I imagine you are in a dither over this being an express, so let me start by saying, no one is in ill health. I have not written to you on family matters in a while, and with some recent developments, I thought I would fill you in, though I am certain Maddie has heard from my ladies often and she has told you of their correspondences.

My leg is getting stronger and recently taking up riding again has been a great strengthening exercise. Though I can feel the cold of winter setting in, it has not stopped me from doing things I have not done in years. At last month's Assembly I was even able to dance with Susannah. Ahhh, the small joys in life! Who would have believed that I, Henry Bennet, would be excited over being able to dance with my wife? You know how much your sister loves to dance, so you can imagine her own joy at such an event.

Having promised her that once I was that strong enough to dance we would start entertaining again, I knew this was coming. She went into a frenzy planning the grandest dinner party I have seen in years here in Meryton. It was a joy to be able to host the neighborhood again, and though I have a feeling we will be doing more again very soon, I am delighted to have it over and done with for now.

As I am sure your wife has already heard, but a few single gentlemen recently joined the neighborhood. Mr Charles Bingley leased Netherfield Park, and he brought with him his two sisters, his brother-in-law, and his friend; his friend's cousin just joined the party, though I am unsure how long he plans to stay. The gentlemen have been here often over this last month, pretending their reasoning is to play me in chess, but I know they are here to court my girls. I am certain Jane is well on her way to having her heart lost to another, and I expect Mr Bingley to be beating down my door any day now, for as my wife is wont to say, 'a single man in possession of a large fortune must be in want of a wife.'

*As for his friend, he has taken a liking to my Lizzy. They sit for hours debating literature and playing chess, and he challenges her in ways I could never hope to do as her father. He is a quiet man, but I have found him to be intelligent and respectable. Last night, he asked for my blessing to marry my Lizzy, and though it saddens me to give her away to someone else, my heart is gladdened with who she has chosen. She has accepted a man worthy of her hand and her heart.*

*He has said his estate is quite large and is in Derbyshire, and I know that both of his parents are no longer living, as he has charge over his young sister. Mr Bingley has assured me that he is an honourable gentleman and well worth the catch, and having met his cousin last night, I was impressed by the family presented to us so far. However, that is about all I know of his home life. I thought perhaps Maddie has heard of him and can give us some information, having come from Derbyshire herself. His name is Mr Fitzwilliam Darcy. Please let us know if you have met him or know anything of him. I have found him to be a great addition to our family gatherings, and look forward to adding another male permanently to the family table soon.*

*I am sure when you have news of our business dealings I will hear from you again. Thank you for all you have helped me with so far, and give your family our love.*

*Sincerely,*
*Bennet*

Gardiner looked at the letter again – *Mr Fitzwilliam Darcy – yes, that is what it says. I must go find Maddie immediately!*

Walking quickly to the sitting room, he saw his wife sitting at her desk writing to Lizzy. He heard Sophia practicing her scales on the pianoforte in the corner of the room and saw Rebecca and David seated nearby going over their letters with their governess. Not wishing to alarm her in the midst of their children, he said, "Dearest, would you please join me in my study? I have received a letter that might interest you."

Maddie heard the anxiety in his voice, and immediately became concerned. She rose and followed him to his study, and when she closed the door she quickly asked, "Is everyone well, Edward? What has happened?"

"No one is in ill health my dear, I am sorry to have frightened you. I have received a letter from Bennet, and I felt you must read this for yourself," he said, handing it to her.

He watched her face as she smiled while reading of the new entertainments Bennet was able to enjoy and as tears of joy welled in her eyes at the knowledge that their niece was to marry. He could tell when she reached the name at the bottom. Maddie dropped the letter on the desk and gasped, putting her hand to her mouth. "Oh NO! What are we to do, Edward? How did they ever meet?"

"I do not know dear, I only know that he is evidently a friend of this," looking down at the letter again, he read, "*Mr Charles Bingley*, who has taken the lease at Netherfield Park near Longbourn."

"I thought not taking her back to Derbyshire, and not going to the Season's entertainments on the west side of Town, would be enough. All these years, and they have never been introduced to each other while here for months at the same time!"

Placing a calming hand on his wife's shoulder, he replied, "I know, dear. We have done all we ever could to keep them from finding out. Now that they have met, and especially since they are soon to be married, they need to know."

Drying the tears from her eyes with her handkerchief, Maddie agreed with her husband.

"So, it seems a personal courier is not needed after all; I can deliver these papers to Bennet myself." He indicated the package ready to be closed as soon as Maddie's letter to Lizzy was added. Meeting her eyes, he quietly said, "I think you need to go with me as well, my dear. I have a feeling Elizabeth would do better hearing this story from you."

"Yes," she replied again, trying to focus on what he said, "yes, I need to be with you."

"My partner, Mr Stone, was already alerted to the possibility of my needing some personal time soon, so maybe this would be a good time to take the family to the country. I am sure the children will love the last of the autumn blooms and leaves that they hardly get to appreciate here in Town. I will make arrangements for us to leave at dawn; can you ready everything by then, my dear?"

Straightening her back, and drying the last of the tears from her eyes, Maddie replied, "Yes, I can have everything readied by then."

<hr>

Alex and Darcy came down the stairs slowly after their late night. They met Bingley in the dining room, and both accepted the offered cups of coffee.

"Drink up, drink up, we must not be late!"

Bingley' enthusiastic effusions were too much for Alex. "Do you plan to show up at their doorstep before they have even had the chance to dress or break their fast? Have patience, Bingley. Your angel will be there waiting for you, but I insist first that we be allowed to have some toast and maybe a second cup of coffee before we go out into the cold."

Darcy chuckled; Alex had such a way with Bingley. "You are just jealous, Alex. You need to find your own girl, then we shall see how happy you will be to pass up the second cup of coffee to be by her side."

Alex rolled his eyes; *if only you knew how much I envy your position, cousin. I very much look forward to visiting the Bennets today, though I will not give you the benefit of knowing that just yet.*

"Do you know what your plans are for the next few days?" Bingley asked.

"I would imagine that will depend upon Miss Elizabeth and her plans," Darcy answered.

Alex joked, "Ahhh, a very noble gesture. You might just make a decent husband after all, Darce."

"Well, I just received notice this morning that if I am able to make it, I am needed in Town for a last minute meeting of shareholders tomorrow, so this afternoon I must leave. I did not know if you needed me to do anything for you while I am there, or if there was a need for you to travel there yourself; if so, we could ride together." Bingley stated.

"As much as I would be loath to leave my lady's side, I do have a few things I will need to speak with my solicitor about. Let me speak with Miss Elizabeth and Mr Bennet this morning, and I will let you know. I may be at leisure to accompany you to Town if it is only for a few days."

"Yes, only for a few days. I do not intend to leave the neighborhood, no matter what Caroline thinks of it; she can always go stay with her friends if she so wishes."

Finishing his last bite, Darcy placed his serviette on the table and stood, "Since we seem to have some time before we leave, I have a few letters that need to be written. I will be in the library when you are ready to go."

Caroline and Louisa came into the dining room a few minutes later, both speaking of the newest fashions. Louisa's tastes tended towards the more conservative side than Caroline's. The two resembled each other so much that others often looked to their attire to determine with whom they were speaking. Alex was always amazed at their resemblance — if only both of their characters were as Mrs Hurst's, then Miss Bingley could have possibly turned his eye many years ago. As it was though, her attitude made him shy away from the slightest association with her, and Alex stiffened when Miss Bingley chose to sit down next to him at the table. Hoping to distance himself, he asked, "May I help you with your plate, Miss Bingley?"

"Oh, my, yes; I thank you, *my lord,*" Caroline said with a sugary sweetness to her voice.

Alex went to the sideboard and chose a few items for her plate. As he set it down in front of her, he said to his friend, "I will be with my cousin when you are ready to leave for Longbourn."

Bingley hurriedly stood, "I am ready; let us leave now." The two left to see if Darcy had completed his letters.

The reminder of what had been announced the night before made Caroline lose her appetite. She must find a way to either break up the new couple, or ingratiate herself to Viscount Primrose. Caroline needed a plan, and unfortunately, she had no idea what to do. She would write to her friend Prudence Morley to see if she could think of something. After pushing the food around on her plate a few more minutes, Caroline excused herself to go write her letter.

*I do not know what you are up to Caroline, but I will find out; I will not let you ruin this happiness for Mr Darcy,* Louisa thought as she stood to follow her sister.

# CHAPTER XIV

The three gentlemen rode to Longbourn in silence, and were received by the master of the house as he came out of the dining room. "Gentlemen, you are up and about early this morning, I see."

"Yes, sir; I hope we are not intruding upon your household too early?" Darcy asked.

Shaking his head and smiling, Bennet replied, "No, the ladies have been up speaking of the latest *on dit* for more than an hour now. They are in the sitting room if you wish to join them."

"I would like to speak to you privately first," Darcy said.

"This way, Mr Darcy," Bennet held his arm out towards his study. "We shall see you in a little while then, gentlemen?"

"Yes, that will be fine, sir," Bingley answered as he and Alex turned towards the sitting room.

"I have a feeling their private chat may be of some time, wouldn't you say?" Bingley asked Alex.

"I do not know; perhaps Miss Elizabeth's presence in the sitting room will lure them back out soon enough."

The gentlemen were announced to the ladies in the sitting room and they looked around to see the three sisters sitting by the window. All three stood, and both gentlemen were greeted.

Bingley and Jane immediately went to the other side of the room for more intimate conversation, which left Alex to the other two ladies. With a bow, he said, "Miss Elizabeth, Miss Mary; it is a pleasure to see you again today." Turning towards Elizabeth, he continued, "My cousin is speaking with your father."

"Thank you, sir." Sitting and indicating for Alex to sit as well, she continued, "We did not have a chance to speak last night, my lord, so I am pleased you chose to visit today."

With a smile, Alex replied, "We are soon to be family, Miss Elizabeth; I would be honoured if you would dispense with the formalities of rank."

With an arch of her brow, Elizabeth answered, "As you wish, sir."

Mary looked down at her hands as the two beside her carried on in their playful way. She listened intently, trying to calm her heart. She did not understand why, but every time he was around her heart would beat violently. If it were not for what she overheard last evening, she could very well fall for his charms easily. She wondered if she should tell Elizabeth what she overheard. Did her sister need to be wary of Mr Darcy's family? He seemed to be all that was charming now, but was this an accurate assessment of his character?

On the opposite side of the room, Bingley and Jane sat side by side on the sofa, speaking of the previous night's entertainments. Suddenly Bingley's face showed worry as he turned his body a little closer to his companion and asked, "Miss Bennet, will you allow me to ask you something personal?"

Jane felt her cheeks begin to glow, but answered, "Very well, Mr Bingley, you may ask."

Looking down at his hands, and trying to dry his sweaty palms without her noticing, he cleared his throat, "Miss Bennet, when I took the lease on Netherfield Park I was not sure what I wanted from this neighborhood. I knew it was a good idea to lease an estate first while I looked for one to buy, but I had not intended to find the neighborhood so accommodating." He smiled and her, and her gentle presence let him know that she wished him to continue. "I know our acquaintance has been only a month, but I am determined to fulfill what my heart desires." Picking up her hand in his, he asked quietly, "Miss Bennet, would you allow me to court you?"

Time seemed to stop for Bingley. *Will she be offended at my offer? Would she even accept the intent of where I am hoping this will one day lead?*

Jane squeezed his hand, and quietly replied, "I would be honoured, sir."

Both smiled and he released her hand before those on the other side of the room saw them. "Thank you, Miss Bennet. I shall speak to your father today. I have some business which must draw me to Town for a few days, but I did not want to leave without speaking with you." Her smiling countenance was telling to him of her joyfulness, and they sat quietly talking for a few more minutes before Mr Bennet and Darcy came into the room.

A short walk was proposed, and the three ladies gathered their hats and cloaks. Darcy and Bingley held out their arms to their ladies and they walked out into the garden, with Alex and Mary following behind. Alex walked beside Mary, but did not offer her his arm – he was not sure she would have accepted it. So far she had not even acknowledged him today.

Mary was cynical and rarely saw the immediate good in any situation. It took a lot to break through the barriers she kept up around her heart, and she was not in the mood to let this gentleman, no matter what his rank in society, cause her to lower her guard again. She quietly walked on behind her sisters, refusing to even look at the gentleman beside her. His insults had cut her to the core, but she would not let him see her cry.

Alex had never met anyone like her before, and he was drawn in by her odd comportment. He had always been fawned over because of his rank and his wealth, yet that seemed to mean nothing to the lady beside him. She stood no taller than the middle of his chest, however she had a look on her face as if she had the strength of a tower. His charming demeanor and likable personality meant nothing to her.

For some reason, instead of being offended at her treatment, Alex was intrigued and found her icy stare and stony countenance a bit comical, almost like that of a petulant child. She would not look his way nor speak to him. That was fine with him, he could learn about her without words. What he already knew of Mary and the Bennets had impressed him. He had seen her yesterday at her most vulnerable, and he knew that eventually she would allow him to see her that way again. He would have to work through the thorns, but he had a feeling he would like the rose at the end.

After their walk, Bingley spoke with Mr Bennet about his intentions regarding Jane. He asked for, and was granted, permission to court his lovely angel, and Bingley left Mr Bennet's study with a smile on his face.

The three men could stay for only an hour, and left before Mrs Bennet or the two youngest came downstairs from their studies. They quickly rode back to Netherfield Park and within another hour were all in Darcy's carriage and off to Town.

"Is there a particular reason you wanted to go with us Alex? After all, you just left Town yesterday morning," Bingley asked.

Alex adjusted in the uncomfortable carriage, "You could not offer enough to induce me to stay, in a house with your sister, without you around, Bingley."

He laughed, "Oh, don't tell me she frightens you? She has been after Darcy for years, and he has come out of it unscathed!"

"Yes, well, I do not wish to push my luck. I would rather ride back with you two. So, what kind of entertainment do you plan to have now that you have a country estate at your fingers?"

"I had thought to have a ball. I know not all here would be pleased to dance," he looked askance at Darcy, "but I myself enjoy the exercise."

"Now that I can dance three sets with Miss Elizabeth, I might find that a ball is just to my liking." Alex and Bingley laughed at Darcy's change of attitude.

"I am sure while you are dancing you will quite enjoy yourself. However, I will have to remember to stay away from your glare when Miss Elizabeth is dancing with others who will, no doubt, ask her for a set." Alex laughed at his cousins' scowl and turned to answer Bingley. "A ball does sound enjoyable though, Bingley. When do you propose to have this grand affair?" Alex asked.

"As soon as may be. I will have the invitations printed while we are in Town, and when I return and speak with my sister, I will set the date. I would hope to have it before the Christmas season begins."

"Sounds good; I may just stay with you for a while then. Is there anything else to fill your winter months in the country?"

Bingley thought for a minute, "Hmm...I *have* always wished to host a fox hunt?"

"Ahhh, yes, the obligatory fox hunt," Darcy said dryly as he continued to thumb through his book. "Well, it *is* the season for such activities."

The two ignored him as they continued to discuss the pleasures which a country estate held. All were hoping this trip would be completed and they would be back in Hertfordshire within a week.

---

"An express has come for you, sir," Mr Hill said to Mr Bennet as he came out of the study to join his family for supper.

Seeing that it was from Gardiner, Bennet thought, *I was not expecting an express in reply; what could be wrong?* "Please tell my wife I will be there shortly, I must not put this one off." Bennet went back into his study, and quickly broke the seal.

> *October 31, 1811*
> *#36 Gracechurch Street*
> *London*
>
> *Dear Bennet,*
>
> *Your letter came at a most opportune time, as I have just received papers that I must pass on to you. Having a few weeks at my leisure, I find that, instead of a courier for your documents, I will be available to deliver them myself.*

*Maddie and I will leave at dawn and expect to be there, with our family in tow, by afternoon tea, or maybe even before — with young children, I cannot determine for certain when we will arrive, as I am sure you can understand.*

*I am positive this will make Susannah happy, as we have not seen her for nearly a year. She will not believe how much Sophia, Rebecca, and David have grown. Please do tell her of our arrival; she would never forgive you if you left her to fuss about after our arrival, setting up bedroom situations and planning meals. I know how much you love a good joke, but for the sake of my nerves after a carriage ride with three little ones, please think on me with compassion and let my sister know this evening of our subsequent arrival.*

*Your Brother,*
*Gardiner*

Laughing at the last paragraph of the letter, and smiling at the opportunity to see his nieces and nephew again, Bennet folded the missive and went to join his family for supper. Gardiner had not indicated one way or the other whether the news he must convey was good or bad, but Bennet was hopeful of good news.

Susannah caught his eye as he sat down at the head of the table, and he answered her unspoken plea, "Everything is fine my dear, it was just an express from Gardiner."

"What necessitated an express?" she asked.

He nodded to the servant, and supper commenced., "It seems our relations are in need of some fresh air, and have decided to join us here in the country for a few weeks. They will be here by tea time tomorrow."

Enthusiastic exclamations were heard all around the table, and Mrs Bennet replied, "Oh, my! Oh, I have so much to do before they arrive! The guest bed will not have time to air out properly, and the nursery is not ready for little ones again," her nerves were immediately on edge; she would be glad to see them, but so many people in the house might prove to be too much for her. She was already in a flutter over one daughter being engaged and another being courted, both by respectable gentlemen of some means, and now to add to that visitors!

She felt faint and began to fan herself with her handkerchief when her husband calmly said, "My dear, I believe you have never failed to impress with your meals, and I think our girls are old enough to determine the sleeping arrangements. I would even guess that there is no need to open the guest chambers either, if our girls are willing to share, as they are often wont to do anyway." When his daughters eagerly agreed, he continued, "See my dear, there is no need to become distressed – your brother and his family will understand if everything is not perfect." Looking at Elizabeth, he smiled, "And I imagine you could use Mrs Gardiner's help with plans for the wedding!"

The rest of the evening was spent speaking of the children and what the elder cousins wished to do for entertainment during their visit. Mary's room was too small to accommodate two people, so it was decided that Jane would sleep with Elizabeth, leaving Jane's much nicer bedroom for their Aunt and Uncle Gardiner. Lydia's recent move downstairs to share with Kitty left the nursery the perfect place for the three young children, however, as their mother pointed out, it was in no condition to house little ones at this time. All five girls went upstairs to the nursery to see to the preparations.

Kitty saw the stack of books Elizabeth pulled from the shelves and was going through. "Oh, Lizzy, is the book of fairy tales I used to love still up here? I am certain Rebecca will like some of those stories."

"Yes, I have that book right here," Elizabeth held it up. Looking over at her sister, she asked, "What are you doing Kitty?"

"I thought I would put out some of my old art supplies. I recently switched to a new medium and these will just go to waste if they are not used. Who knows, maybe David will want to showcase his artistic abilities."

Giggling, Lydia looked up from the handkerchief dolls she was making for her cousins and replied, "Yes, I am sure he could paint the most realistic figures as only a four year old can."

Shrugging her shoulders and straightening the legs on the easel, Kitty replied, "Well, even if his art is not worthy of the gallery wall, I am certain Aunt Maddie will still appreciate his efforts."

The sisters chatted while Jane added details to the faces of the handkerchief dolls Lydia was making. Elizabeth and Mary set out some music and books for the children to peruse while Kitty finished laying out the art supplies she would not need any longer.

It was not much longer before everything was in place. As the girls looked around the room one last time, they were proud of all they had achieved in just a short amount of time. The room looked ready to accommodate the three young children in whatever venture they desired during their stay.

"I remember not too many years ago when all five of us shared this room," Jane said, thinking back to when they were much younger. They all hugged, and Lydia and Kitty retired to their own room for the night.

"You go on to bed, Jane; Mary and I will snuff out the candles," Elizabeth said as she hugged her sister once again. Jane quietly left to go to her room, while Mary and Elizabeth walked around the room extinguishing the candles.

When they started to walk to the door, Mary's hand stopped Elizabeth. "I have not had the opportunity to congratulate you on your engagement. Mr Darcy is very pleasant and admires you greatly. I am so happy for you, Lizzy."

"Thank you, Mary." Elizabeth replied as she picked up the last candlestick for them to see where they were going. "Now that I will soon be married, and will undoubtedly have to be in Town for the season, maybe you can stay with us instead of our Aunt and Uncle."

"Oh, Lizzy, what fun that would be! Although, I would not want to offend Aunt Mattie and Uncle Edward when they have already invited me to join them."

Elizabeth hugged her sister, "I doubt they would see it as an insult." She chuckled and with an air of superiority said, "You know Mama would approve, after all, imagine all the men of such importance to whom you will now be exposed!"

The two laughed. "Thank you, Lizzy. If your Mr Darcy sees fit to invite me, I would be honoured to visit you in Town."

Elizabeth wiggled her eyebrows in an impertinent manner, "I think I can persuade Mr Darcy to do just that."

The girls again laughed as they arrived at Mary's bedroom door. Elizabeth leaned in and whispered, "I plan to make Jane tell me every detail of what happened with Mr Bingley. Would you care to join me?" Mary nodded, and Elizabeth continued, "I shall be back in a few minutes then and we will go to Jane's room. Dress quickly!" Each went into their chambers and dressed for bed before they went to speak with their eldest sister of all that had occurred.

Elizabeth knocked lightly, but when there was no answer, she poked her head into her sister's room. She saw her staring into the mirror while she brushed her hair. "Janie, do you have a minute?"

Slowly turning to see her sister, Jane answered, "Oh Lizzy! Come in, come in — I must speak with you." Seeing Mary behind her, she added, "Oh, you too Mary, come in."

Elizabeth and Mary walked into Jane's room and Mary sat down on the bed, petting her cat, Beatrice, who stayed willingly in her arms. Elizabeth walked over, took the brush from Jane's hand, and turned her around to stroke the golden locks. Enthusiastically she replied, "We have waited all day, Jane, you must tell us everything. Do not leave out even one detail!"

Jane told of all that had occurred that morning, blushing when she recounted how Mr Bingley held her hand. After she finished, she smiled more broadly than Lizzy had ever seen, "I cannot believe it, Lizzy. He asked to court me! Can you conceive of such happiness?"

Elizabeth smiled at her sister's happiness, imaging the happiness she felt with William was much like Jane felt with Mr Bingley.

Jane blushed and turned around, taking the brush from her sister's hand. "Oh, I imagine you can, since you are now to be married!"

"I am so happy for you! You deserve the best, and Charles Bingley is such a wonderful gentleman."

Jane's mien was serious when she replied, "You deserve the best too Lizzy, and I am glad you now have Mr Darcy."

Elizabeth smiled and hugged her eldest sister. Mary put Beatrice down on the bed and came up behind them, joining in the embrace. "You both deserve the best, and I am happy you have found Mr Darcy and Mr Bingley." All three girls talked for another hour about all that had happened to Jane and Elizabeth over the last few days.

As Elizabeth lay in her bed, she quietly whispered, "Good night William," and clutched her pillow. *I hope he is able to finish his tasks sooner than expected and return to me before the week is out*, she thought. *I think I will be glad for the distraction of having our cousins here to entertain for the next week.*

# CHAPTER

## XV

Mary sat on her bed, journal in hand and with her cat Beatrice on her lap. She opened to a new page and began to write:

*October 31, 1812*

*Today was the first day of Lizzy's engagement to Mr Darcy. Not to be outdone however, Mr Bingley asked to court Jane. These two brave gentlemen will, I fear, soon find out of what mettle they are made. Mama was full of anxiety after they left this morning.*

*I wonder — will I ever marry? I know it is the duty of every good daughter to marry and not leave herself open to ridicule and mockery, but I am not certain anyone would want to marry me. I am not the most beautiful, my glasses are thick and awkward, I am short like Lizzy, but unlike her, I do not walk often enough to be as slender.*

*Papa says he will leave the decision of who we marry up to us, but what if I decide I do want to marry and yet no gentleman will have me? I know what torment Charlotte Lucas receives from the neighborhood for not marrying by her age, and I am not certain I could endure such ridicule. Yet it might be my fate with the country's lack of males due to the war.*

Her pencil was stopped by Beatrice, who insisted on being petted, so she set her journal aside. "Do *you* think I will ever marry?" she asked as she picked up the cat and looked into her eyes. Beatrice meowed in response and Mary answered back, "Of course you would say that, you are just trying to cheer me up."

Leaning back into her pillow, she put the cat down across her lap and began to run her fingers through the white fur. "I doubt I will ever find someone who could love me." For Mary's statement she received claws digging into her leg. "OUCH!" She rubbed the spot vigorously, trying to alleviate the pain. "All right, you win; I may *one day* find someone who is willing to love me."

After a minute of silence, Mary asked, "Since you seem to believe such a paragon among gentlemen exists, what do you think he would be like?"

Mary's hand stopped moving too long, and Beatrice nudged it with her head. When that did not produce the desired attention, she jumped up on top of Mary's head. Reaching up to remove the cat from her hair, Mary said, "Oh, you think he should be tall?" At the cat's loud meow in reply, Mary resumed the petting. "If he were tall he could reach books on the shelf that I cannot reach without a ladder, and you know how I feel about climbing on those." Mary opened her journal again and began to write.

> *My list of requirements in a husband, if such a man does exist:*
>
> *1. He must be tall...*

"So, tall he shall be. What next? Do you care about hair color?"

Looking at the cat and receiving no response, she said, "No, I did not think you would. I am certain it would not matter to me either." Mary thought for a minute and then replied, "I think strong eyesight is one feature I would have to insist upon." Beatrice meowed and started to clean her fur while Mary picked up her pencil to write again.

Mary said the next one as she wrote. "While he must be able to see well, he must also not be too concerned with being embarrassed." The cat's tail swished leftward, knocking the pencil from Mary's hand. Chuckling, Mary picked it up again, "Yes, you seem to be as clumsy as me. He must have a sense of humour or it is certain he would become burdened over time."

"I think as far as physically, that is all I shall put. Now we move on to the more important attributes of this supposed gentleman – his character. Do you have anything to add?" The cat immediately stood and began loudly meowing. "He must be talkative you say? Yes, I can see how that would come in handy, since I do not speak much – except to you." Mary settled the cat back down and added that to the page.

After another ten minutes of coming up with characteristics to add to her list, she finally put her pencil down. "Now, let us see what we have, shall we?" she asked Beatrice as she picked up her journal to read.

*"My list of requirements in a husband, if such a gentleman should exist:*

*1. He must be tall, but not as tall as Mr Darcy. I do not want to have to use a ladder to kiss him."*

Mary's cheeks blushed when she read what she had written. Clearing her throat, she continued.

*"2. He must be in possession of strong eyesight; it would not do to have two people with poor eyesight marry – think of our poor children!*

*3. A sense of humour is a must, otherwise my not-so-graceful nature may one day become a burden to his sensibilities.*

*4. He must be able to carry on intelligent conversations and be comfortable speaking. Two quiet individuals, such as Mr Jonathan Lucas and myself would make a very dull house indeed.*

*5. While I am certain Mr Bingley is the perfect person for Jane, I cannot imagine being married to someone who is so fidgety. A calm individual would do nicely.*

*6. Unlike Mr James Lucas, he must be humble enough to admit faults, and yet amiable enough to not point them out in others."*

Putting her journal down, Mary again addressed her feline friend, "Do you think such a gentleman even exists?" Barely above a whisper, she added, "And if he does exist, would he choose to marry *me?*"

### Pemberley, Derbyshire

Mrs Reynolds knocked on the door impatiently – an express from her master to the family was not a common occurrence, and considering his appearance when he left Pemberley, she feared something dreadful was in this letter. After being bid enter, she quickly opened the door and stepped into the room, "My lady, an express has come for Lord Rosebery."

"Thank you, Mrs Reynolds; he had business to attend to at Dalmeny and will be back tomorrow. Just leave it and I will see that he receives it as soon as he returns."

In a quieter, almost quivering voice, Mrs Reynolds replied, "My lady, it is from my master."

"An express, you say? From Darcy?" After receiving a nod from Mrs Reynolds, she replied, "Well, *maybe* it would be best if I opened it myself since my husband will not be available until tomorrow. It is an express, after all."

"Yes, my lady." Mrs Reynolds handed the thin missive to Lady Rosebery, and turned to leave the room.

"Mrs Reynolds," she waited for the housekeeper to turn towards her, "If you would oblige me with some tea, by the time you return I should know what this missive is about," she said with a sympathetic look in her eye.

"Thank you, my lady. I will have your tea shortly." She curtsied and left the room with a small smile on her face. She had always had a soft spot for Lady Rosebery. Not all of the guests that came through the doors of Pemberley throughout the years were as accommodating to the needs of the servants as that great lady.

When the door closed, Lady Rosebery looked over the letter in her hand. The writing was definitely that of her nephew, and his seal was in the wax. Her nerves were steadied when she realized that it was not written or sealed in a hasty manner, but was very neat and precise, just as her nephew always was with his letters. Her nerves calmed a bit, but she was still determined to open it quickly to find out why an express was necessary. She went over to the desk and found a letter opener. Warming it in a candle she slid it beneath the wax seal until she felt it give way. Taking a deep breath, she opened the missive and read:

> *October 31, 1811*
> *Netherfield Park, Hertfordshire*
>
>
> *Dear Family,*
>
> *I address you all, as I know you will all be reading this anxiously, as I intend to send it express. Have no fear; everything is well. Everything is more than well – everything is perfect. I will write you with more details when I have the time, but that will be a few days at least. I go to Town today to take care of necessary business and will not be able to write again until next week. I know, however, that if I delay relating my news, you would surely have my head on a platter.*
>
> *My heart is full to overflowing as I write, and I anticipate your own excitement in this announcement – I am to be married! I know this may come as a shock to you, especially with my having been here only a month and a half, but when you know all the circumstances, I think you will be just as delighted as I am about my upcoming nuptials.*

*Charles Bingley has issued an open invitation to all of my family to join me here at Netherfield Park at your leisure. He has been assured by his housekeeper that rooms will be at the ready for anyone to arrive without notice. Please come as soon as possible so that I can introduce you to the lady who has stolen my heart and will soon become my wife, my Elizabeth.*

*I pray your journey is safe, and I hope the modified carriage I ordered will be comfortable enough for Georgiana. I cannot wait to see you all.*

*With love,*
*Darcy*

Mrs Reynolds hastened the preparations of the tea, trying to steady her nerves as she opened the door and walked to the table with the tray. She looked up and saw the smile on Lady Rosebery's face and her breath caught in her chest.

"He is to be married!" Lady Rosebery held up the letter in her hand. When she saw the housekeeper tear up, she went to her side and helped her to the sofa, handing her a handkerchief. The countess understood that the Darcy children were as close as family to the Reynolds', who had been in service to the Darcy family in some way for nearly thirty years. The last six months had broken the housekeeper's heart to see their dear boy go through all he had without his parents there for support. The two looked at each other, somehow knowing that this was exactly what he needed.

Mrs Reynolds finally dabbing her cheeks one last time, "thank you, my lady. Would you like me to bring you your tea now?"

Lady Rosebery looked affectionately at the housekeeper, "I think we could both use a cup."

Smiling and thanking her, Mrs Reynolds retrieved the tray and the two sat talking. They eagerly spoke of the lady who would soon be the new mistress and made plans for the trip to Netherfield Park.

Lord Rosebery, having completed his obligations at Dalmeny earlier than planned, decided to return to Pemberley that evening since the moon was bright and the night sky was clear; he knew from experience though that the weather could turn at any time. When he arrived at Pemberley, his wife gave him the letter from Darcy and it was decided they would travel immediately in hopes of leaving Derbyshire before the snow began. Georgiana was amendable to this plan, so trunks were packed and they would leave at first light. Georgiana was so excited she could not sleep that night. This would be the first time she had left the walls of Pemberley in over six months.

***

### Longbourn, Hertfordshire

"They have come; at last, they have come!" Lydia excitedly called from her perch on the window seat.

Mrs Bennet looked out the window over her shoulder, nearly as excited as her youngest, "Oh, my, it is them! Come, we must greet them."

By the time the Gardiners carriage stopped, all the Bennets were standing at Longbourn's door. The children's excitement at being released from their confines was evident for all to see.

Elizabeth leaned down to greet her youngest cousin David with a hug. "Do you know what we have in the stable?"

The four–year–olds eyes widened as he asked, "What?"

"Puppies!" Elizabeth had to laugh at his smile. "Would you like to pet one?" She led the group of her sisters and their young cousins to the stable.

Susannah and Maddie went inside to the sitting room to relax over a cup of tea, and Bennet and Gardiner sought the solitude of the study.

"I will never again wish to ride with such young children for so long a journey," Gardiner said.

Bennet laughed, for he too remembered saying such a thing not too many years ago. "I would say a drink will put you to rights. Care to join me, or do I drink alone today?"

"We cannot have you imbibing alone – I think one small glass might do me well."

Bennet poured their drinks and the two settled into the seats by the fire. "I know you wish to discuss what I have discovered, but if you do not mind, I think I need a clear head before we start on that conversation," Gardiner said.

"I understand. I doubt another few hours will matter much. We can discuss it tomorrow after you have rested."

Gardiner leaned his head back into the chair, "Thank you, I appreciate your patience. I will tell you, however, that I do have *good* news."

"Excellent, excellent; that does calm my fears. I am sure we will have plenty of time to go over the finer details of my financial holdings during your visit and possibly come up with a satisfactory amount to offer to Mr Collins. I can only pray that the man accepts the offer. I know that with what I am hoping to offer I could buy any other piece of property, maybe even in better condition than Longbourn, but this land has been in my family for over two hundred years. I must try to save it from falling out of Bennet hands."

"Is Collins anything like his father?"

"Judging from the letter I recently received from him, he is not, but it is hard to determine without meeting the gentleman."

"Do you plan to invite him?"

"I had thought of it, but with Elizabeth's wedding I have decided to wait. It will give us some time to work out the particular details of my offer. Of course, Christmas will be coming soon as well. Perhaps I will be riding well enough in the spring to deliver the proposal to Mr Collins myself without having to endure a house guest for some weeks." He chuckled, "We said we *would not* discuss our business dealings, and yet here we sit doing just that." He waved his hand towards the game board sitting on a side table, "Would you care to be trounced?"

Gardiner smiled, "I always relish a good trouncing."

They settled into a game of chess until time for them to join the others for supper. The children, tired from their long day of traveling, were soon in bed and the ladies discussed at length the newest fashion plates Maddie brought with her from London.

Jane and Elizabeth decided that if the gentlemen most present on their minds must be away, at least they had the opportunity to stay so busy that they would hardly miss them. Of course, this did not actually help; nevertheless, it provided them enough distractions to not daydream too much over the coming days.

*Pemberley, Derbyshire*

The morning they were to begin their travels to join her brother in Hertfordshire Georgiana was dressed and ready to leave when Lady Rosebery entered the room.

"Are you ready, Sweetling?"

Georgiana could not help but smile at the endearment her father used to call her, which all her family now used. "I have been ready for hours!"

"Well then, I shall have to call your uncle in here and he can carry you downstairs. They are still packing some things onto the servant's carriage, including your chair, but I believe our carriage is ready for us."

Georgiana's joy was infectious. She sat on her bed nearly jumping with excitement. She just knew this was a life changing time for her brother, and she was happy to be able to share it with him.

Lord Rosebery peeked his head into the door and saw the ladies speaking. His eyes filled with tears at seeing the excitement on Georgiana's face. He stepped back out of the doorway to dry his eyes and regain control over his emotions. Putting a smile on his face, he pushed open the door and entered singing a song he and Georgiana sang every morning. Georgiana smiled at her uncle and joined in with his singing, adding her alto to his deep baritone. Lady Rosebery saw the pain he tried to hide from others in her husband's eyes, and quietly stood beside him. When the song was completed, Rosebery hugged his niece then lifted her in his arms to carry her to the carriage.

"You need not fuss over me so," Georgiana exclaimed.

"I do not mind, Sweetling. You know how our family can be." He put his nose in the air and said in a haughty manner, "We try to be *excessively attentive* to all the needs of those around us."

Georgiana laughed at her uncle's impression of his sister, Lady Catherine de Bourgh, and she hugged his neck a little tighter. "Thank you, Uncle Hugh; I needed that laugh today."

The three descended the stairs and went outside to the carriage and six waiting on the drive. Darcy had ordered this town coach after the accident last spring; the seating arrangement and dimensions had been specifically designed to better accommodate Georgiana and her needs. There were two bench seats facing each other in the typical fashion, but instead of going all the way across, they only went to the middle of the carriage, just wide enough for two people to sit on each bench. Stretched along the other side of the carriage was a built in bed for Georgiana. The entire side of the carriage opened wide with two doors, making it easy for someone to put her in or take her out without much difficulty. The Darcy crest was emblazoned in the center where the doors came together.

They settled Georgiana into her seat with heated warmers around her feet, and a fur lined blanket over her legs, then they climbed into their own seat, placing the basket from Mrs Reynolds on the bench across from them. "Are we ready to go?" Rosebery asked his wife and niece. Both answered in the affirmative, and he confidently tapped the roof, "Then let us put this carriage through its paces and see how fit it is for our journey!"

The interior had been described to her in detail, but this was Georgiana's first look at the finished product of their vision. Everything was done with such precision and care, and she smiled as her eyes took in all that surrounded her. The exposed wood was waxed and buffed to a brilliant shine. The Darcy crest was everywhere she looked; delicately tooled into the fawn colored leather seats and carved into the wood panels of her bed surround. The bright blue, embroidered crest stood out on the fur lined light blue velvet cover draped over her legs. Even the basket Mrs Reynolds packed for their journey had the family crest woven into its design. Georgiana ran her fingers over the soft velvet of the light blue, tufted walls and curtains, quietly thanking her brother for his attention to every detail. No expense had been spared for her comfort and happiness, but what was most touching was that William was reminding her everywhere she looked that she was, above all, a Darcy.

Tears welled up in her eyes. She pulled out a handkerchief to dry her eyes, and caught sight of one last detail that only William could have put there for her. When she was younger and was frightened of the dark, her father told her that her mother was always looking down on her when he could not be by her side. The two would look outside each night, and he would point up to the stars and say, *'Do you see her eyes? They are shining bright just like yours.'*

After her father's death, she and William would sit outside looking up at the stars every night and say goodnight to their parents. Georgiana ran her hand along the wood where the side of the bed came up high enough so she would not fall out on rough roads. Carved into the side, where only she could see, were stars. Georgiana fingered the rough carving; they were not smooth and perfect like the others throughout the carriage, and Georgiana knew her brother had carved these himself. She was once again brought to tears with all he had done for her over the last few months.

Her sleepless night was catching up to her, so she slid down into the pillows and soft mattress to rest. Her nose was only inches from the stars as she placed her hand on them and went to sleep almost immediately, a quiet peacefulness resting on her face.

Rosebery saw Georgiana pull out her handkerchief and was just about to ask if she was all right when his wife put her hand on his arm. He looked into her eyes and she shook her head slightly. He understood her perfectly, and went back to reading his book. Georgiana did not like all the attention and had told them just last week that if they were needed she would let them know, but she would prefer not to be fussed over so much. Rosebery was trying to be a good uncle and respect her wishes, but he could not stand to see tears from his niece.

Ever since her father's death, when he was appointed as the Darcy's guardian, he had taken her under his care and treated her as he would have his own daughter, if he had been fortunate enough to have one. He felt a great deal of responsibility towards the siblings – after all, if it not for him, their father would still be alive today.

Though he had never told them of his part in the events of that spring, he felt the guilt of what had transpired daily. He was determined to keep the pain of that day from them, even if he had to shoulder it alone for all of his days.

# CHAPTER XVI

Susannah and Maddie sat together speaking privately of the events that would soon change their family's lives forever.

"Oh, Maddie, I do not know how I will handle all this! Oh, I can feel my nerves on edge even just now speaking of it!" Susannah began to feel faint and fanned her face.

Maddie put a calming hand on her sister's arm, "Susannah, look at me." When Susannah's eyes focused on Maddie, she continued, "*You are the strongest lady I know.* I do not say that lightly either. I know quite a few ladies, especially with the circles I am exposed to in London among my husband's business associations. I look at you and see a strong lady who can handle anything that life throws at her. You have been through so much with your marriage not being accepted by your husband's family, having all of your beautiful daughters, and losing your precious Luke. When I saw what you went through with your husband's accident, I was certain it would have made your anxieties limit you, and for a time you let the situation rule your emotions – but Sister," she said, looking deep into Susannah's eyes, "it did not win. Life did not cripple you! You rose from the devastation I know you felt deeply and you faced that situation with a strength of character I have seen in no other lady. You have since grown closer to your husband, and I dare say your daughters' lives are far different from what they would have been if you had not gone through such an experience."

Susannah's eyes filled with tears and her heart swelled with all Maddie was saying to her. *No one had ever called her strong before.* She always found her own strength in having her husband's calming presence right beside her, and when he was almost taken from her she nearly crumbled. Now that Maddie pointed it out though, she realized that, yes, she had faced that trial and had come through it stronger. She dried the tears from her eyes, "Thank you! Oh, thank you for speaking so to me today."

Maddie embraced Susannah, and the two soon had their emotions back under good regulation.

"You are right, Maddie. I can get through this. This is not a tragedy, it is a blessing – for all my girls. I am so proud of Lizzy for finding a man she loves, and who loves her back with such fervor. You have not seen their eyes when they meet, but no one who sees them together could doubt that they possess a kind of love that is rare. It is as if they are connected in a way I cannot explain – drawn together by forces beyond those we can see around us."

Maddie sat quietly listening to Susannah. *Could it be that Elizabeth's love for Mr Darcy is strong enough that they will not be affected by their shared past? More importantly, does he love her enough to not blame Elizabeth for what happened?* She hoped so, but she just did not know. She would have to see them together to make that determination.

"When did you say Mr Darcy and Mr Bingley will be returning?"

"Their plan was to be gone no more than a week. I am certain they will be back in the next day or two."

"Then, we have plans to make! We must have everything organized so that your nerves do not cause you so much trouble. We must not let it take the joy away from you during this special time."

Excitement shone from her eyes, "Yes, I was nearly speechless when Mr Darcy showed up at my dinner party with his cousin – *a viscount!* Can you imagine, Sister, *a viscount was in my home!*"

"I can imagine just how that would excite you."

"*Oh my!*" Susannah put her hand to her mouth in shock of what she just realized. "Oh, why did I not think of this before?" She began to feel faint again.

154

"What is it?"

"Oh, Maddie – if his cousin is a viscount, that means *his Uncle is an Earl!* Oh what will come of me when Mr Darcy's family comes to meet us?"

"Now, Susannah, you know exactly what you shall do. You shall open your doors to them and offer them every comfort they, as your daughter's future family, deserve. It matters not their rank, what matters is that they are the family of Mr Darcy, and will soon be connected to you through Elizabeth. You must be resolute. Do not let this affect you unduly. We shall write up some menus and speak with Mrs Hill and Cook about what need be done in preparation for such a visit. Then when they come, whether that be sooner or later, you will be prepared. I can imagine this will help calm your anxiety."

"Yes, yes that would calm my nerves tremendously. Come, there is not a moment to lose. We must speak with Hill this instant!" Susannah said with a newfound vigor.

Maddie smiled as she followed her sister-in-law to the housekeeper's room.

After they had prepared all that would be needed, they were once again sitting alone and talking in Mrs Bennet's private room. "I am impressed with your ability to face this. I know it is not easy for you, but as the day goes on I find your demeanor calming greatly."

Susannah could not help but smile, "Yes, I do feel much calmer. I dare say I still have fluttering's, but they are nothing that will cause such a stir."

"Your husband would not recognize you!" Maddie teased.

"No indeed, he would not!"

"You shall truly shock him!"

"Yes, I believe I shall!"

The following days brought much activity for the gentlemen of Longbourn. Gardiner and Bennet enjoyed afternoons of shooting and evenings playing chess and talking of all that letters could not expound upon. They pored over financial statements and tried to ascertain the best proposal to buy out the heir to Longbourn. After hours of figuring this column and that statement, they had come to what they thought to be a fair price. Bennet decided he would like Darcy to look over all they had done before they proceeded any further, and Gardiner agreed that it would be best to gain the younger gentleman's perspective on the papers.

The weather cooperated and the children spent several hours each afternoon outside gathering apples and berries, piling up leaves and jumping into them, having picnics, and playing in the wood around Longbourn with their older cousins. Mary, being the most accomplished girl in the neighborhood on the pianoforte, took her cousin Sophia under her tutelage and practiced with her for at least one hour every morning and they played a special duet for the family one evening. Lydia accompanied them on her violin and Elizabeth lent her voice to the evening's entertainment.

Susannah and Maddie planned the details of the coming wedding with the greatest of care. Nothing was too minute to pass undetected from their scrutiny. They spent many hours speaking with Cook about the wedding breakfast and what would be needed for such an event. Pies and meats were chosen, puddings discussed at length, and moulds from Mrs Bennet's dearest friends were listed on a paper for possible use. Soup tureens and dinnerware were inspected and silver was polished to a brilliant shine by the servants. The two ladies enjoyed every minute of the planning that went into such a wonderful celebration.

As a surprise from Darcy, Tuesday morning met with Madam LeFevre, a highly sought modiste, and Mrs Charville, the Ton's premier clothier, arriving on the doorstep of Longbourn, with patterns and sample fabrics in hand. They had orders from Mr Darcy to fashion a complete wardrobe for the new Mistress of Pemberley, including her wedding attire, if that met with Elizabeth's approval. The women spent hours looking over the cloth samples, only to determine that

Maddie was most certain her husband's warehouse had a much finer product. Mrs Charville said that she would gladly go to *'Gardiner's Goods'* and check the available stock, and she would let the ladies know what she found when she and Madam LeFevre returned to Longbourn the following week.

Elizabeth was shocked at all that was determined to be necessary for her trousseau. At least ten morning and ten evening gowns were to be finished before the wedding, with more ordered for the winter season and her London debut in the spring. Patterns were pored over for dresses and gowns, winter cloaks and muffs, chemises and corsets, stockings and nightgowns, and gloves and reticules, for every possible occasion. Of course, shoes to match every outfit could not be overlooked. Madam LeFevre and Mrs Charville left with a good knowledge of their client's needs and what would look best with her coloring and figure. They had a long list to be completed before they returned next week with their team of seamstresses in tow.

Elizabeth finally retired with visions of colorful silks and fur lined coats floating through her mind as she thought of all today had taught her of her intended and the new life she was stepping into with marrying him *How important is this gentleman to the Ton? Could I be an adequate mistress for his estate? What if I do not accomplish what is expected of the Mistress of Pemberley? I am just the daughter of a country gentleman, a simple girl of little means in the world; why did Fitzwilliam Darcy choose me to be his wife? I doubt I will ever live up to all this gentleman deserves.*

On Tuesday, Jonathan Lucas came to visit with Mr Gardiner and Mr Bennet, and he felt so sorry for four-year-old David, the lone boy thrown into the midst all those women speaking of weddings, and fabrics, and lace, and ribbons, that it was decided he would join the gentlemen on their ride that afternoon. David was still too short to ride alone, so he found great joy in being placed in the saddle in front of Lucas. The two soon found a comfortable stride and went galloping across the fields, followed by the other two gentlemen on their mounts. They all returned a few hours later, splattered with mud and weary, but with smiles on their faces from the excursion.

The week the Netherfield Park gentlemen were gone to Town soon passed, and Jane and Elizabeth found themselves counting the hours until they would see the familiar riders coming up the drive again.

At nearly dusk on the evening of Wednesday, the sixth of November, Bennet received a note from Netherfield Park. He opened it and could not help but chuckle at what it contained. They were finally back, and Darcy had written what could only be a journal to Lizzy that the younger gentleman hoped Bennet would pass on to her. He called his daughter into his study and handed her the sealed missive. Having no desire to open it in company, Elizabeth put it into her pocket until she could read it alone later.

After an evening of playing the pianoforte and singing with her family, she retired to her chamber and sat down on her bed. Her hands shook as she opened the rather thick letter from her beloved – her first letter of many, she hoped. He had a fine hand, so even and neat. Flipping through the pages, she smiled – William had written to her every day he was gone. She sat on her bed with her back against the headboard to read.

*October 31, 1811*
*Darcy House, London*

*My dearest Elizabeth,*

*We have finally arrived in Town, and after stopping at our club for a bite to eat, and dropping Bingley at his brother's house and my cousin at my uncle's house, I am finally at leisure to write to you, my love.*

*I wish you were here with me. As we were driving through Town, I made note of so many places I would love to show you. I can picture us walking through the Vauxhall Gardens, your arm resting in mine as we take in the entertainments. I can see the delight on your face as we scrutinize the delicacies of the shop down the street from my house that sells the finest tea and cakes. I can almost catch the sparkle in your eye as we spend hours in the little book shops that are sprinkled around the city. If I close my eyes, I can hear your tinkling laughter as we sit in the theater watching a work of art unfold on stage.*

*As you can tell, I have made many plans for us, and I cannot wait to bring you here and fulfill all my dreams by being the husband you deserve. Please, my love, do not require me to wait long for your hand. I do not have the patience needed to suffer through more than just a few weeks of this arrangement. I long to hold you in my arms as only a husband can.*

*My refusal to end this note until I see it put into your hands compels me to continue to add to it of all the mundane things I think of as this week slowly passes. I love you, my loveliest Elizabeth, and can hardly wait to be in your presence again soon.*

*Affectionately,*
*William*

*November 1, 1811*
*Darcy House, London*

*My dearest Elizabeth,*

*It seems, my love, that the fates are working against us. I had hoped to be able to obtain the necessary papers for a special license today and return back to you before a weeks' time, but it is not meant to be. I will now be required to wait until Monday, and hope it does not delay my return on the appointed day. I have a meeting with my solicitor later this afternoon and I hope he is much more efficient than I have found the Archbishop's secretary to be.*

*For now, I sit here wondering what need be done to prepare Darcy House and Pemberley for its new mistress. I fear we will not make it to Pemberley until after Christmas, so I have yet to order anything done to your rooms there. I have had my housekeeper here at Darcy House, Mrs Tucker, open your chambers to air them, as today is an agreeable day in London. The rooms have been closed up for so long that I fear they will need your excellent touch to restore life to their walls. My mother died when I was not yet twelve and my father had all of their personal rooms at Pemberley closed up at that time. He could not bear to sleep in his rooms without my mother, so he moved to another suite. He did not return to Town without my mother, so his rooms here were left as they were over sixteen years ago when my mother still lived. My father died unexpectedly in an accident during a storm at Pemberley over eight years ago. Since then I have not felt the need to move my items into my father's rooms. I have had the management of everything upon my shoulders since my twenty first birthday, but have never felt as if I were truly the master of the estate. Now that you will be by my side, I feel we can both step into this new world together, as Master and Mistress of all the Darcy name means. I pray that having you by my side will help me heal from the past and put all the difficulties behind me; to do as you have espoused and think of the past only as its remembrances bring pleasure.*

*I apologize for the dreariness of today's writing. It is so very difficult to be so alone, and while I know I will soon have you by my side, for now, I am still quite alone. I love you my Elizabeth. You have truly filled a place in my heart that has remained vacant for ever so long. I do not wish to distress you, so I will end for now. I know I told you only days ago, but I hope you know how much I ardently love and admire you, my love, and I can hardly wait to show you all that you gain when I give you my hand, for only you have cared for my heart and not my holdings. It is why I willingly give you charge of both.*

*With all my love,*
*Your William*

Elizabeth stopped reading and wiped the tears from her cheeks. She did not even realize she had been crying. Her heart broke for all the loss William had been through in his short lifetime. He had not spoken to her the specifics about his past, but she could see how all of these events had molded him into the gentleman he now was. She longed to take him in her arms as she would her little cousin David, and embrace him until the pain of the past was behind them. She knew this was not truly possible, but oh, how she longed to do so for her William.

Elizabeth stood to stir the fire and then settled down in the window seat, pulling the shawl around her shoulders, eager to read the rest of her letter. Page after page she read, and while each was nothing more than the everyday matters that took up his time, with a line thrown in here or there of his love for her, she cherished every word. He finally spoke to her in a way she only dreamed would happen after they were married, and she could not wait to learn all she could of this gentleman from the words, written and unwritten, in his first letter to her.

He wrote of visiting his cousin Fitz and of his winning a game of billiards. An entire page was spent detailing the contents of his mail that required, according to him, mostly just his good aim and a fire. Elizabeth learned of his dull Sunday evening rituals of which his cousins and friend teased him relentlessly; but most of all, she learned of him – his life, his likes and dislikes, and his heart's desires for their future. She knew now, without a doubt, that she had chosen well in saying yes to this gentleman; she could not imagine her life with anyone else. All of her misgivings about her own ability to fit well in his world melted away with her love for the gentleman who had won her heart. She would do everything within her power to fill his days with joy and laughter.

As she turned to the last page, she smiled – *he had written it from Netherfield Park*. Her heart was lifted knowing he was but three miles away and she would see him on the morrow. She could tell from the tone of the last part of the missive that he was looking forward to their reunion as much as she was. She folded her letter and held it to her heart, while gazing out at the dark sky with stars scattered about, thinking perhaps William was looking out at these same stars right now and thinking of her.

Jane came into the room and saw the faraway look on her sister's face and the letter clutched in her hands and held over her heart. She smiled and went up to her side, "Tomorrow, Lizzy; he will visit again tomorrow."

Not turning her eyes from the starry sky, Elizabeth said in a low whisper, "Yes, Janie; tomorrow my William will return to me."

The sisters hugged and without any further conversation, dressed for bed. They had shared much of their hearts over the last few nights together, but tonight it was not needed. They each curled up in bed, pulled the counterpane up to their chins, and closed their eyes for sleep to overtake their tired bodies. Tomorrow, their gentlemen would return.

Sarah Johnson

# CHAPTER

## XVII

Elizabeth awoke the next morning earlier than the rest of the house. She quickly dressed and snatched a warm bun and an apple from the kitchen as she left for a long walk. She was ever grateful for the distraction of the Gardiners this last week, but knowing that Darcy was only three miles away was more than she could bear. She was anxious, and knew that a walk would calm her nerves.

She had been gone for an hour when she saw a rider across the field. Her heart began pounding... she would never forget the sight of her first encounter with her beloved, and she knew now that the silhouette on the other side of the field could be none but his. She saw him slow when he caught sight of her, and she waved her arm in the air. He immediately snapped the reins and crossed the field at breakneck speed, slowing only enough to jump from his mount and crush her to his chest. Elizabeth closed her eyes and felt a warmth spread across her body as she melted into his embrace.

He whispered into her ear, "Oh my Elizabeth, how I have missed you."

Pulling back slightly, she put her hand onto his cheek and looked into his eyes. "I have missed you too, William." He leaned into her hand for a few seconds, then turned his face, he gently placed a kiss on her palm.

"Please tell me we can marry soon. I cannot bear too many more days without you by my side."

"If it were up to me, my love, I would steal away with you to the church this instant." Elizabeth assured him. With a quirk of her eyebrow, she added, "I do not think we would hear any objection from my mother."

"I have no doubt of that, my love." William took her hands in his and stepped back a little. Drawing her hands up to his lips, he kissed the back of each, and replied, "I am ever so glad I saw you this morning. I did not wish to be required to repress myself when I was finally saw you again. I know we will not have much time alone later today when Bingley and I visit Longbourn."

"Especially not with the houseful right now – the day after you left, my Uncle Gardiner and his family arrived unexpectedly to spend some weeks in the country."

Darcy remembered that Edward Gardiner, with whom he was intimately acquainted, was her uncle. "I will be glad to see him again; I have not been at leisure to visit with him in many months. I now have even more to look forward to while visiting Longbourn."

"It has been a great distraction having my cousins to entertain this last week, and my Aunt Gardiner has a way of calming my mother's nerves as no other."

"Your hands are getting cold, my love; let us walk back to Longbourn." Darcy threaded Elizabeth's arm through his and they stepped slowly through the field. He wrapped her fingers in his own, "I have a good idea that I can be blamed in part for your mother's nerves."

Elizabeth lifted one eyebrow, "And what makes you think that, sir?"

"I can just imagine the talk of lace and silks you were made to endure on Tuesday when Madam LeFevre and Mrs Charville arrived at Longbourn."

Elizabeth laughed and looked down, feeling her own insecurities return with the reminder of all she was required to order.

They walked on for a few minutes in silence before Darcy stopped and turned towards her, asking quietly, "What is amiss?"

Tearing up a bit, she continued to look down and said, "Nothing... I... it is just..."

William gently put his hand under her chin and lifted her eyes to his. "Please tell me Elizabeth. Whatever it is, I will use my every influence to make it perfect."

So touched by the compassion in his eyes, she felt hot tears escape her eyes and fall down her cheeks.

Before she could pull out her handkerchief, Darcy wiped them away with his thumb and whispered, *"Please tell me?"*

She tried to look back down, but he would not let her chin go, so she turned her eyes away from his and quietly put her distress into words, "I do not know if I can be all that is required in being your wife."

William immediately embraced her. She felt the strength rise inside her with the confidence he held in her own abilities. After a minute, his arms loosened, "When I was eleven years old, my mother gave birth to my sister Georgiana. Afterward, she was very weak and her body did not recover. I would visit with her every day and we would speak for hours. She only lived a few more months, but during those months, she told me all she wished me to know, but would not have the years in which to pass her wisdom on to me. She told me that, more than anything, she wished me to marry for love. She often said I needed to look for someone who would find joy in life and would balance my naturally reserved and quiet personality. I have found that, and more, in you, Elizabeth. If you had not a penny to your name, I would marry you. I love you for who you are, not for what you can bring to my account or my estate.

"I told you in my letter that I have been, at best, an adequate master, but by no means have I completely grown into the role myself – a role I was reared from birth to one day fill. I cannot imagine how it must feel for you to go from your life here in Meryton into what I am asking you to enter, and yet you are willing to take on all of that for me. You mean more to me than anyone else in this world, and I am willing to do anything to ease this transition for you. We will learn together. Do not be overwhelmed, my love; I chose you because you love me for *me*, not for my house in Town, or my estate, or how many carriages and horses I have to my name. I love you just as you are. If I wanted a lady of the Ton, brought up with her nose in the air and taught to look down on others not of her own station, who cared more for my holdings than the one who holds them, then I have had years to choose such a wife. That is not my desire. I want you. I choose you, with your impertinent and witty ways. You, who finds simple joy in feeding horses a special treat and sitting for hours playing a game of chess just to see a smile on your father's face. You, Elizabeth, who have captured my heart in your gentle hands and have thought yourself unworthy of my affections. You... *I have chosen you.*" He heard her crying still and pulled her tighter against his chest, continuing to speak of his love in her ear.

When she finally calmed, he pulled away, but kept his arms around her waist. "I love you Elizabeth," he said as he looked into her eyes. "Please trust me?"

She quietly answered him, "I know I am not perfect, and I am glad you do not desire perfection, for I could never be that. I *will* trust that you know what you are talking of for our future."

"That is all I ask of you. We will learn together how to mold our separate lives into one." Feeling her shiver, he let go of her waist to grasp her hands, "For now, we must return you to Longbourn, or I fear you shall catch cold and not be well enough to visit with me when I come with Bingley later." He once again threaded her arm through his, grasped her hand that rested on his arm, and turned to walk to Longbourn.

Before they had gone too far, Elizabeth chuckled, "I fear, sir, that your horse has been forgotten and will certainly be lost."

He whistled loudly and looked at her, "Pemberley is too large not to train my mounts to come to my call, madam." They turned to see his white horse bounding across the field towards them. As he neared, the horse slowed and nuzzled his nose into his master's hand. "Madam, may I introduce Whitie. Whitie, this is soon to be your new mistress, Miss Elizabeth Bennet."

Elizabeth laughed and reached out to touch the horse's nose. "Whitie? I envisioned you to be much more imaginative, William."

166

"I did not name him, my sister Georgiana did. He was born right after our father passed away, the first foal of the year, and he was pure white. Another was born just a week later, and he was pure black. I was delayed in returning home, so by the time I arrived at Pemberley a few weeks later Georgiana had already named them *Whitie and Blackie.*"

"Well, Whitie, I am pleased to meet you," Elizabeth pulled the apple out of her pocket and held it in her open palm, "I planned to eat this myself, but I think I will last until we return to Longbourn."

"You have just made a friend for life," Darcy said. Whitie neighed in agreement and the couple turned to take the path that led to the back of the garden at Longbourn, the horse following behind as if he were chaperoning the couple. While still mostly hidden by the wall, Darcy reached for Elizabeth again. No words were needed between the two as they once again gathered strength from the love they shared together in their embrace.

They let go of each other and he watched as she walked to the back of the house and disappeared around the corner. "Well, Whitie, what do you think?" The horse neighed and nodded his head, tossing his long mane around. "I agree completely, old fellow," Darcy said as he mounted and they turned to return to Netherfield Park.

Gardiner awoke to see his wife sitting on the chaise by the window with a sleeping David in her arms. He stood and went to sit beside her, kissing her cheek and looking over her shoulder to what she was watching outside the window. They saw two people embracing at the back of the garden by the wall; he imagined it was probably Elizabeth and Darcy.

Gardiner's thoughts were interrupted by his wife's whispered words, *"We have not spoken with her yet, Edward."*

"I know; with Mr Darcy not in the neighborhood this last week, I did not see the purpose of bringing it up yet. I have not spoken with Bennet about the situation either."

"They look so happy," Maddie said as she watched the two figures separate. "What will happen to them? Will this tear them apart?" She turned to her husband with tears in her eyes.

Gardiner carefully took David from her arms and laid him on the bed, covering him with a blanket and kissing his forehead. Then he turned back to his wife and knelt down in front of her, taking her hand in his and caressing her palm in a calming manner. "We cannot say how they will react, but if they truly are in love, then this will not keep them apart."

"Can we not wait a few more days? I do not wish to ruin their reunion with this news."

"Yes, dear, I believe that would be best. At least give them today free of distractions from their pasts." Gardiner sat beside his wife once again, gathering her into his arms. They both quietly looking out the window until it was time to go downstairs and join the family in the dining room.

---

"Alex, are you certain you will not join us at Longbourn today?" Bingley asked.

"Oh, no; you two do not want to be distracted from your ladies and I will only be in the way. I think I shall wander the grounds avoiding your sister. Perhaps your brother and I will go shooting this afternoon." Alex picked up his cup to refill the much-needed coffee, smirking at the lovelorn looks on the two faces of the other gentlemen in the dining room. "I only ask that you not abandon me all day long. If you are to stay for supper, I would appreciate prior knowledge so as to avoid several dull hours this evening. Fools in love you may be, but I would not wish to be forgotten and fed to *the wolves* prowling about."

"You say that as if Bingley has a dangerous piece of property, Alex," Darcy said with a smirk.

"You know all too well how dangerous some properties can be without the master keeping careful watch over all that occurs." Under his breath he added, "I would almost prefer Aunt Catherine's loud pronouncements to that of the underhanded cunning of *some of the Ton*." No specific names need be voiced for all to know of whom he was referring.

Bingley cleared his throat, "Yes... well, once again, I must apologize for her actions last night. I did not know my sister had set her cap for you so earnestly. I will be speaking with Hurst before we leave this morning to see what can be done. I am just glad you had the foresight to lock your door," Bingley said with contrition, referring to the incident late last night when Alex was awakened to his door handle being rattled.

"*That* I have made a habit of over the years. Some desire nothing more than a title before their name, and I do not wish to be forced into anything," Alex asserted.

William added to the conversation, "It might be best to place a footman in that hallway, just to be certain things do not get out of hand again."

"Yes, I will speak with the butler about doing just that this morning; thank you Darcy."

The three were soon joined by the Hursts and Miss Bingley, greetings exchanged as they filled their plates and took their places at the table. Choosing her usual seat beside the viscount, Miss Bingley beamed, "Good morning, my lord, I pray you slept well?"

Eyeing her warily, he answered, "Well enough, though the country air seemed to be in abundance last night, shaking even the door handles as it howled outside."

Caroline looked down to her plate, "Really? I do not recall being awakened by howling winds or shaking doors."

"Hmmm," Alex answered, "perhaps it is just the guest wing then."

Silence fell on the room as the tension built. Darcy and Alex soon excused themselves, leaving the siblings alone. Alex retired to his room to dress for a much-needed ride and Darcy went to the library to await a proper hour to call on Longbourn.

Bingley stood from the table, "Hurst, if you would, please join me in my study, we must speak." He eyed Caroline as he walked from the room, his brother-in-law close on his heels. As soon as the door to his study door closed, Bingley stated, "Something must be done; I cannot have my guests' doorknobs being rattled at night by my sister."

Hurst rubbed his eyes in clear frustration, "Louisa and I are planning a holiday... without Caroline. My wife needs a break from her sister, so do not imagine that I will be offering to take her with us." Pacing the room, he added, "Perhaps it is time for Caroline to be sent to visit your Aunt Hamilton in Scarborough?"

Thinking of his aunt, who could put even Mrs Bennet to shame with her fluttering nerves and constant need for smelling salts, Bingley smiled conspiratorially, "Now *that* is an idea! I will write to her immediately to ascertain if she is in need of *comfort that only family can bring*." They both smiled, hoping it would not take too long to hear back from her. Bingley sat at his desk to write his letter and Hurst went to find his wife for a walk in the garden.

# CHAPTER

# XVIII

When the time came, the gentlemen went to Longbourn to see their ladies. Bingley was glad to be introduced to the Gardiners, and Darcy relished the opportunity to catch up with friends he had not seen in a while.

Darcy, along with Bennet and Gardiner, were in Bennet's study when they were interrupted by a knock at the door. Mr Hill entered to say a note came for Mr Darcy. It was from his cousin Alex, so he excused himself from the other gentlemen to read the missive.

*November 7, 1811*
*Netherfield Park, Hertfordshire*

*Darcy,*

*Imagine my surprise at looking out the window and seeing your new coach and six driving towards Netherfield Park!*

*My parents and Georgiana have arrived and they wish to meet your Miss Elizabeth. Mother says she is not above intruding upon Longbourn without an invitation, but Father will not hear of such behavior. So for the sake of my own sanity, could you please either procure an invitation for us to visit or invite your intended here so Mother's curiosity can be satisfied?*

*Anxiously awaiting your answer,*
*Alex*

Bennet watched as a range of emotions crossed Darcy's face, ending with a broad smile when he finished the note. "My sister, Georgiana, and my Uncle and Aunt, the Earl and Countess of Rosebery, have arrived at Netherfield Park. They wish to meet Elizabeth, but were not desirous of upsetting your household with showing up uninvited."

"By all means, invite them," Bennet offered. "I imagine we shall be highly diverted this afternoon. My wife was shocked when a *viscount* came to her dinner party; I can imagine she will be quite aflutter with an *earl and countess* visiting her sitting room. I will leave you to write your note while I find my wife. Although I may regret it if there is no fish to be had in Meryton, invite your family and Mr Bingley's family to supper if you think they will not be offended in joining us so informally."

"I do not think they would be offended, sir. Thank you." Darcy sat to write his note while the other two gentlemen walked out of the study.

Gardiner patted Bennet on the shoulder, "I offer you my deepest sympathies for when my sister finds out what you have done." He walked off chuckling and shaking his head.

Knowing her profusions would need a few minutes to settle before she would be fit for company, Bennet ascended the stairs to his chambers and called for his wife. He sat in his chair perusing a book while he awaited her.

Susannah came through the door in a rush, "Henry? Is something wrong? Are you hurt?"

Seeing the look on her face, he felt contrition for sending for her in such a manner. "No, no, my dear, I am perfectly well. I just needed to tell you something and thought it best to do so alone. We seem to be overrun with visitors, so I felt this was the best place." He drew her over to sit in his chair, "I must apologize for the inconvenience which I have caused, and I hope your nerves can manage such news as must now be conveyed."

"Oh? What *have* you done, Henry?"

"Mr Darcy's family have just arrived at Netherfield Park, and I invited them to dine with us this evening."

Susannah found that, just as Maddie said, when faced with the unexpected, she was much calmer because of the plan they had already put into place. She smoothed an invisible wrinkle in her skirt, "I shall be perfectly happy to entertain them at our table."

"My dear, they are his cousin *Viscount Primrose's* parents... *the Earl and Countess of Rosebery.*"

Susannah's face did not change, "Yes dear, I knew of whom you were referring. They are welcome any time."

Bennet stared at his wife, wondering if she had truly gone mad. He had never seen her so calm. "Their coming this evening is agreeable to you? *With no prior warning?*"

"Yes dear; my sister and I already discussed that Mr Darcy's family would likely be coming into the neighborhood at some time before the wedding, and we have already planned for several meals. The butcher in Meryton is aware we may need a last minute order of fish or pork. Which do you think they would prefer?"

Still in shock, he mumbled his answer, "Fish would do, I think."

"Is that all, my dear?" Susannah asked while rising from the chair. When her husband nodded, she kissed his cheek and excused herself to speak with Cook.

Bennet stood there watching his wife exit the room, an odd calmness surrounding her. *Gardiner will never believe what has just taken place*, he thought as he left the room to find his brother-in-law.

---

Alex read the note back from Darcy, "You are in luck, Mother. Mr Bennet has extended an invitation to supper, if you do not mind it being an informal, family affair."

"What better way to meet the family than with a simple supper?"

"Georgiana will be happy to be introduced tonight. She has been all anticipation for days now," Rosebery added.

Alex stood, "I will have the carriage readied. Is there room inside for me to join you, or do I need to ride separately?"

"Darcy thought to make it as large as possible, so there is enough room to comfortably fit four others besides and Georgiana," his mother answered.

His father added, "He even thought to make enough leg room for those of us in our family with longer legs."

"Then I look forward to seeing the inside of this carriage." Alex left the room thinking to himself, *I am glad; I did not wish to smell of horse tonight.*

He ordered the carriage readied, sent a maid to Georgiana's room to inform her of the plans and that he would come for her in a few minutes, then went to change into his new green waistcoat. His family joked often about his fastidious appearance, but he took it as a compliment. As he opened his drawer to retrieve a new handkerchief, he saw Mary's glove that he found near her glasses the day they met. He picked it up and looked at it carefully, laying it out on his own hand. The ends of the cloth fingers only came to the middle of his own. She had such dainty hands, yet such a strong spirit. He sighed and put the glove back in the drawer; *maybe the separation while we were in town was enough to soften her thoughts towards me.* He hoped tonight he would have the opportunity to exchange at least a few civil words with the young lady whom he was not able to forget since seeing her sitting on that log waving her arms that fateful day. With one last look in the mirror, he pulled down the bottom of his jacket and left his room to retrieve Georgiana and carry her downstairs.

The Hursts' and Miss Bingley were invited also, but the Hursts', not wanting to overwhelm Longbourn with so many guests, declined the invitation. Miss Bingley would remain at Netherfield as well. She had stayed in her chambers all day, supposedly with a headache, though Alex had a feeling it was just her sulking that her plan with him was thwarted. He would not doubt if she were trying to come up with other such plans to catch him, and he would not have been far from the mark, for Caroline truly was trying her hardest to think of a way she could attract his attentions and garner his hand.

During the carriage ride, Georgiana and Alex spoke of all the details inside the carriage that were put there for her comfort. The only thing she kept to herself was the presence of the stars on the inside of her bed frame. By the time they arrived at Longbourn, Alex knew all he wished to ever know of the numerous cloth samples they went through to find the perfect color of blue velvet that lined the carriage walls. He was willing to endure anything though, if it meant his cousin was happy.

Darcy met them outside with a smile so big his rarely seen dimples were on display. The minute the horses stopped, he opened the doors on Georgiana's side of the carriage and embraced her. The siblings shared a hug for over a minute as the other occupants of the carriage looked upon the pair. As Darcy gathered Georgiana into his arms to carry her inside, he greeted his other family members and told them of his arrangement to introduce Georgiana to Elizabeth in private.

Alex assured Darcy he would introduce his parents to the Bennets, and before they could descend from the carriage, Darcy was already inside with Georgiana.

With practiced ease, he made his way to the back of the house and into Mr Bennet's study where Elizabeth awaited them.

He was worried about Elizabeth's reaction. He had yet to tell her anything of Georgiana other than that she was much younger and was left to his care when he came of age. His apprehension melted away when he entered the room and Elizabeth immediately stood with a sincere smile on her face, not showing any outward reaction to the fact that Georgiana was carried into the room in his arms. Darcy placed his sister in a chair by the fire, settling her into the seat as he tucked her blanket around her legs.

When he was finished fussing over her, he quietly asked, "Are you ready, Sweetling?" With a nod of her head, Darcy stood to his full height. Turning, he walked to Elizabeth and gently took her hand. Kissing the back of it, he then led her forward. "Georgiana, this is my intended, Miss Elizabeth Bennet. Elizabeth, my sister, Miss Georgiana Darcy."

Elizabeth stepped forward and curtsied, "I am pleased to finally meet you, Miss Darcy."

Bowing her head since she could not curtsy, Georgiana quietly answered, "It is a pleasure to meet you as well, Miss Bennet. My brother has not told me much of you," she looked conspiratorially at Darcy, "but I have been looking forward to meeting you for many weeks now. I have a feeling you were the reason my brother wrote of his pleasure, for once, in dancing last month, for I have never known him to find much pleasure in that particular exercise."

Elizabeth was touched he would have told his family of her so early in their acquaintance. "I was not aware of his dislike of dancing." Looking at Darcy, she quirked her eyebrow and continued, "William asked for a set immediately upon our being introduced."

"In the past I have avoided certain situations which may have placed me in a position of showing favoritism to any one individual."

Squeezing his hand slightly, Elizabeth met his eyes and replied, "I am glad to have had the rare opportunity, sir, to be asked by you upon our introduction, then."

Darcy squeezed her hand back.

"If you need to greet the rest of your family, please do not feel obligated to stay here with us. I am certain talk of bonnets and lace is not to your liking."

William looked into her eyes; she had just challenged him, as she often did while playing chess, but this time it was not a game. Did he trust her enough to leave her alone with Georgiana? Looking at his sister to see if she was agreeable to this plan, he saw her stifling a laugh. Darcy smiled and bowed, acknowledging that he would meet her challenge, "Yes; well, then I shall leave you two to your devices. How long do you need?"

"An half hour will suffice, sir," Elizabeth answered confidently.

Looking at the clock, he replied, "I shall return at the appointed time then." Instead of releasing her hand when he turned to walk away, he drew her over to the door with him. Shielding her from Georgiana's view, he leaned down, he whispered into her ear, "Please be gentle with her; she has been through so very much."

Elizabeth cupped her hand on his cheek, "William, you asked me to trust that you know I can be the wife you need, and I have chosen to do so, even though it is very difficult for me to even imagine how I will fit with your society. Please trust me now in my own knowledge of what a sister's role is and what Georgiana needs from my new place in her life. I look forward to learning anything and everything she is willing to share with me in her own time. For now, I think she just needs a friendly companion, and *that* I can be."

William placed his hand on the outside of her own hand resting on his cheek and drew her palm to his lips, "I trust you, Elizabeth." He let go of her hand and quickly turned and left the room.

Elizabeth returned to the seat next to Georgiana. "Would you like some tea Miss Darcy?"

"Yes; thank you," Georgiana answered quietly.

Elizabeth ordered the tea and the two spoke of inconsequential things for the next half an hour. By the time Darcy returned, with Alex in tow, the ladies were calling each other by their first names and Georgiana bore a smile the likes of which Darcy had not seen in many months.

Sarah Johnson

# CHAPTER

# XIX

The door opened to the sitting room, and Mrs Hill announced the visitors. "The Earl and Countess of Rosebery and Viscount Primrose to see you, sir," she said to Mr Bennet.

The family were all introduced, and smaller groups quickly formed throughout the sitting room. Mrs Bennet, Mrs Gardiner, and the Countess of Rosebery sat next to each other and soon found themselves engrossed in a conversation of lace and silks and other such wedding necessities.

Mr Bennet, Mr Gardiner, and the Earl of Rosebery struck up a conversation about the political changes on the horizon with the new inventions that were changing the world around them so very drastically. The Earl said he had already spoken with his steward about some changes that would, they hoped, increase the land's usability in the harsh Derbyshire environment where his estate was located. Mr Gardiner added that he felt the new steam engines could be the future for shipments of goods being distributed and that it might one day do away with horse travel completely.

Alex joined Bingley on the other side of the room with the Bennet sisters and sat in a chair near Miss Mary and Miss Kitty. Mary was not looking at him, but at least she was not ignoring him like the last time he saw her either.

"Do you know how long your parents will be staying in the neighborhood?" Bingley asked him.

"I do not believe they have any fixed plans. Everything will be greatly dependent upon when the wedding is to take place and what Miss Darcy will need at that time."

"I am glad they are come. I know Darcy has been worried about his sister, and having her here where he can see to her welfare will help tremendously." Bingley saw the confused looks on the ladies faces and explained, "Miss Darcy was in a carriage accident a few months ago. Her recovery is most important to her brother."

"Oh, my!" Jane replied in shock, putting her hand to her mouth. "Was she badly injured?"

Looking down and clearing his throat, Alex said with much emotion, "Yes, she was. She is getting better, but we are still unsure how much more she will recover." He looked up and caught Mary looking at him as he continued quietly, "They are uncertain if she will ever walk again."

Mary closed her eyes as the remembrances of her own father's near demise filled her heart. "I will pray daily for her continued recovery."

Alex replied, "I thank you, Miss Mary – with all my heart, and on behalf of my family, I thank you."

Kitty felt the tension of the moment and could stand it no longer, so she tried to lighten the mood by asking, "Since Miss Darcy is now visiting the neighborhood, what does she like to do?"

Alex cleared his throat, gaining control of his emotions once again before he answered. "She plays the pianoforte and the harp, though I do not know how strong her hand is at present. When last I saw her, she had just received a pianoforte for her rooms so she could begin practicing again, but did not have enough strength yet to even grip a pen with confidence. I have recently heard from my cousin that he has received several letters from her, so her hand is strengthening. I am certain with practice she will once again play as beautifully as she did before."

Mary smiled, "I am teaching my cousin Sophia while my Uncle and Aunt Gardiner are visiting. Perhaps Miss Darcy would like to join us some days with our practice?"

Smiling, Alex answered, "I am certain she would welcome the diversion. Thank you, Miss Mary."

Kitty spoke up, "Does she paint, or draw? Or perhaps she enjoys playing games? I would love a challenger for *backgammon*, if she would be like to join me."

Bingley now replied, "She does love to play games and I have seen some of her charcoal drawings. She is very talented. I would love her to do one of Netherfield Park for me, but I would not wish to have her exert herself until she is stronger."

"I have not been very successful with charcoal," Kitty said, "but I have used watercolors for years and am now trying my hand at drawing with pencil. Perhaps she would be able to join me sometime."

Darcy entered the room, interrupting the conversation. He greeted his Uncle and Aunt then joined the younger people.

"Mr Darcy, we were just discussing your sister," Lydia spoke up. "Your cousin has told us of her unfortunate accident, and we were trying to decide what diversions she would enjoy while she is visiting the neighborhood."

Smiling slightly, he looked at Alex, then back to the group, "I believe just joining in with whatever you are doing will help. Physically she will get stronger with time, but she needs friendships that flourish in order to face the difficulties life now has for her.

Jane quietly replied, "She will not just be our friend, sir, she will be our sister. I look forward to adding another one to my life, as I am sure all my sisters will agree."

William's heart swelled with the generosity of this family. He knew Elizabeth was special, but he was finding out that she was special because of her family. Their hearts led them all, and being a recipient of their care was touching.

The half hour passed quickly, and Darcy and Alex soon left to retrieve Georgiana and Elizabeth. Alex picked up his cousin to carry her back to the sitting room to meet the Bennet family, leaving Darcy and Elizabeth alone for a few minutes.

Elizabeth felt Darcy's arms envelope her, "How was your little chat with Georgiana?"

A small smile formed on her lips, "Your sister is a very sweet girl, William. I am certain we shall get on perfectly well together." Elizabeth pulled back from his tight embrace and her eyes found his as she asked, "When was she hurt?" Darcy immediately began trying to pull away from her, but she would not have it, tightening her grip. "The day you and Mr Bingley walked with us to feed Mr Goulding's horses you agreed to tell me about her, and you have mentioned Georgiana in several conversations, but you have never told me of her physical limitations."

He could not look at her as he replied, "She was in an accident last spring and it has left her without the ability to walk, possibly for the rest of her life." He once again drew her to his chest as his arms encircled her, "Please do not ask any more from me right now."

"Only if you promise you will tell me later," she replied.

"I promise, when the time is right, you will know all." Pulling back from her, he put his arm out, "Are you ready to meet my uncle and aunt?"

Elizabeth smiled and confidently placed her hand on his arm, "Yes, I am ready."

Georgiana had been introduced and was already seated with her cousin and the Bennet sisters when Darcy and Elizabeth came in the sitting room. They all stood for the introduction to Darcy's intended. Hugh Fitzwilliam looked at the back of the brunette woman standing beside his nephew as she was introduced to his wife. When she turned to him, he bowed, and as he rose, he caught hers – *eyes he would never forget for all of his days*. Flashes of images filled his mind and his face immediately paled. He stumbled, and was quickly led to a chair, not hearing anything else around him until he saw his son, only inches away, asking if he was well. He looked back up at the others gathered around him and heard Mr Gardiner say, "I believe the earl may need some air. May I escort you outside, my lord?"

Rosebery nodded and was led outside by Mr Gardiner. When they were in the garden they found a bench, and Rosebery sat down, still trying to process what he had just seen.

"I was not sure if you would remember or not, but clearly you know who my niece is."

He looked up at Gardiner, "*YOU!* That is why you look so familiar – *you were there with her?*"

"Yes, my wife and I were visiting relations in Lambton and our niece was traveling with us. She has no knowledge of what took place. When she awoke she had no memory, and thankfully it has not come back to her all these years."

"What is to be done?" Rosebery said, not really asking, but trying to understand all he had just learned.

"For years my wife and I have tried to keep their paths from crossing when our niece visited Town, but we never thought they would meet here in her own neighborhood. We were told of the arrival of some gentlemen to the neighborhood, but by the time we knew of her suitor's name, they were engaged. We came here with the intention of telling them of the connection, but we have yet to do so as Mr Darcy has been in Town for the last week. My wife and I thought we would give them a day or two for their reunion before we bring up such matters. We are not certain how either will react to this news."

Shaking his head, Rosebery exclaimed, "NO! No, they *CANNOT* be told! Absolutely not – *I FORBID it!* They cannot know!"

Gardiner saw the panic in the earl's face. "If you think it is best, then we will not tell them; but, my lord, is there a reason you are against their knowing? What if my niece remembers sometime in the future?"

Standing, the earl began to pace. "If she remembers, we will deal with her knowledge at that time. Until then, we must not say a word." *I cannot believe the one girl in all of England with such a connection to us could end up being his intended! How could this happen? What if they find out what I have caused? Will they ever forgive me?* He thought for a few seconds and came up with a viable excuse that he thought would appease Mr Gardiner. "My nephew has been through too much this last year with almost losing his sister in the carriage accident, and I would prefer to keep as much from him as possible at this time." Looking up, he continued, "When my wife and I received word we were needed at Pemberley, we never thought we would see the sight before us. Darcy would not leave Georgiana's side and was not eating or sleeping properly. He was sent to Town for a few weeks and then he came here with his friend Bingley to recover. I do not know if he could handle this kind of news at this time."

Gardiner nodded in understanding, "We will not tell our niece. If she remembers though, I do not know if Elizabeth will like that we have kept this from her for so long, especially considering who she is to marry."

"We will handle such a situation if it arises. For now, they must *not* be told," Rosebery said again.

"I can promise we will not say something at this time, but I will not lie to my niece if she asks us," Gardiner stated firmly.

"I would not expect you to lie to her, but I feel this is the best option before us."

The two men agreed and returned inside to the others waiting in the sitting room, assuring them of the earl's good health. The evening continued with much success and the Darcy carriage left that night with much praise of the Bennet family being discussed by all.

When he finally retired that night, Gardiner told his wife of all that had been said outside. She was uncertain of their silence being what was best for the situation, but she was willing to keep quiet about the events of the past – for now.

When they were back at Netherfield William took his sister upstairs to her room. They sat beside each other on her bed when he asked, "Are you better? Please tell me you are?"

Georgiana saw the worried look on his features as his eyes pleaded with hers, "My strength is returning.. Some days are harder than others, but I will be well, William."

He held her tightly for a minute before pulling away. "I have spoken with Mr Bennet about what happened." When he saw her face fall, he put his finger under chin and lifted her eyes to his again. "He will not judge you, Georgiana. He was in a carriage accident a few years ago and nearly lost his life as well. I know there are difficulties I will never understand about your injuries. If you ever feel the need for wise counsel, and do not think I will understand, please speak with him. I know you are a private person, but he wishes to help in any way he can. He will soon be an integral part of our family and I trust in any advice he would give to you. He truly is a good gentleman. Please promise me you will think about what I have said?"

With a small smile, she replied, "I will keep your counsel in mind if there is ever a time I need a sympathetic ear."

"That is all I ask," Darcy said as he hugged her once again. "Sleep well, Sweetling."

As he left the room, Darcy knocked on Mrs Annesley's door, alerting the nurse to her charge's presence. When she immediately came in and stepped over to Georgiana's side, he could not help but smile at her caring manner. He trusted her so much more than Mrs Younge, who had proven to be an unworthy companion for sure. Mrs Annesley was nothing like her predecessor and he was grateful to have found her.

The next day the residents of Netherfield Park prepared to visit Longbourn once again, this time with the Hursts joining them. They all broke their fast and were soon off, with no intention of returning for many hours as Mrs Bennet had already invited them to stay for supper.

Caroline, having already retired when they returned the evening before, and once again not downstairs when they left this morning, was once again not amongst the party. She was beginning to get the distinct impression that she was unwanted on these visits to Longbourn. *Tomorrow I will not allow them to abandon me again*, she thought. Her plans to wed Mr Darcy had obviously fallen through; she would not give up on her newest venture – to capture his cousin instead. She had to put her newest plan into action soon. Having finally heard from her friend, Prudence Morley, Caroline once again spent the day going over the rather brazen schemes her friend suggested. Luckily, she was not above being brazen.

Bingley spoke with Louisa about his plan for a ball and his desire to have her act as hostess for him. They agreed on a date of Tuesday, the 26th of November. Bingley assured her of his confidence in her determining every other detail of the ball. Though she appreciated his trust in her abilities, she looked forward to discussing it with the other ladies, especially eager to utilize the expertise of the Countess of Rosebery.

Having already printed the invitations while in Town, Louisa only need fill in the particulars and Bingley could deliver them to the neighborhood and send them to the few friends he would invite from Town

With many preparations in need of the ladies' scrutiny, it was decided the gentlemen would leave them to their devices and go shooting. Sir William Lucas and his eldest son, Mr Jonathan Lucas, were also included in the day's excursion, and they arrived soon after the Netherfield Park visitors had disembarked from their carriage and horses.

Mr and Mrs Bennet, along with Darcy and Elizabeth, were speaking privately while the others gathered.

In Mr Bennet's study, Darcy stood before his intended's parents, feeling his stomach churn in anticipation. He and Elizabeth talked of their desire to have the wedding sooner rather than later, and they each preferred a small, private ceremony to that of a grand affair. When Darcy arrived this morning he was able to convey to Elizabeth the date of the ball. They both agreed it would be the perfect time to wed, if only her parents were amenable to the notion of the wedding taking place in a matter of just a few weeks' time. Mr Bennet would surely not relish his favorite daughter moving away so soon, and Mrs Bennet was certain to want the first wedding of one of her daughters' to be a large and elaborate affair. Darcy only hoped the date was possible.

"Sir, madam, I am grateful your daughter has chosen to accept my hand, and I am ever thankful you have given us your blessing and so easily accepted me as a part of your family already." Looking down and twisting the ring on his finger, he continued, "Elizabeth and I have spoken of our own wishes, and we would prefer the wedding to be a small, family affair."

Susannah started to say something and Bennet put his calming hand on his wife's arm, "How small are you thinking?"

"Only those presently represented in the house. All of you, of course, the Gardiner's, and my Fitzwilliam relations, as well as Bingley and his family. Elizabeth has also requested that her dearest friend, Miss Lucas, and her family also be included."

"Surely you have other family and friends you wish to invite as well?" Susannah replied, surprised by the small list he gave.

"I and my sister are all that remain of the Darcy's. I have one other aunt on my mother's side, but due to her persistence that I wed her daughter, and the split my decision not to do her bidding has caused between us, I feel it would be best if Elizabeth and I are wed without my Aunt Catherine having any prior knowledge."

After hearing his explanation, they both understood a little better his reasoning. "The banns can be read beginning Sunday, so that would make your wedding date no sooner than December. Perhaps a Christmas wedding is in order?" her father suggested.

Elizabeth took Darcy's hand in hers. She had more experience with her parents and felt she could negotiate on their behalf better than Darcy could alone; she knew just how to garner her mother's support. "Mama, William has visited the

Archbishop to obtain a special license, so we could be wed at any time and in any location."

Mrs Bennet's hands rose to her mouth in surprise, "A special license? *OH MY!* Mr Bennet, our daughter is to be married by *special license?*" She looked at her husband with tears in her eyes.

Smiling at his wife, Bennet turned to the young couple, "Well, it seems you have convinced your mother."

Elizabeth and Darcy shared a look, and Darcy once again spoke, "Bingley has long talked of hosting a private ball, and just this morning he finalized the date with his sister, Mrs Hurst, who will be acting as hostess for him. It is to be held on the twenty-sixth of November. Elizabeth and I thought it would be the perfect opportunity to celebrate our wedding as well. With a special license, we are free to marry whenever and wherever we desire, and the ball would offer the others in the neighborhood, as well as a few of my friends from Town, the opportunity to join in the celebrations with us without being at the ceremony itself."

"So, you propose to wed in two and a half weeks?" Mr Bennet asked, looking between the two in front of him.

"Yes, sir," Darcy answered with confidence.

Looking at his wife and seeing the pleasure in her eyes, he turned back to his daughter, "And this meets with your approval, Lizzy?"

"Yes Papa, it does," she looked up into the face of her intended, love evident on her every feature. "I think it would be nice to have an intimate ceremony and then be introduced beside my husband at the ball immediately following."

He could not deny his daughter's wish. With a resigned expression, he replied, "Then let me not stand in your way." He continued with a hint of sadness in his eyes, "I will have no surprise weddings, is that understood? The event must be planned. It will not just occur without prior knowledge of all those involved. I want no scandal coming from such a short engagement." Turning to his wife, he displayed his unusual wit as he teased, trying to overshadow his own emotional response to Elizabeth's wedding. "My dear, this shall be your finest hour, do not let me down."

"Oh, Mr Bennet, you do take delight in vexing me," Susannah said with a gleeful smile. "Lizzy, we have so much to plan!" She threaded her arm around her daughter's and spoke animatedly as they all left the room to join the others.

Sarah Johnson

# CHAPTER

## XX

Saturday held many various activities for all, and they formed into their respective groups about midday. There were invitations for the ball to be delivered by some, while others were required to pore over the marriage contracts and ensure all the legalities were in place before the ceremony in just over two weeks' time. While the gentlemen fulfilled their duties, the ladies were invited to join Mrs Hurst at Netherfield with the intention of inspecting the common rooms of the house for the ball's preparations.

Mr Darcy sent his carriage to Longbourn early in the morning with orders to convey the women to Netherfield Park, and not to leave without them *even if* Miss Elizabeth insisted on their own equipage being adequate for the three sisters, her mother, and her aunt. Johnson received his orders with practiced ease, but he thought to himself, *who would not wish to ride in this fine carriage?*

Upon his arrival at Longbourn, he was met by Mr Bennet coming from the stable. Johnson informed Mr Bennet of his orders to wait on the ladies and return to Netherfield Park when they were ready. The older man answered and walked away smiling and shaking his head as he mumbled something about his daughter under his breath. Within a few minutes, a young lady he assumed to be said daughter came outside and approached him, "We are not in need of your assistance. Please thank Mr Darcy, but we have two serviceable carriages here and can easily make the small distance in them."

"Madam, my orders are to stay here even if you refuse the ride."

Rolling her eyes and huffing, she said petulantly, "We will do as Mr Darcy says, but do not think he has won this round!" Elizabeth turned to go back inside. She stopped at the door, twisted around, and said, "We will be a few hours still, if you would like to unharness the horses and take them to the stable. If you knock on the kitchen door, I am sure you will find something to eat while you wait." With that, she turned and went back inside.

Johnson chuckled to himself and led the horses away. *Oh, she will be the making of Mr Darcy for sure,* he thought. He was impressed with the lady who would soon become his new mistress. He and the footman on the back of the carriage unharnessed the horses and were soon seated in the kitchen with a bowl of soup and a crust of bread.

A few hours later, the ladies of Longbourn passed the gentlemen from Netherfield Park on the road. Elizabeth cocked her brow and smirked at Mr Darcy when he smiled at seeing her inside his carriage.

*I am sure I will pay for that stunt, but somehow I doubt I will mind,* he thought as he tipped his hat to the ladies and trotted on down the road.

The ladies arrived at Netherfield Park and were announced, greetings were exchanged, and tea commenced. They naturally broke up into smaller groups throughout the room.

Miss Bingley tried to ingratiate herself to the countess, proving to Lady Rosebery that she was only trying to earn her acceptance for some nefarious reason. Lady Rosebery would not be taken in by this one. For years she had seen Miss Bingley pursue her nephew, trying every way she could to garner his attentions. Now it seemed – with Elizabeth in the picture and soon to be Mrs Darcy – Miss Bingley was trying to attach herself to the family by other means, those *other means* being her eldest son. The countess was wary of anyone willing to be as underhanded as the tales she had heard of Miss Bingley, and she would not allow her to taint the Fitzwilliam's good name.

Bored with talk of weddings amongst the older ladies, Caroline decided to find out what she could of the other Bennet sisters. Not having been around the residents of Longbourn very often, she set out to determine just whose *fine eyes and pretty face* the viscount said he was taking great pleasure in when they were at the Bennet's dinner party a few weeks ago. Looking at the group of ladies sitting together, she began to think. The youngest two were not yet out in society, and the eldest two were pretty well spoken for, so she could not imagine the viscount being taken with any of them. If what he said at the party indicated that his eye has been turned by one of them, then it had to be the middle sister. *What was her name again? I cannot remember. Oh well, it is no matter – I will just refrain from having to address her by name,* Caroline thought as she strode over to the young lady sitting quietly on the sofa.

Caroline took a seat beside Mary and feigned disinterest in what Elizabeth was saying to Georgiana. After a minute, she leaned over to Mary and asked with a sigh, "What do you do for entertainment around here? I find the society unvarying and it has become quite tedious."

Mary was not sure what to think of what Caroline said. "I have rarely been outside of the neighborhood, so I cannot imagine what would keep your interest beyond what Meryton offers already."

"No, I imagine you would not," Caroline said with disdain. "I suppose there are not very many local young gentlemen?"

"A few, but not many. We are an area blessed with many young ladies, and the war has taken some others from our streets."

"Then I imagine you do not have much experience with gentlemen in general?"

Not certain where this conversation was going, Mary answered, "To what do these questions tend?"

Caroline leaned in closer and with a raised brow, she quietly replied, "I only wish to determine if I should do my duty *as a lady* to warn your family of the *ungentlemanly* that hide amongst the upper classes."

Her emphasis on certain words made Mary's skin prickle. "I cannot imagine that those of the Netherfield party would be *as you say*."

"Can you not? Well, believe you me, they do exist. *Some* in the *upper classes* consider it a rite of passage to see how many *conquests* they can make in a new neighborhood." She placed her hand on Mary's arm in feigned sincerity, "I do not mean to frighten you, but you should consider that I know of whom I speak *very well*. I have seen a side of him for many years that those outside of his *intimate circles* cannot have recognized."

Mary looked down at her hands, "I understand and thank you for your concern, Miss Bingley."

With a smile of accomplishment, Caroline rose and indicated to Louisa that they should start the tour of the house soon.

Jane stood, thinking of all she had overheard Miss Bingley say. *Of whom could she be speaking? Surely Mr Darcy is not such a gentleman? Lizzy would never have fallen prey to someone of that nature, and Papa is a great judge of character – he would not allow a marriage to someone with such a reputation.* She thought of the other gentlemen who were absent from their company today. Mr Bingley told her once that his sister did not know the viscount very well, so she doubted that was to whom she referred. Another thought ran through her head – *could she be telling Mary this to have her warn me off Mr Bingley? Surely not! Nevertheless, she did say she was in this person's intimate circle. That could only be her own brother! Oh, what am I to do? I must speak with Lizzy tonight!*

Not wanting Georgiana to feel left out, Mary suggested the two of them remove to the music room during the inspection of the rooms. They had been speaking of composers yesterday, and Georgiana was eager to go through some music sheets with her new friend, so she found the suggestion agreeable. Thus, it was decided that Jane and Elizabeth, along with the older ladies, would tour the house with Bingley's sisters as guides. It would be an inspection of all the common rooms as well as the guest chambers to see what was needed to accommodate those who would be staying overnight from Town after the ball. As she left the drawing room, Lady Rosebery told her niece she would send someone to help her to the music room.

Within a few minutes, the viscount walked into the room with a smile on his face. "Good afternoon ladies," he said with a deep bow. "I have been told my assistance is needed to escort you two lovely ladies to the music room?"

Georgiana giggled at her cousin's exaggerated gallantry, "You are too kind, my lord."

Alex walked over and scooped her up with ease, then turned to Mary, "Miss Mary, it is a pleasure to see you again today."

"Thank you, my lord," Mary quietly answered, avoiding his gaze. Having been around Mr Bingley and Mr Darcy quite often, she knew they could not be the *ungentlemanly* of which Miss Bingley spoke. That only left the viscount. She needed to think more on what was said, and, thinking all the others were gone, she did not expect to see him walk through the door.

Walking across to the door, he could feel her eyes staring at his back. His thoughts were once again consumed by her. *I believed whatever was troubling Miss Mary was ended; she was much more amiable when I returned from Town. Yet today she is once again diffident.* He was confused about what could have caused her glaring glances.

Alex settled Georgiana into a seat, tucked a blanket around her legs and asked if she needed anything else.

"Yes, I had thought to bring my music sheets down this morning, but I have forgotten them in my room. If you would not mind, could you please send someone to retrieve them for me?"

"I will go myself," he offered. "I will return shortly, my fair ladies," he bowed low again and left the room.

Mary was taken aback at the viscount's treatment of her. *When he went out of his way to find and return my spectacles it seemed as if he were singling me out in a gentlemanly manner. Now though, as I see how he interacts with his young cousin, I begin to think it must just be his usual behavior.* He puzzled her greatly. Was he the knight in shining armour he first appeared to be, was he the proud man who chose to emphasize her inferiority to his cousin in the middle of the dinner party where she or anybody else might overhear, or was he the ungentlemanly rake Miss Bingley suggested today was his known character among the Ton? She became concerned as her mind tended towards the latter. *Is this gallantry just his way of wooing his prey, just as Miss Bingley indicated?* Mary was determined not to fall victim to such wiles.

Georgiana saw Mary's contemplative face and wondered what she was pondering so intently. Interrupting Mary's thoughts, she asked, "Have you had the opportunity to see an opera?"

Mary focused back on her friend, "No, I have only been to Town to visit family, and that rarely. I am meant to visit my Aunt and Uncle Gardiner for the coming Season though."

"You will be in Town for the Season? Oh, that will be such a joy! I have grown up going to Town every year with my brother, and he and my cousins treat me to many wonderful sights and exhibits. I am certain we will be there again this year. I must speak with William about taking you with us on our excursions."

"I look forward to it, Miss Darcy."

"Oh, no, we are to be sisters; I cannot have you calling me *'Miss Darcy'*. *'Georgiana'* will do nicely, and I shall call you *'Mary'*, if that is agreeable with you?"

"Yes, that is perfectly agreeable, Georgiana," Mary said with a small smile.

Georgiana had a sudden thought and excitedly asked, "I would like to spend more time with you, but my recovery is not well enough to travel to Longbourn every day. I wonder... would you like to stay here at Netherfield? I am certain Mr Bingley could be easily persuaded to extend an invitation, and my aunt would gladly watch over us."

Mary could not help but smile at her new friend's suggestion. "If Mr Bingley extends an invitation, I would like to stay here with you."

When Alex returned, he caught the end of their conversation and watched their exchange from the doorway. With Georgiana, Mary was the quiet yet genuinely friendly lady he had encountered on the road, not the cynical and standoffish one he met with at other times of their acquaintance. *One day – one day soon, I hope, but definitely one day – she shall be that comfortable with me also*, he determined.

Alex gave Georgiana the music sheets and informed her he would be in the billiard room right next door if she needed anything else, then he went to pass the time until the other gentlemen returned. He soon found that the close proximity of the two rooms made it easy hear the music from the master at the pianoforte. *Georgiana is not strong enough to play like this yet, so it has to be Miss Mary.* Closing his eyes, he was lost in the sounds for a few minutes. When the song changed, he decided to forego the game of billiards for a greater pleasure.

Putting the cue stick away, he poured a drink and settled into a seat, leaning his head back and closing his eyes as he listened.

As he sat entranced for the next hour, the heavenly sounds filtering through the door, he realized this young lady, who was barely civil to him at times, had completely stolen his heart. How she had done so he could not say, but she had done so nonetheless. He had gone from intrigued to attracted, from attracted to captivated, and from captivated to in love with her in such a short amount of time that his mind was in a whirl. *Do I truly love her? Yes, there is no doubt of it.*

He would relish his time here in her neighborhood and hope his cousin's marriage to her sister would bring them together more in the future. *I will win your heart, Mary Bennet; and one day I will win your hand as well,* he declared to himself.

Bingley smiled, talked, and drank more tea than he thought possible as he delivered invitations to the ball he was to host.

When they returned home, he was delighted to see his angel in the sitting room. He noticed she was upset and he immediately looked over at his sister Caroline. It was evident from the sinister look in her eye, the one he knew never to trust, that something had taken place. Just what, he did not know. He needed to discover just what had occurred. Caroline's machinations could cost him his angel, and *that* he was not willing to lose. In the past, he let his sister control his life a little too freely, and she had a way of warning off those she did not deem *worthy*. Bingley, however, wished to carry his suit as far as *he* intended without respect to what anyone else decided. He hoped his Aunt Hamilton would soon receive his letter and invite Caroline for a visit. For some odd reason, she was the only person who thought the world of Caroline. He would never understand his elderly aunt, but he appreciated her all the more knowing that the invitation would come soon enough.

With the presence of the others surrounding them, Bingley was unable to speak with Miss Bennet before she and her family departed. Frustrated, he decided to see if Caroline would reveal anything about the day in her ramblings after supper. Unfortunately, after hours of listening to her prattle on, he heard nothing to confirm she was behind Miss Bennet's despondency. He retired hoping he would find a time tomorrow after church services to speak privately with her.

When they retired that evening, Elizabeth followed her sister, determined to find out what had happened. All she knew was Jane's demeanor had been forlorn since their tea at Netherfield Park.

Dressed in their nightgowns, they climbed into bed and Jane began to tell her sister what she overheard Miss Bingley say to Mary earlier that day. Jane could not put into words her own fears of *who* this person was Caroline had spoken of, but Elizabeth did not need to hear the words escape her sister's lips to know from her demeanor why Jane would be sad at such a revelation. She determined to speak with William on the morrow about his friend's intentions.

# CHAPTER

# XXI

The following morning Darcy and Elizabeth sat together during church, sharing a prayer book. His deep baritone and her lilting soprano rose in perfect harmony in praise to God. They were the talk of the neighborhood. The announcement of their engagement was the most exciting event to happen in Hertfordshire in many years. After service, the two found themselves being moved from one group to another as each neighbor wished to give their congratulations of the coming nuptials.

When they were finally free to speak with rector privately, they sought him out, finding him inside the church.

Reverend Hughes heard the couple enter. He smiled and walked towards them, congratulating them on what was clearly on the lips of everyone this morning.

They accepted his good wishes and sat to discuss the finer details with him, telling him of their desire to wed on the twenty-sixth, as well as informing him they would wed with a special license.

When he asked when they would like the ceremony to take place, Elizabeth mentioned a fanciful idea of it happening just before the ball. Darcy was eager to agree to such a simple request. Reverend Hughes joked that it would be the affair of a lifetime for him, as every wedding he had performed was constrained by the dictates of having to take place before noon. However, if they had the special license that would allow them to marry at any time, why not utilize it to its fullest potential? The time was agreed upon and the couple took their leave from the minister

By the time Darcy and Elizabeth exited the church, the rest of the Bennets and Gardiners were already well on their way back home, so the pair set out to walk towards Longbourn alone.

Having already received permission from Mr Bennet, Darcy suggested they take the path along the river. They were soon alone with only the bare autumn trees surrounding them. The crunch of leaves beneath their feet and trickling sound of the river caused a peacefulness to envelope them both.

Finally, after they had walked in quiet companionship for a while, Elizabeth spoke. "Thank you William; only you could know that with such an onslaught of the neighborhood, I would need some time alone today."

Smiling, he drew her into his arms, "Elizabeth, it seems I know you more and more every day, and even in ways I do not understand myself."

Neither wished to join the others just yet, so they found an old log and sat down by the water. The sounds and smells in the autumn breeze were mesmerizing and replenishing to their souls as they sat together, hand in hand.

Elizabeth finally broke the silence, "William, I need to ask you something about Mr Bingley."

He turned to look fully into her eyes, "Yes my love, what is it?"

She looked down, not certain how to form such a question about his friend. Gathering her courage, she finally asked, "Has Mr Bingley... been known to... well, to break hearts wherever he goes?"

Bingley was friendly to all. He had never even singled a lady out as he had Miss Jane Bennet. However, Darcy misunderstood what Elizabeth meant in her question. Thinking she was just asking if he had spoken with many ladies in the past, Darcy replied, "Elizabeth, my friend has always been amiable... to both gentlemen *and ladies*. I cannot say for certain if he has broken many hearts, but he is not unknown among society."

Elizabeth was not sure she wished to know more, so she let the conversation end. It seemed it was possible Miss Bingley was speaking of her brother. How was she ever going to tell Jane such news?

After a few more minutes, the two set out for Longbourn where Darcy only stayed long enough to pass on the invitation Bingley issued, on behalf of his sister, for Mary to join them at Netherfield until the wedding. Mr Bennet spoke with his daughter and it was decided it would be best for her to stay at Longbourn until after Madam LeFevre returned on Tuesday for the last fitting. Then she would remove to Netherfield to join Georgiana on Wednesday.

Darcy took his leave and returned to his sister to tell her the news of her friends visit.

While the others were about their own devices, Jane and Elizabeth decided to take a stroll among the flora and fauna that remained in the garden.

Jane asked, "Lizzy, were you able to speak with Mr Darcy yet?"

Elizabeth's heart fell. She did not want to have this conversation with her sister, but she knew it was necessary. She took a deep breath, "Yes Janie, I did. He said Mr Bingley is *not unknown* among their society."

Jane's countenance fell with those words. She now knew she would have to do the hardest thing of her life and end her courtship with Mr Bingley. Not wanting to upset Elizabeth with her decision, Jane hugged her sister then returned inside alone.

When they retired that night Jane was quiet and went to sleep without much interaction with Elizabeth; neither sister thought to tell Mary of all they now thought about the overheard conversation.

---

The next morning Bennet was sitting at the table with Jane and Elizabeth when Mr Darcy and Mr Bingley were shown into the dining room. He knew from the looks being cast about by all four of the young people that they wished to not be in his presence too long. "I dare say it is a pleasant morning. Why not go for a walk? Perhaps Mr Bingley and Mr Darcy would like to see Oakham Mount?"

Looking directly at Miss Bennet, Bingley immediately spoke up, "Yes sir, I would like nothing better than to see it." She would not even look up at him and his stomach lurched. *I have a very bad feeling about this,* he thought.

Jane felt the walk would provide enough privacy to have her talk with Mr Bingley, so she agreed. She and Elizabeth left to gather their bonnets and pelisses, leaving Mr Bennet with the young gentlemen.

Having seen the distressed looks on his eldest daughter's face for two days now, he had a feeling it had something to do with Mr Bingley, though he did not know what exactly he had done. He decided to expend a little bit of advice to the gentleman who was nervously pacing around the table. "Mr Bingley you are making me dizzy, please have a seat." Waiting until he sat, Bennet then continued, "My guess is that you have done something to upset my eldest?"

"Me? No, sir! Nothing of which I am aware, that is."

Bennet stood slowly to leave the dining room. "Let me give you a piece of fatherly advice, Mr Bingley; it will always come back to *you* being at fault. Whether that be you having said something, or you having not said something; you having done something, or you having not done something; you having remembered something or you having forgotten something. If there is just a little bit of wisdom I can pass on to you this morning before your walk, it is this – listen to what she has to say and apologize even if you do not see the connection to you. It will take you far with ladies sensibilities." Bennet turned and walked out of the dining room to relax in his study for a few more minutes before he would go upstairs to join his wife.

The ladies came back down the stairs and the couples left for their walk. While Bingley knew something was bothering his angel, and he had a feeling it had to do with his sister, he was still unsure what it could be.

Darcy was a bit confused by the forlorn demeanor of the usually smiling Miss Bennet this morning; she looked sad and lonely, and he wished to alleviate whatever problem caused her distress. He had a feeling, because of Mr Bennet's words, that Bingley was behind the looks, so he determined himself that if she was not smiling again when they returned from their walk, he would have to speak with Bingley.

Elizabeth was prodding him to walk a bit faster this morning, and he saw no reason to disappoint his intended. Having seen the view from Oakham Mount already several times, he would like nothing more than to stand there at the top and look out over the Hertfordshire landscape with Elizabeth held tightly in his arms. The two soon out-paced the slower couple and were alone at last.

Darcy and Elizabeth quickly strode up the mount, stopping only once to see if Jane and Bingley were following them. Elizabeth hoped Bingley would assure her sister of his affections and clear up this misunderstanding — at least she hoped it was a misunderstanding. Feeling Darcy's hand on top of her own made her focus again on her surroundings.

*William* – Elizabeth looked up at her intended and smiled. He was the most handsome gentleman of her acquaintance, but above all, she felt he was meant just for her. He loved her even with all her faults. *I wonder what life will be like after we are married?*

Her musings were interrupted when they reached the top and Darcy leaned down to whisper into her ear, "I love you, Elizabeth Bennet."

Looking into the deep pools of his eyes, she nearly lost her footing and started to slip when he caught her and pulled her into his chest. She felt at home in his arms. *What more could I want than this?* she thought.

Darcy's heart was pounding so hard he could hear the steady thumping of it in his ears. He held this wonderful lady was in his arms, as close as he could without their embrace being completely inappropriate, and yet he still felt she was not close enough. *I cannot wait until we are married*, he thought.

The wind swept around them and eventually they pulled away from each other. Darcy cupped Elizabeth's rosy red cheek with his hand, "There is no place I would rather be right now than here with you."

Elizabeth smiled, "I can only think of one place better – in front of Reverend Hughes."

"Soon," he answered, "very soon." He ran his finger along her cheek. "I hope these preparations are not too trying on you?"

"William, I am quite used to my mother's nerves. Believe me when I say, there is nothing I want more than to be your wife, and if I must endure a few weeks of torture, then it will be worth it."

"If I could grant you one request on our wedding day, what would it be?"

"I wish to have the opportunity to dance with my new husband before the day is over," Elizabeth said with a smirk as she spun around.

Darcy's breath caught as he watched her twirling in the sun dappled leaves. Before he could even think, he stopped her and crushed his lips to hers. *Their first kiss.* He felt her soft form as it molded into his embrace, fire overtaking his entire body. As he pulled back he saw that her eyes were closed, the smile on her face telling of her pleasure in his abrupt action.

Elizabeth could not help herself; she was so happy she felt she would burst. Grabbing William's hands she whirled them both around until they were dizzy.

Darcy was laughing so vigorously at her enthusiasm he could hardly stand up straight. "I must catch my breath Elizabeth," he said as they stopped spinning.

"Have you seen the view from up here before?" Elizabeth asked when they had both calmed.

"Yes, but not with you in my arms," he led her closer to the edge of the rocky hill and stood behind her.

Bingley, taking what Mr Bennet said to heart, addressed his companion, "Miss Bennet, I do not know what I have done, but I am truly sorry your face does not hold its usual smile this morning. Is there a way for me to assuage whatever is bothering you?"

Jane felt sympathy for him. He truly was an amiable and caring gentleman —
she could not picture him being a rake! Jane knew they must speak about what
Miss Bingley said, but did not know how to begin such a conversation.

Bingley saw an area just off the path that would be a good resting place, so he
veered that direction. Jane did not even notice until he was urging her to sit
down. When she sat, she looked down at her hands.

Bingley stood in front of her waiting. When she would not even look up at him,
he decided to ask again. "Miss Bennet, please tell me what is bothering you?
What did my sister say that has upset you?"

Startled to hear him say that, she looked up. "How did you know it was
something Miss Bingley said?"

"If there is anything I know about my sister, it is that she is always scheming. I
did not miss the downtrodden look on your face the other day when I returned
home, just as I did not miss the look of a fat cat full of cream on Caroline's face
either. I know she is at the crux of this. Please tell me what happened?"

Jane gathered her courage and finally spoke, "Miss Bingley said nothing to me,
she was speaking with my sister Mary, but I overheard the hushed conversation.
She was warning her of your *intentions* and whether they were sincere... *or not.*"

He thought deeply, trying to determine, from the limited words spoken, what
the real problem was. It finally dawned on him. "She said I was a *rake!*"

"She did not use any names, and nor did she use *that word* specifically, but that is
what I took it to mean by what *was* said. Then when Mr Darcy told Lizzy
yesterday that you have a past with ladies, it was my natural conclusion."

Bingley was shocked, "Darcy! What exactly did *HE* say?" Bingley was pacing
furiously now. "I shall strangle him! I shall strangle them both! Miss Bennet,
you must tell me everything that was said by all involved."

Jane explained, to the best of her remembrance, what she had heard Miss
Bingley say, and how Elizabeth offered to speak with Darcy to determine if
there was any truth to such a rumor.

Bingley was furious. *How could Caroline do this to me? How could Darcy do this to me? No, no, I must not blame Darcy. More than likely he did not know what Caroline said and just gave the wrong response to Miss Elizabeth. All the blame for this must be placed directly at the feet of my sister.*

Jane watched as he agitatedly paced back and forth in front of her. He was balling up his hands and his face was a deep red. She tried to get his attention but he was too preoccupied to hear her, so she stood, thinking the movement would pull him back to the present. Instead he nearly plowed right into her, but she managed to step out of the way just in time to not be run over. "Mr Bingley!" she chastised firmly and loudly.

Bingley finally saw her standing there, "Oh, I apologize for my inattentiveness, Miss Bennet. Here, let me help you," he led her back to her seat on the stump. "I must apologize for my sister's actions as well. She had no right to say such things, and I will certainly be speaking with her."

"Oh, no, I would not wish you to be upset with your sister on my account. I am certain she had good reason to say what she did." Jane was too kind-hearted to think so ill of even Caroline Bingley.

"No, madam, she did not. You cannot make me think pleasantly of my sister in this situation. She had no right to say such things of anyone, especially me, and will be taken to task for her words." Bingley was firm in his opinion. "However, I must also apologize to you on my own behalf. I should have done more to assure you my intentions towards you are sincere."

Jane looked up into his eyes and saw the pain there. Her heart swelled and she knew without a doubt that if he asked for her hand right now she would say yes.

Bingley bent down in front of her. "Miss Bennet, I want you to know – my intention is to one day ask for your hand; not today – there are some issues I must attend to first within my family before I can ask you properly. I also do not want the day I ask you to be one filled with anguish as this has obviously been for you. I want it to be a special memory we can think back on with much pleasure for years to come. I also do not wish to overwhelm your family. The happiness of my friend in finding your sister will sustain me until after they are wed, and then we shall see when the right opportunity presents itself. Know this, Miss Bennet, I will ask you one day, and it will not be too far in the future. I know my heart in this, and I pray I have been able to correctly read your own heart as well."

Jane felt a flutter in her stomach as a small smile appeared on her lips. "I will wait for your question with all anticipation, sir."

"I hope you are not offended because of my wish to wait a little longer?"

With understanding, Jane replied, "I too do not wish to overwhelm my family. I am a patient person and will wait until you feel the time is right."

Bingley stood and held his hand out to her, "Thank you, Miss Bennet." He threaded her arm through his and they both began walking towards Oakham Mount, both in agreement that the betrothed couple had been left alone long enough.

"I understand you are upset with your sister," Jane said as they walked, "but for my sake I ask that you please have mercy on her. She did not say these things directly to me, and she never mentioned your name. I do not want you to blame her for my own misunderstandings. I should have never listened to the conversation."

It took everything in him to agree, but he did finally answer her plea. "Only because you ask with the purest of intentions will I forgive her. This is not the first time her scheming has caused problems, and I dare say it will not be the last, but because you ask this of me, I will let this time go without interfering."

As they came upon the final turn of the path at the top of the lookout, they saw Darcy standing with Elizabeth in front of him. Both were facing out over the landscape beyond, their eyes closed and their hands held out like wings, the wind from the elevated mount rushed all around them as it stirred the dead leaves on the ground at their feet into a whirlwind of activity. Bingley chuckled at his friend and was grateful Miss Elizabeth was bringing out a side of Darcy he had not seen in many years.

The two couples enjoyed a few minutes of quiet contemplation on top of the mount before they turned back to Longbourn. The men left not long after their return; Mr Goulding was hosting a shooting party and they would be gone the rest of the day.

As they rode away, Bingley sighed heavily, "Darcy, sometimes I could strangle you!"

"What? What did I do?"

"Did Miss Elizabeth happen to ask you about me yesterday?"

"Yes; yes she did. I told her you were amiable to all and were well known among the Ton."

Bingley shook his head and chuckled, "I had a feeling your part in this was something of that nature. You, my friend, are not the best at sketching people's intentions. It seems you only confirmed what my sister hinted to on Saturday about my being a *rake of the highest order* amongst the Ton."

"She said *WHAT?*"

"Yes, that was my reaction as well." Bingley could see the surprise in his friend's face. "Oh do not distress yourself, I have already written my Aunt Hamilton to ask if Caroline can visit her. I have a feeling she shall be on an extended trip to Scarborough very soon. Hurst and I already decided after the incident last week with your cousin's door handle that we would not be inviting her back to either of our homes again for some time. She will have one more chance, and that only because Miss Bennet asked that of me. If Caroline is involved in one more scheme, I will have her out of my life immediately."

"Does she have any prospects for marriage?"

Bingley sighed, "No one will approach her in Town. Not even her substantial dowry is enough to entice gentlemen to our doorstep these days. My father arranged for both my sisters to marry. Louisa was happy to have found such a good gentleman in Hurst, but I have held off on pushing such a situation on Caroline despite my father's wishes. She has never even been informed of his choice for her husband."

"You are thinking of contacting this person to see if he is interested?" Darcy asked.

"Louisa was lucky in that she and Hurst have a mutual affection for each other, and I want that for Caroline as well, but she may leave me no other option than to marry her off to whoever will take her."

"Perhaps she will meet someone in Scarborough," Darcy offered.

"Yes, I can always hold out hope my aunt will have someone in mind."

Before long they were riding through the gate at the Goulding's and both remembered the first time they came here with the Bennet sisters to feed the horses. It seemed such a long time ago, yet barely six weeks had passed. So much had happened for both of them in that short amount of time.

When they returned to Netherfield Park that evening, Bingley informed Hurst privately of what Caroline said. He did not confront her only because of his promise to Miss Bennet, but the two brothers knew Caroline's scheming would not end and they spoke of what they would do if further action was needed.

Sarah Johnson

# CHAPTER

# XXII

The days flew by and the next thing Mary knew she was packing her trunk to stay at Netherfield Park. She and Georgiana were becoming close. They were both looking forward to when they could become even better acquainted as Mary stayed at Netherfield Park for the weeks leading up to the wedding of their siblings. The two would share a bedroom, and Mary anticipated late night talks with her new friend and soon-to-be sister.

In her excitement, she failed to remember until today that the viscount would also be in residence. Picking up her cat Beatrice, Mary sat down on her bed beside the pile of dresses laid out to be packed. Burying her face into the white fur, she asked her feline companion, "What am I to do Beatrice? I do not know how I feel about him, but I am afraid he may be what Miss Bingley suggested. He is very attentive when I am around, but I know someone of his rank would never be drawn to someone like me." Holding Beatrice out to look into her eyes, she continued, "Maybe he is only drawn to the challenge I present?" While on one hand she was becoming quite fond of their little battle of wills, on the other hand she was afraid of what this would mean to the rest of her life if she gave in to his attentions. She was determined to stand strong and not show him any preference for his presence, even if she was becoming quite fond of him. Putting the cat back down onto her lap, she whispered, "I will just have to avoid him as much as possible."

Mary finished packing her trunk while she thought of all the changes these next weeks would hold for her and her family.

Mary followed Lady Rosebery into the room she and Georgiana would share and was immediately impressed with its size.

"My niece was so excited to have you stay that she insisted upon sharing a room. I hope you are amenable to such a decision? If not, we can easily have another room prepared."

"Oh no, it is perfect. I have shared a room with my own sisters, and I look forward to having another to call my sister very soon." She looked around and nodded, "This is a lovely room. Thank you."

Lady Rosebery explained that Georgiana would be up in a few minutes, then she excused herself.

Mary removed her bonnet and laid it on the bed, then walked to the middle of the room to inspect her surroundings more fully.

There were two beds pushed against opposite walls with large canopies hanging from the ceiling over each. Light pink, silk fabric draped down over the two ends of the beds and was pulled back to the corners in the front and tied. The cocoon it formed looked very inviting with its pink counterpane and soft white pillows stacked against the back of the bed. Georgiana's bed was identical to Mary's but pushed against the opposite wall leaving a large open space in the middle of the room. By the large window sat a wooden table with two chairs. The fireplace was angled in the opposite corner with a small side table and two wingback chairs of pink velvet positioned nearby.

A small dressing table was between two doors which led to the dressing room and the room Georgiana's nurse, Mrs Annesley, was given.

In the far corner, mostly hidden by the canopy of her bed, sat Georgiana's large, black bath chair, its front wheel jutting out beyond the confines of the corner in which it was placed. It was obvious this room was chosen because of the space available to move about easily in the wheeled contraption, though she did not remember ever seeing Georgiana use it.

The feelings of grandeur the room had evoked in Mary died instantly when she recognized the reality her friend had to live with each minute of the day. The times they were together Mary tried to encourage Georgiana in her pursuits; she now had a greater understanding of why Georgiana was sometimes unreceptive of her encouragement. Unlike her father, who was always given hope of regaining most, if not all, of his prior abilities, her friend was given little hope of recovering to the point of even being able to walk again.

Mary removed her spencer and pulled the gloves from her fingers, laying them next to her bonnet already resting on the bed. She heard the maid in the dressing room unpacking her trunk, and she quickly closed the door, hoping to gather her thoughts in private. She sat on the edge of her bed looking around the room, seeing the tiny details she recognized so well from her own father's ordeal – bottles of medicine on the table, a cane leaning against the chair by the fireplace, a stack of books in easy reach of Georgiana's bed. Mary felt tears well up in her eyes.

Georgiana quietly knocked on the door, hearing Mary answer, "Enter."

The door opened to reveal the viscount standing there with his young cousin in his arms. Seeing the tears in Mary's eyes, he quickly took Georgiana to sit her at Mary's side as he asked, "Miss Mary, is something amiss?" He pulled out his handkerchief and handed it to her.

She took the offered item, drying her eyes, "No, I am sorry, I was just brought to tears over... something." She did not wish to make Georgiana uncomfortable. "I am recovered now."

Georgiana saw where Mary's eyes trailed, "You saw my bath chair?" Mary nodded her head, and Georgiana replied, "I cannot bring myself to use it. It is almost as if, when I do, I am giving in to the reality of not ever walking again." The two girls closed their eyes with the gravity of emotions that washed over them.

Alex could stand it no longer. He did not want to see either ladies' eyes filled with tears again, so he jovially responded with a deep bow, "And thus she employs my arms to carry her about from place to place as if she is a high and mighty queen."

Georgiana chuckled, "Well, I cannot very well put my trust in the puny footmen Mr Bingley employs. They would surely drop me in an instant."

Alex tweaked her nose and smiled at her, "I do not mind, Sweetling; you know that. You are as close to a sister as I shall ever have, and someone must bear the load in order to free up your brother and allow him to enjoy this special time with Miss Elizabeth."

"I truly appreciate your strength, Alex." Turning to Mary she said, "I have found over the last few months just how strong my brother and cousins are. You cannot imagine how many times I have had to rely on being in their arms to get around."

Mary blushed and glanced at Alex, "I believe I do know how that feels."

Alex smiled shyly at her, then turned back to Georgiana, "My mother has informed me we shall have tea in..." he pulled out his watch and continued, "a little less than an hour. Will you need my assistance once again at that time?"

"Yes, please; I do not want to become a bother to William."

Shaking his head, he replied with confidence, "You could never be a bother, dearest. I shall leave you for now and will return shortly."

When the door closed, Georgiana leaned over to Mary, "You and I have some planning to do. My brother is amenable to allowing me to attend the ball, but only for a little while."

Mary smiled, "He is a good brother."

"Yes, he is the best brother I could hope for."

"When I first met him I thought him to be aloof."

"Oh, gracious, no. Shy is more like it. He can be lively enough in the right company, and I dare say your sister brings it out in him as I have never seen with any other."

"Yes, Elizabeth seems to do that with me also," Mary said. She sat back and sighed, "I will miss her greatly when she is gone."

"Are you close then?"

"Not as close as she and Jane are; they share confidences and experiences from their visits to Town. However, I would say she is the one sister who best understands me. She draws me out and helps me see things in a way that does not come naturally for me. I tend to be a bit too cynical at times, seeing the harsh instead of the good in most situations."

"Ahhh, I understand. William has a tendency to be that way at times. He is always blaming himself for things that are none of his doing," Georgiana looked down at her hands, thinking of what had happened over the last year of her life.

Mary saw the forlorn look on her friends face, so she smiled and changed the subject, "I have never had the pleasure of a private ball before!"

"Truly?"

"I have only been to a few of the local Assemblies since my coming out last year."

Georgiana gleefully asked, "Do you know what you will wear?"

She shrugged her shoulders, "I have brought a few choices with me, but I must add some trim to either one of them. What will you wear?"

Georgiana went on to describe her dress. Even though it was modest in cut because of Georgiana not yet being out, Mary was impressed with the description.

"It sounds like a lovely gown."

"Oh it is! I chose it because the color matches so perfectly with a necklace my father gave me." She leaned forward so she could point to the dressing table, "Do you see that box? If you will bring it to me, I will show you."

Mary retrieved the box and handed it to her friend as she sat back down beside her on the bed. Georgiana opened it and pulled the top tray out to search through the bottom section for the necklace. Mary could not help comment about the beautiful jeweled comb that lay in the sectioned tray. She fingered it gently, "This is lovely Georgiana."

She paused in looking for the necklace and turned to see what Mary found so appealing. When she caught sight of the jeweled comb her brother had given her just a few weeks before her accident, she replied flatly, "Yes, just lovely."

"You should wear this in your hair as well. It has so many colors, I imagine it would match anything beautifully."

"I don't think so," she replied sharply. She finally found the small box that contained the necklace and she pulled it out, opening it to show Mary. Immediately her voice softened, "My father gave this to me when I turned seven years of age. He said it was too fancy for me to wear all the time, but I did not care – I did so anyway. Then one day the clasp broke and I lost it while out riding with him. When we returned home and I discovered my misfortune, I knew it must be found. So later that day, when my father was busy with his steward, I went out alone in hopes of retrieving it." Georgiana had pulled the necklace from the case and was lovingly running her finger down the chain and across the small jewel draped across her palm. "I did not realize how late it was in the day until it was already too dark to see properly and return home safely. I was so upset I just sat down beside a tree and began to cry. Everything seemed so hopeless."

Mary recognized the feeling as she remembered the day the viscount rescued her from her own misfortunes. "You needed a rescuer," she said quietly.

"Yes. My brother was expected home any day, and it was providence he happened along at that moment. He scooped me up and we returned home safely. My father had just found out I was gone and was gathering the servants to begin searching for me. He embraced me so tightly I could hardly catch my breath." She closed her eyes as if she were being held even at this moment by her father's arms. Sighing deeply, she opened her eyes again and continued with her story. "When I told him why I was out so late he was understanding and assured me he would replace the necklace. The next day William spent all day searching for it, and when he finally found it, he brought it back and gave it to me. My father had the clasp replaced, and I promised I would only wear it on special occasions in the future." Her voice dropped to nearly a whisper as she said, "When I have it on, it is as if his arms are around me once again."

Mary reached for her friends hand and squeezed her fingers lightly. No words were needed. Georgiana put the necklace back in its case and then into the jewelry box. When she replaced the top tray, Mary noticed the jeweled comb was turned over. She was curious about it, but did not wish to distress her friend by asking. Instead, she decided to change the subject back to her dress, "Perhaps you could help me choose which gown I should wear and which trim I should add to it?"

"Oh yes!" Georgiana was once again excited. "I am certain your trunk is unpacked by now. Go and retrieve your dress and we will see what it needs."

Mary did as she was bid, returning the jewelry box to the dressing table on her way to retrieve her dress and the trimmings. She returned and the two discussed the possibilities for a while. The dress was chosen, then they pulled out the trims.

"Hmmm...I just do not think any of these trims would look best."

"I happen to agree with you," Mary replied. "I think that is why I have been unable to decide before now."

"Perhaps my cousin would accompany us to Meryton to choose some other trim?"

Mary smiled at her friends willingness to go with her, "If it is not too difficult a journey for you?"

"Oh, no. William has had a special carriage made just for me. It contains a bed on which I can lay and be very comfortable. You will be impressed with the artistry of the details. It is quite lovely."

Mary smiled, "Then it is settled – we must talk your cousin into taking us to Meryton tomorrow."

"Yes, we must!"

The two continued to talk of the wedding and ball until they heard a strong knock at the door.

"Come in," Georgiana called out.

The door opened to reveal two men, the viscount and a slightly shorter man with reddish blonde hair and a much wider frame.

"FITZ!" Georgiana squealed with delight.

# CHAPTER
# XXIII

The unknown gentleman came into the room and engulfed Georgiana in his arms. "I have missed you tremendously, Sweetling."

"Oh, how I have missed you also," she answered. "I did not know you were coming."

Chuckling, he pulled back, "I did not know I was coming either. I had some time off and Mother informed me the family would be most appreciative if I could join them, so here I am." He stretched his arms out wide as he said the last part.

Mary saw movement beside her and noticed the viscount as he came to stand at her side. "Miss Mary, may I present my younger brother, the Honourable Richard Fitzwilliam, Colonel in His Majesty's Army."

"Miss Mary, I have heard much about you over the last half hour and am pleased to meet you." Fitz bowed and Mary returned it with a curtsy and a quiet greeting. *How could he have heard much of me? I am sure he means he has heard much of my family, not of me personally,* she thought.

Fitz turned back to Georgiana, "Are you ready to go downstairs for tea?"

"Yes, we have been waiting for Alex to return for me," she answered.

"I dare say that is only because you did not know of *my* arrival. I know you prefer me to my brother any day," Fitz said with a wink. He leaned down and easily positioned Georgiana in his arms. "We shall see you downstairs," he said as he spun around a few times then took quick steps towards the door making Georgiana giggle. Fitz could get Georgiana to forget her own inabilities more quickly than anyone, and she enjoyed it when he carried her. Darcy and Alex were too careful, but Fitz made her heart flutter as it used to when she rode her horse. She missed riding most of all.

Alex turned to Mary, "You must excuse my brother; he has not seen our cousin in two months and has been very worried about her. He and Darcy were appointed charge over her after my uncle died and they came of age, and the three of them are very close. When we left Pemberley a few months ago Georgiana was not even leaving her rooms yet."

"I know how it feels to see your loved one go through a tragedy such as she has had to endure, so I understand his trying to cheer her, my lord," Mary said with much emotion in her voice.

Alex put out his arm and asked, "May I escort you, Miss Mary?"

"Yes, thank you," Mary placed her hand timidly on his arm and the two left the room.

"I am glad you were able to join my cousin here at Netherfield and I hope you have a pleasant time during your stay."

"Thank you, my lord," Mary answered.

Stopping at the top of the stairs, he turned to her and asked, "Miss Mary, before we join the others, may I ask you a question?" Curious, she nodded her assent and he continued, "May I have the pleasure of your hand for the first dance of the ball?"

Shocked, Mary did not know what to say. She was flattered that anyone would ask for her hand in a dance, for she was forgotten most of the time by the local young gentlemen. However, she was hesitant because of who it was asking. Knowing if she did not answer in the affirmative then she could not dance at all that night, she finally nodded, "Yes, you may, my lord."

Caroline Bingley observed the exchange from further down the hall, hidden from their sight. *Yes, it seems I did judge correctly who has caught his eye. I will have to speak with Miss Mary once again,* she thought to herself. As the pair made their way down the stairs, she followed, watching them intently.

Later that afternoon, Georgiana went to her chambers to rest and Mary chose to practice in the music room. Caroline heard the pianoforte and glanced into the room. Seeing Mary alone, she saw this as the perfect opportunity to speak with her again, so she sat down on a chair until the song was finished. With a false smile she said, "That was well performed, Miss Mary." Caroline did not agree with the words coming out of her own mouth, but she knew she would have to be nice in order to garner Mary's trust.

Mary was not expecting anyone to hear her and jumped when Miss Bingley spoke. "Oh," she said, gathering her music sheets, "thank you, Miss Bingley."

When she stood to put her music back in order, Caroline sauntered up to her. Quietly, she leaned in and said, "Miss Mary, I saw your little *exchange* upstairs with a…" raising her eyebrows, she whispered, "…*certain person*." Mary paled immediately, not knowing where this was going. "No, no, do not worry – I will tell no one of it; I am just so worried about your own reputation, knowing what his is. Now, I personally do not care one bit what he does to his own reputation, but I cannot stand by and see him ruin yours. I would not have my *dear friends* destroyed because of someone of his ilk taking advantage of an inexperienced girl who does not know how the society of the Ton works."

Mary was trying to find a motivation for not believing Miss Bingley, and so far none had come to her. Since she was now speaking with her yet again, Mary thought she must be correct and had better distance herself as much as possible from the viscount. "I thank you, Miss Bingley. I was caught unaware earlier, but in the future I will remember your words and try to discourage his attentions." With that, she picked up her music sheets and left the room.

True to her promise, Mary avoided the viscount all evening. When he tried to speak with her, she cut the conversation short. Alex was once again curious as to what had changed. *Could she be offended by my asking for her hand during the first dance? Maybe she does not like the exercise and only felt obligated to accept me? I will just have to build her trust in me.* Alex could not sleep until very late that night, thinking of ways to gain her trust.

Rosebery took one last sip of his drink, looked at the young men surrounding him. "Well, gentlemen," he said, "I can no longer keep up with you young sprites. If you will excuse me, I will see you all tomorrow." They exchanged farewells and he left to join his wife.

As soon as the door closed, Fitz looked at Darcy, "Now that the old man is out of the room, you must tell me all."

Bingley immediately spoke up, glad to provide what information he could of the Assembly dance and all that happened over the last two months. Fitz learned years ago that he could glean quite a lot from Bingley's form of jumping from one subject to another in a conversation. One thing he picked up on immediately was when Bingley mentioned that Darcy met Miss Elizabeth *before* the dance.

When Bingley was finally finished speaking of the beauty of the Bennet's, especially Jane, Fitz looked at his cousin. "Well Darcy, are you going to expound upon that story?"

"Why should I? You would only pester me about it forever."

"Please do tell him, Darcy" Alex implored. "We all know this story already, so you might as well let Fitz in on it as well. If you do not, he will not let one of us leave until he has us staggering to bed from too much drink."

Fitz smiled at his brother, "You know me all too well, Alex."

"I have awakened with a headache from your methods of loosening my tongue one too many times."

Darcy finally gave in. "I met her in a field. She was lost and I pointed her in the proper direction. She then thanked me and went on her way." Putting down his drink, he continued, "I will never forget the smile that came over her face when my eyes found hers at the Assembly a few days later. I hoped she would remember me and would feel the connection I felt from our first meeting, and it turns out she did." No one moved when he stopped speaking, and he quietly finished barely above a whisper, *"I could feel my parents leading me out that day, and I am now convinced they were leading me right to my Elizabeth."*

The room was quiet for a few more minutes, no one knowing quite what to say. The gentlemen slowly excused themselves one by one to retire for the night.

When it was just the two of them left, Fitz said to Darcy, "From what I have heard of Miss Elizabeth, your mother would approve. She makes you smile, and I have not seen that in many years."

Darcy sighed heavily, "I am glad you found the time to come."

"Well, my investigation is not making much progress, and I wanted to check on my father. How is he? Is there any sign of distress I should know about?"

"I know why you ask – you have been worried for his health ever since he was frightened enough to turn Georgiana's guardianship over to us when we were one and twenty."

Fitz shrugged his shoulders, "I know he has assured of us his health, but there is something he is holding back. Perhaps it is time Alex and I discuss relieving him of some of the duties which keep him traveling from Derbyshire to London so often during the year."

"I do not envy either of you your positions when this conversation must be had with your father," he smirked.

"No, I would say you are lucky to not have to be involved this time." Drinking down what was left in his glass, he stood, "If that is all, I will retire."

"Actually, I have one more request of you," Darcy looked down at his hands. "I cannot remember a time in my life without you."

"That's because I am only three months younger, and I doubt you remember the first three months of your life," Fitz added jokingly.

Darcy chuckled, "That is true." Becoming serious again, he continued, "When we were growing up, you tortured me and pushed me to do better than I wanted at the time, but it was always for my own good. In the end, you were usually right in pushing me. You have been beside me through family tragedy, and I wish you to be standing right beside me in the triumphant moments as well." Looking up with much brotherly love shining from his eyes, he continued, "That is why I want you to stand up with me at my wedding."

"I would be honoured to stand up with you," Fitz answered sincerely. "I look forward to meeting your intended tomorrow, especially after Mother's comments."

"What did she say to you?"

"She said Miss Elizabeth is the perfect match for you in every way and she can see your mother choosing her for you." After a minute of silence, Fitz said, "I will see you in the morning Darcy," and retired to his chambers.

Darcy sat alone for a few a while thinking of all this next week would hold for him. *In six days, I shall be married.* He soon retired, with Elizabeth and their future life together on his mind.

Mary awoke to Georgiana's screams of pain. She stumbled in the dark over to her friend's bed. "Georgiana? What is wrong? What can I do to help?" When she did not answer, Mary ran to the adjoining door and knocked loudly, "Mrs Annesley, Mrs Annesley, wake up!"

The nurse came through her door and immediately ran to her patient's side. She began smoothing Georgiana's hair out of her face and rubbing her legs, calmly saying, "Miss Mary, would you please fetch us a bowl of warm water and some rags? I keep a pot of water near my fire; it should be warmed nicely. The rags are stacked in the corner." She pointed to the corner where the bath chair sat, then turned back to soothingly speak to Georgiana while Mary poured some water into a bowl and brought it and the rags to the bedside. "Please help me with her other leg." Mrs Annesley's tranquil voice instructed Mary, "Wrap this rag around her muscle, yes, just like that, and rub. No, no, that is too light, you must rub deeply. Yes, that is good." She again addressed Georgiana, "Is that starting to feel better now?"

Georgiana was finally able to mutter out, "Yes, thank you."

The two rubbed both of Georgiana's legs for the next few minutes until her muscles relaxed once again. Looking over at the table, Mrs Annesley chided her charge, "I see you did not drink your tea tonight."

Georgiana winced in pain, "I just could not tolerate the taste, although I am regretting not drinking it now."

"I will see if there is something we can add to make it more palatable, but whether you like it or not, you must drink the whole cup every night."

"I will from now on, I promise," she said.

Mrs Annesley prepared a fresh draught and Georgiana drank it without complaint. Mrs Annesley sat beside her gently running her fingers through Georgiana's hair until she fell back asleep.

Standing, she waved for Mary to follow her back into her room, then the nurse closed the door, "I thank you Miss Mary; you helped me a great deal tonight."

"What happened?" Mary enquired.

"Miss Darcy has not been able to use her legs since her accident back in May; sometimes they cramp up, especially when she is extremely tired or has had a lot of activity during the day. When that happens to you or I, walking around or moving the affected muscles will help, but Miss Darcy does not have that ability, so she is unable to stop them from hurting without someone rubbing them," Mrs Annesley explained.

Mary felt sorry for her friend, "Does this happen often?"

"It depends on her activity level. If she does a lot during the day, she tends to have more episodes at night. She usually takes a special tea every evening before bed, but as you heard, she did not take it tonight. It would have helped prevent her cramps, I believe."

"Do I need to stay awake and watch her?"

"Oh, no, my dear, you need your sleep. The drink I gave Miss Darcy will help her relax, and she should sleep peacefully the rest of the night. I will stay near in case she needs anything." Mrs Annesley started leading Mary back to her bed. "Do not worry, Miss Mary, all will be well in the morning. We will just need to do some deep rubbing every night because of her recent increase in activity."

Mrs Annesley helped Mary back into her bed, "Now close your eyes and go to sleep. You will have a busy week and we must not spoil it for you." Mrs Annesley stayed by Mary's bed for a minute more, before she went to check on her charge. When she saw that both girls were fast asleep once again, she pulled a chair over to Georgiana's bedside, retrieved a blanket, and settled in to watch over her as the house slept for a few more hours.

When morning finally came, the household buzzed with activity all around once again. In only a few more days they would host a wedding and a ball, and every available concession was being made for both events.

Mr Bennet came to discuss the last details of the marriage contract with Darcy, and as he was leaving he saw his daughter sitting alone in the garden. He went to sit beside her. Noticing the sad look on her face, he drew his arm around her shoulders and pulled her closer, "What is wrong, my dear? Please do not tell me you are becoming maudlin over your sister leaving home?"

Mary sighed slowly. "Papa, I am worried for Miss Darcy."

"Why? What has caused your concern?"

"She awoke last night with cramps, and Mrs Annesley and I had to rub her legs to get her to settle again." She turned to face her father, "Did you have leg cramps as well after your accident?"

He had always tried to keep as much from his family as he could, but he knew she needed the truth now. "Yes, and from what Doctor Jones told me, it is common after such an injury."

"I am so sorry, Papa. I never knew."

"If I knew you could do something for me, I would have told you, but I knew it was something I must bear on my own. Please do not be distressed on my account." He looked around, "Where is Miss Darcy today? It is unusual to not see you two together when I am here visiting."

"She decided to stay in her room today."

He stood, "Let us go and check on her then."

Mary stood and thanked her father for listening to her concerns, then walked beside him as they went to her room. When she peeked in the door, she saw Georgiana sitting beside the fire.

"Are you up for a visitor?"

"Who is it?" Georgiana asked.

Bennet stepped around his daughter. "Hello Miss Darcy. I thought perhaps you and I could talk for a few minutes."

She nodded her head and Bennet kissed Mary on the cheek before he whispered to her, "Everything will be well. Why don't you go downstairs and practice your music and I will find you when I am finished here."

Mary took her leave and did as he suggested.

Bennet walked over to the fireplace and sat in the empty chair. "I know how you feel."

"Do you? Somehow I doubt anyone could know how I feel."

"Yes, I truly do. I went through the same emotions after my accident as well. I may not have your particular burdens, but there are a lot of things I had to come to terms about after my accident a few years ago. It is difficult sometimes, but everything will be well. You will see."

Georgiana could hold her tears in no longer and she burst out in sobs. Bennet drew his chair closer and held out his handkerchief to her.

When she calmed, he told her of the accident he had. He even told her of things he had never told to anyone else, such as the thoughts that ran through his head as he was trapped beneath the carriage, and the anguish he kept from his family as his body healed. Georgiana spoke of her experience as well, and was finally able to put into words what she had held in her heart for so long.

It was nearly an hour later when Bennet descended the stairs and went to find Mary. He stopped at the door to the music room and could not help but smile at the masterful way in which she displayed her talent. When the song ended he clapped and walked over to her, giving her a hug as he kissed the top of her head. "That was lovely, my dear."

Mary could not keep the worry from her features. "Is she well?"

He nodded, "Yes, she is well. In fact she will be down shortly. She has a desire to practice the pianoforte with you. Her cousin should be bringing her down in a few minutes."

As if on cue, Alex walked in the door with Georgiana in his arms. He settled her on the bench beside Mary.

Georgiana reached for her friends hand and squeezed her fingers in a showing of appreciation. "Let us play," she smiled.

Alex and Bennet both stepped over to the doorway and could not help but smile at the two ladies as they chose a piece and began to play the simple duet.

Bennet saw the way the viscount looked at his daughter, and if he did not know better, he would say it was with a great deal of affection. *I will have to see what comes of this,* he said to himself before patting the younger gentleman on the shoulder and taking his leave.

# CHAPTER

## XXIV

Elizabeth awoke before anyone else in the room stirred. She carefully climbed out of the bed where her two cousins, along with Jane, were all still fast asleep. She wrapped a blanket around her shoulders and curled up in the window seat, looking out at the few stars still shining in the early morning sky as they peeked out from behind the clouds that quickly formed.

*This week has gone by so quickly, yet at the same time it has felt as if this day would never come,* she thought. *Today, I am to be married. I will give up the name of Bennet and leave it behind for my husband's name, to forever be connected, in life and death, to him. I have lived for twenty years with this name, and yet when next I lay my head on my pillow, I will no longer hold it as my own. From this day forth, I will forever be known as Elizabeth Rose Darcy.*

Rubbing her arms as chills ran through her body, she recollected a conversation she and Darcy had only a few short hours ago.

*"Do you see those stars, Elizabeth? When my mother died, my father used to tell us she was looking down from above and that is why the stars twinkle. My father used to comment that it was that very same twinkle in her eyes which first caught his attention. We would go outside and say goodnight to my mother every night."* Darcy moved to stand behind Elizabeth and wrap his arms around her. *"Then when my father also passed away, Georgiana and I continued to say goodnight to both of our parents every night. My sister says she is too old now, but sometimes I see her looking out from her window and waving to the sky."*

*He tightened his hold on her waist, and whispered in her ear, "I know my parents are looking down on us, and I think they are saying they approve of our marriage." He pointed up to the sky, "Do you see that bright one right there? That is the Pole Star. It helps ships navigate through the night, just as the sun helps them navigate throughout the day. They can set their direction by that star. That is what I feel my father has done for me. He gave me everything I needed in the time he was here to set me off in the right direction. Since he has died, he continues to guide me. The day I first saw you in that field, I knew it was my parents leading me to you. It was the anniversary of my mother's death, and I found great comfort in coming across you on that particular day."*

*Elizabeth leaned into his chest closer, "I love you, William."*

*The two stood looking at the stars for a few more minutes before Mr Bennet came to escort Elizabeth inside. "Tomorrow, you two; you will gain your privacy tomorrow, but for now, Darcy, I must insist my daughter get her sleep."*

Elizabeth smiled at the memory and leaned her forehead against the cold glass. Rain drops began to slowly trickle down the other side of the window. A few minutes later when lightening flickered through the dark sky, she jumped a little. Leaving the window seat, she climbed back into the bed with the others, pulling her young cousin closer as she tried to ignore the rumblings that were building outside.

Elizabeth did not even realize she had fallen asleep again until she was awakened by Jane's gentle prodding. "Lizzy... Lizzy, wake up. Papa says we are to leave for Netherfield Park soon, and you are not even dressed yet."

She groggily sat up and looked around, still hearing the rain as it poured outside. "What do you mean? We are not to be there until later today."

"He feels it would be safer if we leave now. Mr Bingley has sent a note assuring him of there being rooms readied for us to dress before the ceremony, and Papa knows how you are when it storms."

A boom of thunder made her jump and she quickly stood, "Yes, I would feel much safer when we are there and not having to travel in a carriage."

The Bennets and Gardiners were soon safely at Netherfield. The children and their nurse were ensconced upstairs in the room set up for their use during the ball, and the ladies were just about to enjoy a hot cup of tea when the other gentlemen began to joined them.

The sudden clap of thunder caused them all to jump, Elizabeth going pale. Darcy noticed and was at her side in an instant. He sat beside her, placed her hand in his, and looked into her eyes, "Are you well?"

For a few seconds Elizabeth did not hear anything around her. She had always hated storms, and it seemed the last year that fear was nearly crippling her when they occurred. She finally realized her surroundings and looked to the nervous eyes of her family as the color was finally returned to her cheeks. "Yes, yes I am fine. Thank you. Perhaps it is best if I rest for a little while." She stood, pulling Jane up with her, and turned to leave the room. As they were passing Lord Rosebery, another clash of thunder sounded, the flash causing them all to jump once again. Elizabeth closed her eyes and felt herself fainting, though she could do nothing about it.

Was William holding her? *She thought it was his familiar arms, and yet there was something unfamiliar about them as well. She felt the water pelting against her face, her hands gripped tightly to something rough as the arms tried to coax her to let go.* "No, I cannot let go," *she kept saying to the gentleman who tried to persuade her to do so. Her eyes were closed so tightly she could see bright flashes in the dark abyss. He kept telling her she must let go. She recognized the tenor of his voice and the accent with which he spoke. It sounded so very familiar.*

*She could not bring herself to open her eyes. The arms were so memorable, and all she wished to do was sink into their comfort and rest. Yes, she would rest. The chaos around her would stop and all would be well. Her grip finally relaxed and the arms wrapped tightly around her, pulling her to his chest.* Ahhh, this is just where I want to be, *again thinking it was Darcy pulling her into his arms. When she finally opened her eyes, she saw the face of the gentleman who held her. It was not her intended, yet he resembled him in many ways.* "Who are you?" *she asked firmly, trying to pull away again.*

*"No, no, you must stay close to me. Hold onto my neck and I promise I will get you down safely."*

Sarah Johnson

*Elizabeth gripped his neck tightly as she looked around. They were in a tree, and she was not an adult. She did not recognize this place.* What is going on? Where am I?

*Slowly he climbed down the tree, her small and lithe body firmly held in his arms. Elizabeth looked at his features. He looked so familiar, and yet she did not really recognize him. When they were safely back on the ground he pulled her away just a little, examining her for any injuries. When he looked back up at her, he looked very much like an older version of her intended.* "William?"

*"I am sorry? Did you say something?"*

*"Who are you?"* she asked.

*"I am George Darcy, miss. And who might you be?"*

George Darcy? No, it cannot be possible, *she thought.* "I am Lizzy."

*"Well Lizzy, we must get back over the river, then you can safely rejoin your family. Now I need you to climb onto me and hold on as tightly as possible. Can you do that?" At her nod, he helped her get into the right position.*

*"I am so scared," she said as she began to tremble.*

*"There is no need to be frightened, Miss Lizzy. I will get you to safety if it is the last thing I do. I give you my promise," he assured her.*

*"My Papa says I must pray and put on a brave face when I am frightened."*

*"Your Papa is a wise gentleman. Would you like me to pray with you?" At her nod he called out to the Lord asking for guidance in returning the girl safely back to her family. When the prayer was completed, he turned back to her. "I hope one day my own daughter is as brave as you have been today. Now – hold on tight."*

*He slowly made his way through the rushing water, trying to keep his balance and also trying to sooth the girl that held on for her life to his back.*

*"You have a daughter?" she asked through chattering teeth.*

*He smiled, "Yes; and a son."*

"I have four sisters."

"Well, when you return home you can tell them all of your adventurous tale; how you were rescued from your treetop perch by a knight in a gold waistcoat and blue jacket," he said with a glint of humour.

Lizzy giggled, "I like you."

His eyes met hers, "I like you as well." He turned back around, holding onto the tree that guided their way across the river. "Hold on tight, Miss Lizzy. We will be crossing where it is very deep and I will have to let go of your legs to guide us along on the downed trees."

"Are you scared?"

He stopped and turned his face to look at her, rain pouring down all around them. "Now is not the time to let fear grip either of us; we must be brave."

He saw an amazing change in the little girl who could be no more than twelve years of age. Her jaw jutted out, her shoulders squared, and her grip tighten around his neck as courage rose in her little body. Finally she took a deep breath and replied, "I am ready."

He smiled at her, "One day you will grow up to be a lovely young lady; one whom I would be proud to have in my own family. Now hold on tightly and do not let go, no matter what happens. Can you do that?"

She nodded and tightened her already firm grip even more before closing her eyes.

George Darcy then turned towards where he knew the other bank of the river to be, even if he could not see through the sheets of rain pelting down upon them. Hand over hand he slowly made his way across the raging water. Several times he felt the mud sliding under his feet, and it took all the strength in him to keep their heads above water, yet Lizzy did not let go or make a sound.

Finally he could see the bank where another gentleman awaited them, along with the girl's family. The gentleman's firm grip took ahold of her and Lizzy heard Mr Darcy say, "It is time to let go, Miss Lizzy. My brother has you now."

*The girl crawled into the arms of the other gentleman, wrapping her arms and legs as firmly around him as they had been around her rescuer.*

*Mr Darcy reached for his brothers hand and the two locked their hands on the other's forearm. Just as he was about to be pulled from the river, a log, caught up in the swift current of the river, came rushing towards them, hitting him and knocking him unconscious.*

*"DARCY!"*

*Lizzy heard the other gentleman yell out, then she felt him yank hard, pulling his brother from the river enough for the others to take over. When she tried to lift her head from his shoulder he held her tight, "No, stay there – you are safe."*

*Lizzy did as she was told, but she could not help but listen to the others as they rushed to assist Mr Darcy. When the gentleman who was carrying her turned around and began to walk away from the river bank, she finally saw her uncle guiding his pregnant wife along behind them and several footmen carrying Mr Darcy, all fighting against the rain that still poured from the sky overhead.*

*"Will he be all right?" she asked.*

*With much emotion in his voice, she heard Mr Darcy's brother answer, "I hope so." He then repositioned her so she could not see over his shoulder any longer, pulling her across his arms, her head resting against his chest.*

*She was finally able to look up into the face of the gentleman who held her and she recognized him immediately.*

Elizabeth's eyes flew open and she looked around at the faces of those in the sitting room at Netherfield, where she now lay upon the sofa. She finally caught the eyes of the Earl of Rosebery and could not turn away from him. *"My Lord?"*

His eyes filled with tears when the look of recognition washed over her features.

*"You were there,"* she whispered. At that moment she felt the familiar arms of her intended lift her, and, at the insistence of her father, they took her upstairs to rest. The gentlemen were quickly dismissed from the room and her mother and

aunt settled her on the bed, Mrs Bennet calling for the fire to be stoked and tea to be brought up for her daughter.

Elizabeth's mind was in a whirl. She remembered everything so vividly now, the depth of the memories giving her an instant headache. She heard her mother discussing details with the maid, then she felt a cool cloth touch her forehead. Elizabeth looked up into the telling eyes of her aunt. *"You knew?"*

Maddie took a deep breath, letting it out slowly as she turned away from her niece and addressed her sister, "Perhaps it would be best if you speak with Mrs Hurst about which herbs are available to add to Elizabeth's tea?"

"Yes – yes, you are correct. I will be back shortly," she said as she followed the maid out of the room.

When they were alone, Maddie turned back to her niece. "I am so very sorry Elizabeth. Your letters were evidently dropped in mud, and I was unable to read them. By the time I knew of your suitor's name, you were engaged. We have tried for years to keep you two from meeting, but it seems fate stepped in and brought him directly to your doorstep. When we found out from your father who you were to marry, we rushed here to tell you of your shared past. Then Mr Darcy was gone for a week, and when he returned you were both so happy. We just did not know how to tell you."

Elizabeth began to tremble, "What will he say? Oh, how will he react when he finds out *I* was the cause of his father's demise?"

Maddie sat on the edge of the bed and took her niece's cold hand in her own. "Elizabeth, look at me." When she did, Maddie continued. "It was truly an accident. We were to take a trip to visit my relations one last time before my confinement would bind me to Town for a while. Your Granny Bennet had passed on and you were taking it so much harder than the others. When you found out we were going on an extended trip to the north, you begged your father to allow you to travel with us. He easily gave in, and you were such a joy to have along on the journey."

"I do not remember anything of that time."

"No, my dear. You were so distraught that you forced it from your memory. You remember more of the good times with your grandmother than you do her last days."

"Please tell me everything, Aunt Maddie?"

"When we were in Lambton you befriended the maid at the hotel and she spoke so fancifully of the pleasure gardens at the nearby Pemberley that you would not allow us to leave without touring such a wonderful estate. The family was in residence though, so when we arrived and spoke to the housekeeper, we told her of our desire to only tour the gardens. Of course, she agreed, and we walked around the park for a better part of the afternoon. You had such fun that day. It was the first time we saw you smile since before your grandmother died.

"Just as we were about to turn back to our carriage, you wandered off. Then the storm came upon us so quickly. Mr Darcy and Lord Rosebery were out riding and were alerted to our distress when they heard us calling for you, so they joined the search as well. By the time we heard your cries the river had already risen so high we were cut off from you. Mr. Darcy knew the risks when he set out across it, yet he would not hear of any others going after you. He felt responsible for your safety on his land. Your uncle, as well as the Earl of Rosebery, tried to talk him into letting them help as well, but he would not hear of putting more lives in danger. He returned safely with you clinging to him and we all thought the worst was over."

Maddie sat down on the bed beside her niece as she continued the tale, "Then a log, caught in the mighty current of the river, knocked into him and caused him to hit his head. He never awoke after that, and we heard from the earl later that he had passed on. We sent our condolences and left as soon as we could from the area. It was such a traumatic few months for you – first with the death of your grandmother, then with this accident – we believe you blocked it from your memory, as you never once brought it up to either of us. We did not wish to distress you, so we did not bring it up either, especially after learning of Mr Darcy's demise."

Elizabeth was grateful for her aunt's confirmation of what little she remembered after she was finally out of the river. Tears left hot streaks down her cold cheeks, and she did not know how to react to the pain in her chest at such a knowledge. She curled into a tight ball on the bed and was soon fast asleep.

Sarah Johnson

# CHAPTER
## XXV

Darcy and Bennet returned downstairs to find Gardiner and the Earl of Rosebery alone in the sitting room, the others having left to do various other things in preparation for the wedding and ball this evening.

When they entered the room Darcy could not help but hear what his uncle said to Gardiner, "I hoped she would never remember crossing paths with me. I truly did. How am I to tell him such news on the cusp of their wedding?"

Neither realized he had entered the room, and he stepped over to join them. "What news must you tell me?"

Gardiner looked at Darcy, then at his brother, before he turned back to the earl's lowered eyes. He knew what he must do, so he insisted the gentlemen sit, and he relayed to them the events neither had been privy to until now.

Darcy was in shock. "Why was I never told?"

"I did not wish you to despise me," the earl answered.

"Despise you? Why would I do such a thing? It was not your fault my father lost his life that day."

"Darcy, it was my arm he gripped. If I had pulled him out of the water sooner, the log would never have caused him to hit his head."

Darcy leaned closer to his uncle, wrapping his arm around the shaking shoulders of the earl. "Uncle Hugh, I do not blame you. The good Lord knew what was to take place, and yet He allowed it for some reason. We are never to know why things happen, just that they do. I see this more as a sign of good things to come than as something to shackle us to the past."

"What do you mean?" he asked his nephew.

"I have felt from the moment I arrived in Hertfordshire that I was being guided by my parents. Then when I met Elizabeth, I knew why I was here. Now to learn my own father had such a hand in saving the life of my intended – I cannot help but rejoice in the knowledge that my father saved her *for me*. He promised me years ago he would help me choose the right person for me to marry when the time came, and this is just confirmation that he has done just as he said he would."

Darcy looked back to Bennet, "I must speak with her. I can imagine the distress she is under if she has remembered these events on her own. I must see her."

With a nod of understanding from her father, Darcy turned and followed Bennet back upstairs.

The concerned father knocked on the door to Elizabeth's room and was informed by Mrs Gardiner that Elizabeth was asleep. When he questioned whether his wife knew of the circumstances yet, she said no. Feeling such news should come from him, he asked Susannah to join him for a private discussion while Darcy spoke with Elizabeth. Maddie agreed to sit on the other side of the room, giving the couple their privacy.

Darcy sat on the edge of the bed and looked down at the curled up body of his intended. He could tell just from the way she slept how distressed she truly was. He gently shook her shoulder, and when she groggily looked up at him, he could not help but run his finger down her tear stained cheek. When tears once again welled in her eyes, he helped her sit up and whispered, "All will be well, my love."

"You know?"

"Yes, I have just spoken with my uncle and yours. They informed me of everything that took place."

"*You still love me?*" she whispered.

"Oh, Elizabeth," he encased her face in his hands as he met her eyes, "I could never stop loving you. My father promised he would help me choose a wife, and he did – in his own way. He chose you. He saved you for me."

When she began to sob he pulled her to his chest and wrapped his arms gently around her shoulders. "I will still be waiting beside the minister this evening, and if you will have me, I would like nothing more than to exchange our vows and then dance the night away with our family and friends. Will you still marry me, my love?"

Elizabeth tightened her grip ever so slightly and sighed deeply as she began to calm her tears. "Yes, I still wish to marry you, William."

"Then we shall marry. Nothing can keep us apart, my love."

Elizabeth's parents came into the room once again and Darcy let go of Elizabeth and stood. He lifted her hand to his lips. "Until tonight," he said with a bow before he left.

Mrs Bennet immediately wrapped her arms around her daughter and calmed her as only a mother can. When they were both ready, she pulled back and tucked a stray curl behind Elizabeth's ear. "Now, we have a great deal left to do if you are to meet your gentleman at the altar in just a few hours' time. We have not a moment to lose." She turned to the maid who stood by the door, "We need some cucumbers for these puffy eyes, some hot water as well, and please inform the other ladies that we are ready to begin our preparations if they wish to join us."

The maid curtsied and disappeared to do as she was bid, and within a few minutes all the other ladies, including Lady Rosebery and Georgiana, were gathered in Elizabeth's room to do what the Bennet sisters always did before a ball – assist each other with their hair and gowns.

After they were all dressed with their hair fashioned appropriately for the private ball, Elizabeth turned away from the mirror, and looked at the ladies gathered around her. Her best friend Charlotte would stand beside her as she exchanged her vows. Jane, Mary, Kitty, and Lydia were the best sisters she could have ever desired. They had grown close, especially over the last few years, and she would miss them terribly. Georgiana was such a wonderful young lady, and Elizabeth felt her heart swell with love for the dear girl who was now to be her sister as well. She turned then to the three older ladies – her mother, her aunt, and William's aunt. She had grown to love Lady Rosebery just as much as she did her own relations over the last few weeks.

Tears threatened to spill out of her eyes, until Charlotte's sensible words not to become too sentimental made them all giggle. She hugged her sisters and friend, and stood before the mirror one last time. As she looked at the visage reflected there, she hardly recognized herself.

Squaring her shoulders and lifting her chin, she took a deep breath, "It is time for me to marry."

Georgiana could not help but smile as she saw the loving family. She had always wanted sisters, and after tonight she would have five.

<hr/>

When they were trying to find the perfect place for the ceremony, Elizabeth commented that if she had to choose any place other than a church, she would love to be married where nature surrounded them. Of course, it was too cold and the weather too unpredictable outdoors, as was proven earlier with the storm, to hold the ceremony there.

It was then that Bingley suggested they use Netherfield's orangery. When Elizabeth first stepped inside she was enchanted. The sweet smell of the citrus, oleander, and gardenias permeated the air. The tiled marble floors underneath her feet were warmed from the two fireplaces on the long wall. Greenery of every height she could imagine surrounded them – everything from dwarf myrtle to the tall ficus tree in the opposite corner that branched out overhead, its limbs festooned to the walls and over the large Palladian windows. Elizabeth could imagine them opened up in the summer to let the fresh breeze flow through the flora and fauna within these walls. The beams overhead were covered in ivy and moss, making her feel as though she were in one of her favorite hideouts – the branches of a tree. Immediately it was decided this was it – *the perfect place.*

William now stood in Bingley's study, pacing furiously as he waited for the signal that everyone was ready.

"Calm down or you will wear a hole in Bingley's rug," Fitz said with a firm pat on the back.

"I cannot calm down. Having never been in my shoes, you just have no compassion."

"No, and I never hope to be in your shoes either. If I ever get married, I will elope without telling anyone where I have gone. I will then just show up on the doorstep one day with a wife on my arm," Fitz joked.

"Somehow I can see that of you," Alex remarked to his younger brother. Looking out the window again, he finally saw Bingley give the signal that all was ready. "It looks as if it is time, Darcy; let's go get you married!"

The three walked down the hall, past the common rooms of the house where their friends and neighbors had already begun to gather for the ball that was to follow directly after the private ceremony.

He stepped from the warmth of the house into the cold autumn wind outside and could not help the chill that ran down his back as he hurried through the garden to the orangery. The rain from earlier had subsided, leaving everything wet and shimmering in the moonlight. Darcy found the cold helped to ease his nerves, and when they finally reached the orangery and the sweet fragrance filled his nose, he thought of his mother and the flowery scent she always wore. He could not help but look up through the glass overhead to the stars beyond, smiling when he saw them twinkling brightly.

When he looked back to those gathered, he noticed his sister was looking up as well. They shared a moment of silence across the room, then Darcy walked over to her and leaned down to kiss her cheek. "You look lovely in your new gown."

She smoothed her skirt with her hand, "Do you like it?"

"Yes – very much so. It matches the necklace Father gave you perfectly."

Georgiana blushed and ran her fingers lovingly across the chain and stone that hung around her neck. She turned to look at the other side of the room and something caught Darcy's eye. When Georgiana looked back at him he wore the biggest grin, his rare dimples on display.

"What has you so amused, William?"

He gently touched his finger to her chin, turning her head so he could see the back of her hair. "You are wearing it – the comb I gave you for your last birthday. I have not seen it since..."

He did not finish the sentence as she lifted her hand to grasp his. "I needed all of my family with me tonight"

"I am curious to know what you have that was Mothers?"

She lifted the curls that covered her ears, showing off the small pearl earrings she wore.

Darcy sighed, "I remember those well. They were her favorite pair."

"Yes, you told me so when you gave them to me."

He looked into her eyes. "Are you well Georgiana?"

"There is no need to fuss over me, William. I am well."

Darcy nodded and lifted her hand to his lips, bestowing a simple kiss on the back, then he went to stand next to his cousin and the minister as he awaited his intended.

When the doors opened and Elizabeth stood there on her father's arm, everyone around faded away and all he could see was her. She wore a light blue cape with white fur lining the edge. Underneath he could see small hints at the color of her dress – his favorite color, dark blue. How she found out he did not know, but he knew it was intentional. He smiled when he realized his sister must be behind it, as she insisted he wear a dark blue waistcoat this evening.

Mr Bennet walked between the family and friends gathered and stood in his place behind the couple, giving his daughter's hand to the gentleman who stood beside her when the proper time came, then he joined his wife to watch the rest of the ceremony.

Even when the particulars of the day were forgotten with time, all who attended the ceremony would remark of the beauty and peacefulness that rested in this place as vows were exchanged between the two lovers.

Darcy and Elizabeth received the congratulations of their families, then everyone went back inside to perform their duties for the ball, which would start in just a few minutes. The couple followed the group, then Darcy led them into a small room off the corridor where they could wait until they were to be announced.

Elizabeth pulled the hood of the cape off her hair carefully, then untied it. William stepped behind her and removed it from her shoulders. He laid it across a nearby chair and reached for her hand and spun her around so he could see her gown. The smile on his face showed his approval.

Elizabeth reached up to touch the choker she wore, looking down at the dark blue velvet and silk gown. "Do you like it?"

"Yes, very much so."

"My aunt and your aunt both insisted on this cut being the height of fashion right now in Town."

He could tell she was a little uncomfortable with the fit. Darcy stepped forward and drew his arms around her waist, "It is perfect. You are the loveliest bride I could ever imagine. The cut is all that is fashionable, or so I would assume if that is what my aunt has said. The color is my favorite, though I suspect you know that."

She smirked, "Yes, that little detail was revealed to me by your sister."

He reached up to run his fingers lightly across the sapphire choker she wore as he whispered, *"My mother's necklace."*

"Yes, your sister insisted on bringing this with her to give to me, with your aunt's approval of course."

Bringing her hand to his lips, he quietly whispered, "You are more lovely than the stars in the heavens, Elizabeth." Darcy drew her to his chest. "Thank you, Elizabeth. Thank you for marrying me. Thank you for loving me." He pulled back from the embrace and drew his finger down the side of her face. Slowly his lips descended upon hers and the two were lost to everything around them. Finally he pulled away, "I have longed for the day I could call you *my wife*. Now that it is here, I intend to keep you by my side for all time."

"I love you William," Elizabeth choked out, with tears filling her eyes.

He gently pressed a handkerchief into her hand, "Please do not cry, my dear."

Smiling, she dried the last of her tears, "I will try, but your love is overwhelming me today."

"You deserve so much more than I can give you," he said quietly.

"I desire what only you can give, my love." She leaned into him and the two were once again lost in a lover's embrace.

Eventually hearing the chiming of the clock as its bells rang out, he stepped back, "It is time for us to leave." With one more kiss, he placed her hand on his arm and entwined their fingers as he led her from the room.

She did not recognize where he led them, but soon she could hear her father on the other side of the door speaking loudly to those gathered in the ballroom. They stood listening to him until he finally said, ". . . and so, I am very proud to present to you this evening, *Mr and Mrs Fitzwilliam Darcy*." The doors opened, and the crowd parted for the couple to walk through. Applause broke out and all eyes followed them as they took their place beside the Bennet and Fitzwilliam families. Bennet spoke once again, "Let the festivities begin!" The music began and couples formed on the dance floor for the first dance of the night, led by the Darcy's.

Sarah Johnson

# CHAPTER XXVI

Darcy did not want his sister to miss out on the celebration, especially with there not being a wedding breakfast, so it was decided certain allowances would be permitted for the young ladies who were not yet out and therefore could not fully participate in the ball. The room right off the ballroom was set up for them with refreshments and chairs set all around, the middle of the room cleared for dancing.

Georgiana had been looking forward to this night for many days now, ever since her uncle approached her and asked for her first dance. She had teased that he was getting too old to carry her around, at which time he lifted his brow and said he would not be required to lift her. She was intrigued, and further investigation revealed that Elizabeth's two youngest sisters had conspired to find a way to allow her to dance. She was unable to find anyone willing to reveal their secret though, so the knowledge had plagued her for days.

After the Darcy's were announced and the dancing was to begin, Fitz lifted his cousin from the chair on which she sat and waited for the signal that the ladies were ready for her.

When they entered, Georgiana was enchanted with the decorations all around the room. Kitty and Lydia stood in the corner near a chair the likes of which she had never seen before. Hanging from a frame was a seat almost like a swing, with a high back and straps attached so she would be safe from falling off. Georgiana could not help but laugh at the innovation of such a contraction.

Fitz carried her over, placing her in the chair as his father held it steady. "Your throne awaits, my lady."

Lydia and Kitty wound the sashes of material around her waist, tying her securely to the seat, then stepped back to see how she felt.

"I knew this would work," Lydia said with confidence.

Kitty explained, "When Lizzy was younger and would often fall out of trees and hurt her ankle, she used our swing for all manner of activities. She once tried to convince my father she needed him to put another swing up so she could go from one to the other, but luckily he did not give in to her request."

They all laughed and Georgiana thanked them for such a gesture.

Her uncle came up in front of her. Bowing, he extended his hand and asked, "May I have this dance, Sweetling?"

The girls giggled as they watched Lord Roseberry swing Georgiana around in his arms to the beat of the music filtering through the door. Maria Lucas, Charlotte's younger sister who was not yet out, and Lydia soon began dancing together, with Kitty, the youngest Miss Long, and the other young ladies from the neighborhood joining them. They were all determined to enjoy every minute of the two hours they would be allowed to join the ball before they would retire.

Unbeknownst to those in the room, Jonathan Lucas watched from the doorway. His sister Maria twirled around the room, and Jonathan remembered dancing with her when she was much younger. *She has grown up so much since I left Meryton a year and a half ago*, he thought.

As the dancing continued, his eyes were drawn to another in the room – *Miss Katherine Bennet*. After Mr Bennet's accident, he would go to Longbourn every day to help with the estate business. At first it was to help his father's best friend, but it turned into quite the learning experience for him. His father was not born genteel, and it showed sometimes in his lack of knowledge of the running of an estate beyond just the basics. Mr Bennet had taken Jonathan under his care though and for the next year he taught him everything the younger gentleman would one day need to know to better develop his father's land. They established a strong friendship.

Then the time came for him to do as his father desired and tour England with some acquaintances. He would have preferred to stay here in Hertfordshire, but he did as his father wished and was gone from the neighborhood for a year.

He was now returned, having come back just before the ball at which the couple they celebrated tonight was introduced to each other. In the two months he had been back he could not help but realize just how much Miss Katherine Bennet had grown. They used to play backgammon and talk almost daily, and he had looked on her as he did his little sister. Now her lovely features were becoming more evident to him every time they crossed paths, though they had not found much time to speak. He knew what he felt for her was becoming much more than friendship, but she was not out yet.

Mr Bennet walked up behind him, seeing where the younger man's eyes looked. Placing his hand on Jonathan's shoulder, he said, "I think we need to speak."

Nodding, Lucas followed him to the Library. As the doors closed, Mr Bennet walked over to the decanter to pour himself a drink. "Would you care for a drink?"

"No thank you."

Turning to watch the young gentleman in front of him, Bennet took a swallow and walked over to the sofa. "Have a seat, Mr Lucas."

"Yes, sir," he answered nervously, doing as the older gentleman asked.

"You have been gone a long time."

"Yes sir, I have."

"A great deal has happened since you left."

"Yes."

"I have seen the young girls of the neighborhood grow up before my eyes," Bennet continued.

Looking down at his hands, Lucas chose not to say anything in response.

"I know you and my daughter Kitty had a special friendship before you left, but it cannot continue as it was now that you are back," Bennet stated firmly.

"I realize that, sir, and have chosen not to further our friendship at this time for just such a reason."

"I will not have my girls' reputations put into jeopardy."

"I would not wish to see that of your daughters either, sir."

"Good then." Mr Bennet stood to leave. When he had his hand on the doorknob he turned to say, "She will turn eighteen next year, Mr Lucas, and I have a feeling she would accept your attentions at that time."

A smile formed on his lips, "Thank you, sir."

"So we will speak again when it is closer to her birthday. Do I make myself clear?"

"Yes sir, perfectly" Lucas replied. "I will wait as patiently as one can until her birthday in September."

The two left the room and joined the dancers in the ballroom once again. Lucas had been trying to build up the nerve to speak with Mr Bennet for weeks, and he was glad the interview was over. Now he only needed to wait until next year when she came out and he could ask to court Miss Katherine Bennet.

Fitz enjoyed his dance with Mary; she was light on her feet, though not as confident in her own abilities as she could be. He had heard all about her from Alex over the last few weeks. Even though she was staying here at Netherfield, he had not found much time to really get to know her. She was such a quiet person when they were in company together, but he could see why she attracted the attention of his brother, with her quick wit and dry sense of humour. Alex's quirky personality would draw her out of her shell, if only she allow him the opportunity. She was young and had not been out long, and Fitz could tell it would take a while for her to accept his brothers suit. *Alex is a patient man, and I think it will take all the patience he possesses and some he has not yet found to reach her heart*, he thought as he led Mary to supper.

She was mesmerized by the room when they entered. Round tables were set all around, with flowers and candles in the middle of each. Chandeliers above sparkled with light, and the bare windows reflected the room like mirrors. Richard led Mary to the table where her name card was placed and pulled out the chair for her to sit, bowing as he said, "I thank you for the dance, Miss Mary." With her nod of acknowledgment, he turned to find his own seat, and was soon lost in conversation with the gentlemen already seated at his table.

Mary sat thinking of the last few hours. The dance she shared with the viscount was quiet; he did not say anything to her, and she, likewise, chose not to speak to him. As they executed the steps with much poise, she could not help but notice the dark look in his eyes. Words never escaped his lips, but his eyes never stopped speaking. What they were trying to communicate she could not say, but the emotions they reflected ran deep. She ruminated on what had taken place until she felt her skin tingle as *he* came up behind her. Why was she reacting so to someone she did not wish to be around? After the insult she overheard and all that Caroline Bingley told her of his reputation among the Ton, she knew she could not let him affect her. Yet all it took was his presence, and her heart began pounding uncontrollably. She tried to ignore the sensation by looking around, then her eye caught something. *How could I not notice, until now, the place card next to me which reads 'The Viscount Primrose'?* Mary blushed and looked down at her hands as he pulled out his chair and sat down.

"Miss Mary, I am happy to be seated next to you for supper. I hope you are enjoying this evening?"

Trying to still her shaking hands, she replied quietly, "Yes, it is quite enjoyable, my lord."

"Must we be so formal? After all, we are practically cousins now," he said with a hint of humour to his voice.

Annoyed with herself and her own reactions to his presence, she snapped in her response, "You are cousin to my sister's husband. I do not see how that makes you my cousin. I prefer to stay with formality, my lord."

Alex was hurt by her tone, but taking a deep breath, he tried to hide his own disappointment. He knew he would need to give her time, and yet here he was rushing her. *One day, when you are ready, I will be waiting*, he determined silently once again.

Leaning slightly closer to her, he said quietly, "I am sorry, Miss Mary; if you wish to keep with formalities then I will honour your request. It was not my intention to make you feel uneasy."

Mary did not know what to say, but was spared a response when he smiled and asked, "Would you like some wine?" At her nod of acceptance, he waved a servant over to fill both of their glasses. The two sat alone sipping their wine until others joined them. The conversation flowed for the next hour as food and drinks were served, but Mary never said another word to him. He caught her glancing at him a few times, and that was enough to bolster his spirits for now.

When they stood to return to the ballroom, he asked, "Miss Mary, may I have another dance tonight?"

Mary would not look up as she replied, "I am sorry, my lord, but I have a headache and wish to retire."

Disappointed in her rejection, he saw her turn to go and took a step to stop her. "Then may I escort you?"

*She could not say no.* "Thank you, my lord," she answered stiffly as she put her hand on his arm and walked beside him. Her head was starting to hurt so much that his arm was appreciated, even if she would not admit as much to him.

When they passed the stairs she asked, "Where are we going?"

"Darcy has a surprise for your sister, and I thought you might wish to see it before you retire." Alex led her over to a chair, "Sit here; I will return in a minute." He disappeared, leaving Mary in the hall.

Confused by the increased pounding behind her eyes, she sat down and, leaning her head into her hands, started to rub her temples, certain all she needed to cure this pain was sleep. She knew what the cause was – she had misplaced her glasses and spent half the day today straining her eyes. Now that it was well past her usual bed time, she was beginning to regret not resting this afternoon when she could.

Elizabeth watched Mary leave the room on the arm of the viscount. Her face seemed a bit pale and Elizabeth stepped into the hallway to follow them and ask if her sister was feeling well. Suddenly she felt a hand grab her from behind and pull her into a dark room. As the door closed she felt that same hand cover her mouth and the person behind her whisper, "*Shhhhh.*" Shivers ran down her spine as she recognized the voice. Almost as soon as his identity registered in her mind, he spun her around and captured her mouth in a sensual kiss. She felt herself melting in the arms of her husband as the world all around them faded away.

After a few minutes, Darcy broke the kiss and leaned his forehead against Elizabeth's. "I love you," he whispered.

"I love you too," Elizabeth said back. "I do not think I can ever say it enough."

"I shall never grow weary of hearing those words from your lips," Darcy said.

Elizabeth's hand went to her neck as she fingered the necklace that hung there.

"All evening I have seen you playing with that necklace, and I could not take it any longer," he said, as he drew her hand to his mouth and kissed her fingers.

Smiling, she replied, "You do not mind that your aunt gave it to me to wear, do you?"

"No, my dear; these jewels are meant for your lovely neck." He said as he ran his fingertips lightly across the dark blue stones. "If you want to wear them every day, I would not mind. There is a story behind them, but I do not have the time now to tell you."

"I think they can spare us a few more minutes," Elizabeth said, "but I have something besides story telling in mind," as she wound her hands up around his neck and kissed him again.

Darcy was lost to everything around him until he heard the clock chime. He immediately broke the kiss. "Come," he said as he pulled her to the balcony doors. He placed his greatcoat around her shoulders and ushered her outside.

Looking around at the garden below, Elizabeth saw others coming outside as well. "What is going on William? Why is everyone coming outside?"

He did not have time to say anything before a loud boom sounded and flashes of light filled the night sky. Darcy stood behind her and pulled her back into his chest as he circled his arms around her and threaded his fingers through hers. He looked sideways at his wife's face, watching her eyes follow the fireworks and her smile grow as each explosion of light filled the heavens above. He kissed her cheek and whispered, "*I love you, my Elizabeth.*"

She hugged the arms that surrounded her and Elizabeth quietly answered back the three words that would fall from her lips every day for the rest of her life – "I love you."

Alex soon returned to the hall wearing his greatcoat and carrying a cape. When he saw Mary leaning over rubbing her temples he hurried to her chair and knelt in front of her, "Miss Mary, are you feeling well?"

She looked up into the eyes just inches from her own and memories of the last time she was this close to him flooded into her mind. The compassion she saw that first time was present again now, but there was something else she could not identify. Her cheeks flushed and she felt his hand lightly touch her arm.

Blinking to clear her thoughts, she mumbled, "Yes... yes, I am well; my head just hurts a little."

Alex saw the look in her eyes but did not know what the reason was. "Do you wish to return upstairs immediately?" he asked with concern.

Mary shook her head slowly, "No, I am well enough to see this surprise first."

Not wanting to frighten her again as he had in the past, he stood and held out his hand to help her from the chair. She quietly accepted his assistance. "I borrowed this from Georgiana as I did not know where yours was," Alex said as he draped the cape across her shoulders. "Darcy's surprise is outside," he added when she seemed confused.

Mary knew she mumbled something in response, but was not aware of what she said. She could not get the look of his piercing green eyes out of her mind. It was almost as if she was in a fog and could barely hear what was taking place around her. She felt a weight wrap around her shoulders and then the viscount placed her hand on his arm and led her outside. The cold air hit her face and helped her mind snap back to reality. Mary looked around at the people coming outside and was about to ask what Darcy's surprise was when the dark sky above exploded in a cacophony of light. She had heard about fireworks, but never seen them. Drawing her hands to her mouth in awe, she quietly replied, *"Oh, how beautiful!"*

Alex stood beside the young lady he was certain he loved more each day, watching her eyes brighten and her features lift as she discovered this new and wondrous event for the first time. He heard her quietly say *'Oh how beautiful'*, and before he could stop himself from remarking on the lovely sight before him, he whispered, *"Yes – beautiful!"* Suddenly remembering where he was, he turned his gaze to the sky and hoped she did not hear his comment or notice him staring *at her* when he said it.

After the fireworks ended, Mary found herself being led up the stairs, once again on the viscount's arm. When they came to her door, he stopped and turned to her, "Would you mind if I help my cousin back into bed before I leave you? She was watching the fireworks from the window."

"No, I do not mind," she said as she let go of his arm and opened the door. She saw him go over to the chairs by the window where Georgiana and Mrs Annesley sat. He bent down to speak with Georgiana and Mary went into the dressing room. Closing the door, she leaned her back against it, her head beginning to hurt even more. She soon heard the chamber door close on the other side. *I am glad he has gone quickly*, she thought.

Mary was trying to find her bedclothes when Mrs Annesley appeared at the door with a cup in her hands. "Viscount Primrose said you were ready to retire and that you have a headache, Miss Mary?" At Mary's acknowledgement, she placed the cup in Mary's hands, "Here, drink this and I am sure you will feel better soon.

After Mary drank the bitter, warm liquid, Mrs Annesley helped with her clothes and she was soon ready for bed. She thanked the nurse for her assistance and went back into the bedroom. When she found that Georgiana was in her bed with the curtains drawn, Mary was thankful she would not have to talk tonight. Mary climbed into her bed and snuggled under the counterpane, ready for sleep to come, but her mind whirled with all that had taken place.

*What was that look in his eyes? I have never felt what I feel when he is around me, but how am I to know his intentions are honourable? Miss Bingley has told me several times of his reputation, and I cannot imagine her lying about such an important person. What would be her motivation?* Her mind wandered back to those eyes. *What am I to do?* Mary lay awake hearing the far-off sound of music as it filtered through the house. When she finally found sleep, her dreams kept disturbing her with the same thoughts she had whirling around her mind after the ball.

Mary woke the next morning to an empty room. Still unsure of what she felt about the events of last night, she packed her trunks. She was ready to go home just to be away from the gentleman who confused her so wholly and whom she could not seem to stop thinking about.

Caroline retired when the ball was over, but sleep would not come easily for her. She kept on thinking of the numerous interactions she witnessed between the viscount and Mary Bennet over and over again. She had to find a solution to this problem. It was obvious her conversations thus far had not changed Mary's mind, so Caroline knew she would need to go much further to prove her point. Now to figure out what exactly was needed. *Luckily, Viscount Primrose will be leaving tomorrow, and I doubt he will see Mary Bennet again for several months,* she thought. *By the start of the Season, I will have her believing exactly as I want her to believe about the viscount and he will never have a chance with her.*

Sarah Johnson

# CHAPTER

# XXVII

Darcy awoke to Elizabeth watching him. It was now half past seven and even though she was still exhausted, Elizabeth was so excited for their day that she could sleep no longer. She smiled as she watched her husband, turning her body to better see his face. She drew her finger over the rough stubble on his jaw and he opened his eyes.

"Good morning, *my husband*."

"Good morning, *my wife*," Darcy drew her into his arms, kissing her soundly. Pulling back, he asked, "It is too early yet, why are you awake, my love?"

"I was too excited to sleep any longer. I have never spent the Christmas season in London, and I cannot wait to see all the shop windows and the festive colors. Christmas is my favorite holiday, and I am so very glad I will be spending it with you."

Smiling, Darcy pulled her head down to his chest, "Rest, my dear. We do not leave for London for several more hours, and you need your sleep after last night."

Laughing, Elizabeth cuddled into his chest and was soon asleep once again. Darcy found that playing with her hair helped her relax, just as it did for Georgiana when she was younger. His own breathing evened out as sleep overtook them both for a few more hours.

Mary was sitting at the table as other guests filtered into the dining room. She did not recognize some of them and she assumed they were Mr Bingley's guests from Town. When she saw her sister Jane sitting beside their host, she could not help but think of what a lovely couple they made. The two were obviously besotted with each other, and she would not be surprised if their intentions to marry as well were not announced soon.

She was pulled from her reverie when someone asked, "Is this seat taken?"

Looking up to see Lord Rosebery with a plate of food, she smiled, "No, my lord, it is not taken."

"Capital," he said, as he sat beside her. "Georgiana has told me how much she has enjoyed sharing a room with you these last few weeks. Thank you for all you have done for her."

"I too have enjoyed getting to know your niece. My only regret is that she must leave our neighborhood so soon."

"Actually, it was decided just this morning that she and my son will be staying for another month, giving her brother some time alone with his new wife. The Darcy's are to return for Christmas, then Georgiana will join them after that. My wife has not spoken with you yet? She was to extend an invitation from my niece for you to stay with her here at Netherfield Park for another month complete."

Swallowing the bite of food in her mouth, Mary answered, "No, I have not seen Georgiana or spoken with Lady Rosebery this morning. I thank you for the invitation, my lord."

Bennet came up behind his middle child and leaned over to kiss her cheek, "Good morning, my dear, I hope you slept well?"

"Yes, Papa, I did," Mary answered.

Bennet sat in the chair on the other side of Mary. "What is this I hear of an invitation?"

Lord Rosebery spoke up, "Georgiana has asked to be allowed to stay here at Netherfield Park for a few more weeks since Darcy and Elizabeth will be coming back for Christmas. She wishes to extend an invitation to Miss Mary to stay with her, if that is acceptable to you, sir."

"I think it to be an excellent plan. Our house is a little full at the moment with my brother and his family visiting." Turning to Mary, he asked, "Would you like to stay with Miss Darcy?"

*What am I to say? I cannot possibly offend Georgiana by saying I do not wish to stay with her, but how am I to avoid the viscount while we are in residence together? I do wish to stay though. It might not be as bad as I think.* Mary answered with a small smile on her lips, "Yes, I would like that very much."

"Capital," Lord Rosebery exclaimed, "I am certain my sons will take great pleasure in continuing the acquaintance as well. They have both spoken highly of you over the last few weeks."

Blushing, Mary looked back down at her plate, moving the food around with her fork. She did not know how to take such a comment and it unsettled her, but the decision to stay was made, so stay she would.

Caroline overheard the conversation and was livid. *Now what am I to do? My brother is determined to send me to Scarborough to visit my aunt for the winter, and he insists I leave today, all the while* she *will be here with the gentleman I have determined to marry?* She excused herself from the guests to speak with her brother.

The conversation did not go as smoothly as she planned, and when both Charles and David refused to hear her pleas, she stomped off. They both insisted that within the hour her carriage would be readied, and she was expected to not cause a scene. She knew such an example as she wished to give would flow through the sitting rooms in London within just a few days, so she had no alternative than to do as her brothers insisted. Within the hour she was in her carriage, accompanied by her maid, and on her way to visit her Aunt Hamilton in Scarborough.

They said a tearful goodbye to all of their families, and Darcy ensured that Georgiana was happy to be staying at Netherfield Park until Christmas. Alex assured him he had no fixed plans and could stay with Georgiana. Elizabeth hugged her family multiple times, and finally stopped only after Mr Bennet personally handed her into the carriage. Darcy caught sight of the tear in Mr Bennet's eye as he kissed his daughter's cheek one last time.

Elizabeth now sat next to her husband and watched as the town of Meryton passed by the window. When Meryton was far behind them, the movement of the carriage and lack of sleep the night before made her nod off easily. Darcy pulled her into his side so she could rest against him as he closed his own eyes and leaned back into the corner of the carriage, both sleeping until they reached Town a few hours later.

Elizabeth woke with a start and when she realized how close to their new home she was, she frantically began pinning and tucking errant curls that had fallen during the ride. "I should have never fallen asleep; now my hair will look quite the mess."

"Your hair looks beautiful, my love."

Smirking, she replied, "*You* would say that if every pin were falling out."

Darcy smiled, "I happen to like your hair down."

"Yes, well, I prefer to meet your servants looking like their new mistress, not like some hoyden."

"You need not worry, Elizabeth; Mrs Tucker would not allow me to employ anyone who could think so of their mistress."

"What if Mrs Tucker does not like me?"

"She will love you. She has worked for my family for over thirty years and is the most loyal servant of my employ, though Mrs Reynolds comes in a close second."

"Mrs Reynolds is the housekeeper at Pemberley?" Elizabeth questioned.

"Yes; Mrs Tucker was the housekeeper there for nearly ten years. When her husband suddenly died, she wanted to move to a new area where his memory would not haunt her, so my father talked her into running his house in Town, and Mrs Reynolds took over as housekeeper at Pemberley. The two are the best of friends and communicate so efficiently I find there is no need for me to worry as they keep both places running smoothly with little intervention."

Elizabeth said nervously, "I hope I am able to be the proper mistress of your home."

"Elizabeth, look at me." Darcy waited until her eyes were focused on him. "I employ servants to help where they are needed. If you wish to do nothing more than be my wife and stay by my side all day long, then that is what you have the freedom to do. My housekeepers can handle everything, as they have had those tasks added to their list of duties since my mother died sixteen years ago. Give yourself time, and allow yourself to step into this new role of mistress as slowly as you need. I would not expect anyone to take over everything all at once. I know how that feels, and I do not wish to put such a burden onto your shoulders, no matter how capable I know you are."

"Thank you William," she said as she brought her hand up to cup his cheek.

He reached for her hand and kissed her palm. "I love you, Elizabeth."

"I love you too," she echoed.

The carriage turned along the side of a large four-story house. When it stopped at the side door, Darcy exited and held his hand out for Elizabeth to take. They entered the main entrance hall and Elizabeth looked around at the light colors. "Oh, William, this is beautiful," she said in awe.

"I am glad you like it. My father avoided Town after my mother died, so many of the rooms were in need of updating when I took over at the age of one and twenty. Georgiana thought this would be too dull, but in the end she was glad I went with such subtle colors."

"It has a very serene and peaceful feeling when you walk in," Elizabeth replied. "I like it very much."

# Sarah Johnson

Elizabeth was introduced to the staff and just as her husband said, they were eager to meet her. Mrs Tucker assured them that, per Mr Darcy's instructions, supper would be provided in their sitting room at the appointed time, and water was already heated and ready for their baths.

William put his hand out to her, "Mrs Darcy, will you join me in our chambers?"

Elizabeth blushed and placed her own hand in his much larger one, "With pleasure, Mr Darcy."

The two walked up the stairs leaving a smiling Mrs Tucker in the hall. She prayed silently, *thank you Lord for finding him someone who can make him smile and laugh, and who has brought him back to the youthful person he was always meant to be.* After her small prayer, she returned beneath stairs to do her job and ensure that no one disturbed the couple until they were called.

They had been married for two days now, and Elizabeth was pleased with her new life and the servants. The two newlyweds now sat on a blanket in front of the fire, feeding each other from the tray of food provided and going through the small box of treasures Elizabeth's aunt and mother had given her before they left Hertfordshire.

Included in the box were drawings she had made as a small child, some poems she wrote years ago, a pair of baby shoes and bonnet she wore as an infant, and other such items.

One item she recognized immediately when she pulled it from the trunk was a small quilt she and Granny Bennet made together when she was a child and fell out of a tree, injuring her foot. She remembered dearly the hours they spent together cutting the pieces and stitching them together. When she brought it to her nose and took a deep breath of the cloth, she could still smell her grandmother's favorite scent on it.

266

As the two pulled out each item, stories unfolded, and Darcy learned more about his wife's life.

When the trunk was packed away again and the food on the tray was eaten, Elizabeth had a sudden thought. "William, what did your uncle give to you just before we left Hertfordshire?"

Remembering the envelope, he replied, "Oh, I forgot all about it. I put it in my pocket and did not even look at it. If you will excuse me," he said with a kiss to the back of her hand, "I will retrieve it now." He stood and left their fireside repast to retrieve the envelope as Elizabeth put everything back onto the tray and placed it on the table. When he returned, he sat down on the sofa and Elizabeth curled up beside him, pulling her feet underneath her and leaning on his shoulder. He opened the letter and another sealed letter fell out of the inside. The note read:

*November 25, 1811*
*Netherfield Park, Hertfordshire*


*Darcy,*

*This was left with your father's will to be delivered when you married. I am very proud of your choice of wife and know your parents would be as well. I think back now to those days long ago when I had charge of you and Georgiana, and I cannot but smile at the strength of character you possessed even then. It was my delight to turn over your sisters charge to you and my son when you were both of age, if only because I knew you would make the best guardians for her. I was always better at being your uncle than I ever was at anything else. Our assistance was rarely needed, but your Aunt Helen and I have always tried to help when we could. However, I know it is not the same as having your parents here still. Your strength astounds me, and I am forever grateful to have you as my nephew.*

*With all our love,*
*Lord & Lady Rosebery*

Darcy broke the seal on the other letter and immediately recognized the writing as belonging to his mother. Tears welled up in his eyes and Elizabeth asked if he would like her to read it aloud to him. With his agreement, she took the letter and began:

*"July 17, 1795*
*Pemberley, Derbyshire*

*My Dearest William,*

*I sit here looking at you curled up in the chair near my bed, a book in your lap and you fast asleep, and I cannot imagine all the events that will take place in your life before you even read this missive. I know I will not be here to see you grow up, and it breaks my heart to have to leave you. My own mother passed away when I was not yet ten years of age, and I have missed her every day since, especially on special occasions and holidays.*

*I would have given any amount of money to have one last letter from my mother, so even though my strength is waning, I am determined to write to you in hopes you will one day appreciate all the love I pour out with each word.*

*I can imagine you and your wife curled up before the fire reading what my hand pens for you today and it makes my heart swell with joy. I hope you know how much I love you, my sweet William.*

*I remember my own wedding day as if it was just yesterday. My father did all in his power to make it special for me even though he was too weak to perform the duties of his role. My brother, then Viscount Primrose, led me down the aisle to my father waiting at the front next to George. I now know what great amount of strength it took for him to stand there that day, and I am grateful he was able to bear the pain. As he took my hand and placed it into the waiting hand of your father, he said to me, 'I love you more than you will ever know'.*

*As I sit here now, I think I have come the closest to understanding his words that day as I can now tell you the same — I love you more than you will ever know William. My own father was able to see me well settled, and he passed on just a month later with a peacefulness I had not seen in him in many years. Although I know I will not live long enough to meet your wife, I know she is a special lady…"*

Elizabeth continued to read the pages as Darcy closed his eyes and listened with great intensity to his mother's words. At the end of the final greeting, Elizabeth realized there were several more pages in another person's hand. She showed her husband and asked if he wanted her to continue reading, and at his affirmative response, she continued.

"September 29, 1801
Pemberley, Derbyshire

Dear Son,

Today is your eighteenth birthday, and I know the day will soon come when I will have to pass your mother's letter on to you. If there is anything I have learned from my wife, it is to listen to what you feel deep inside even when it makes no sense. As I now feel the great need to add my own words to this letter of your mother's, I must listen to her own words of wisdom and do just that. I hope to be here to see you wed, but if I cannot you will at least have this last communication to read on that special day.

I promised I would help you choose your wife, and if you are reading this, I have not been able to fulfill such a promise. I apologize, son. You doubt your own judgment too often, and yet I am certain the lady sitting beside you right now is worthy of the moniker of 'Mrs Fitzwilliam Darcy'.

I am certain she is lovely, and I hope she has a lively character, as your mother has always said you needed someone who could make you laugh. If I could choose just one final wish before I pass from this earth, it would be to look upon the face of the lady who has captured your heart ..."

Elizabeth stopped reading and looked at her husband, the knowledge that he did, indeed, look upon her face just before he died was too much for either of them, and they both felt the tears falling down their cheeks. Darcy embraced his wife as they both mourned for the loss of his parents. Elizabeth knew the pain she would have felt if her own father had died in the carriage accident, but it was not until this moment that she realized just how lonely her husband truly was for all these years. She felt a little closer to the in-laws she would never meet, and could not help the love that swelled in her chest for her husband, *her William.*

When the letter was completed and put away and the tears both shed were finally dried, Darcy suggested they go for a walk.

The chill of the London air made Elizabeth's cheeks blush to a healthy pink and Darcy could not help but offer a smile to everyone they passed, an unusual sight for those who knew the gentleman.

"William," Elizabeth said as they walked along the path through Hyde Park, "what do you think will become of your friend and my sister?"

"What do you mean?"

"Do you think they have found love just as we have? Do you think they will marry?"

He could not help but chuckle at his wife. He dearly wished to reveal all, but he had promised his friend he would not. It became even more difficult with his wife specifically asking his opinion now. He looked around to see if they would be seen by anyone else. He was glad for it not being the fashionable hour, as they were quite alone in this alcove. He wound his arms around Elizabeth's waist and pulled her to him. "I suppose it is possible they will one day marry, but I must tell you, I doubt anyone could find the love we have for each other."

Darcy's face slowly lowered until their lips were touching, the soft movements they made drawing them both into a passionate embrace not appropriate for the park. He broke the kiss, his voice cracking as he said, "Let us return home, *Mrs Darcy.*"

Elizabeth opened her eyes, seeing the love he held for her burning within his own gaze. "With pleasure, *Mr Darcy.*"

## TO BE CONTINUED...

# ABOUT THE AUTHOR

Sarah Johnson is a freelance writer and longtime lover of the written word. Her love of the classics began early, with Jane Austen becoming a clear favorite by her early teen years. When the world of fan fiction was introduced to her, she was happy to find so many wonderful stories based on the dearly loved characters. It was a few years before a new writers challenge, posted at one of the Jane Austen Fan Fiction forums, drew her to put pen to paper and begin creating the stories that have always unfolded in her mind. What began as a picture has become a muse that will not stop forming ideas for more stories. After fifteen years of military life, she and her husband, along with their six children, have now settled in Texas, where she continues to write of an era gone by and of characters that will forever live in the hearts of Jane Austen's admirers.

# CONNECT WITH SARAH JOHNSON

E-Mail:
sarah.johnson.jaff@gmail.com

Twitter:
@SarahJohnsonPL

Facebook:
https://www.facebook.com/SarahJohnsonAuthor
https://www.facebook.com/sarah.johnson.jaff

Website & Blog:
http://sarahjohnsonbooks.com

Goodreads:
https://www.goodreads.com/author/show/8118710.Sarah_Johnson